THE HOLLOW

NICOLE BARRELL

For Mike, not Mischa.

Phantasmagoria: A sequence of real or imaginary images like those seen in a dream.
– Oxford Dictionary

Contents

1

Marshside

If you looked beyond the coastline and peeked inland, ignoring the abandoned flea market lots and the bumper boats, you'd see Marshside was just like any other boring little town. It had one stoplight, one movie theater, and even a Dunkin' Donuts, despite a hard-fought battle by the purists at the Cape Cod Historical Society.

Marshside had its secrets, just like any other place; the police log was peppered with domestic disturbances and there was a growing opioid issue. But it was nothing like two hours north, outside Boston, up in Stabbin' Hill or Murderpan. Far from it. A few years ago, Marshside was even voted "Happiest Seaside Village" in the *Globe*.

Upon graduating college, I resolved to never live on that quaint, "happy" little peninsula again. My mother thought I was being a snob, like those summer people who slapped pink whale's tails on their bumpers and Yelped in outrage over sand in their steamers. I insisted this wasn't the case—though part of me feared becoming a townie like my father had been. (He'd opted for a "Marshside: A Quaint Drinking Village with a Fishing Problem" bumper sticker.)

Home on college breaks, I was well on my way to becoming the town drunk; how often I was hauled out by the elbows at last call, I'll never know. But it wasn't just the memories of me yakking into bushes outside the Lighthouse

Pub that kept me away from Marshside. There was something else, something I didn't acknowledge, or couldn't acknowledge, buried deep in my consciousness that served as an invisible repellent. I only crossed the Sagamore Bridge when my mother guilted me or if I needed to pick up my birth control at the pharmacy I was too lazy to change, prescribed by the doctor I was too lazy to change.

One of these trips, in April of 2009, is where I'll start my story. This is when I saw Maxine Lang. A boatload of other weird stuff started happening, and soon, I was so hell-bent on figuring out what was lurking in my memories, trying to claw its way out, that I didn't stop to ask myself if it was something better left buried. Better left alone.

***

I was in the parking lot of Dunkin' Donuts when I noticed a brunette waving madly at me, the straw to her iced coffee jammed urgently between her lips, like she couldn't bother to take two seconds to stop sucking.

I recognized this person. It was Jenny Cummings. And that double entendre held: she truly did suck.

My first impulse when people from high school cropped up like termites in a parking lot or the grocery store was to pretend not to see them; I'd adopt a dulled expression as if lost in thought and float in the opposite direction like a butterfly. So when I saw Jenny, off I went, veering westward towards the pharmacy. For good measure, I put my head down to dig through my bag like there was something extremely important in there, but in doing so I floated smack into a station wagon. Fortunately it was a parked station wagon. Unfortunately there was a dog inside and it began barking maniacally.

"Ellie! You all right over there?" Jenny called across the lot, loud enough so I had no other choice but to look up and wave back.

I took my time ambling over to her, smoothing my sweatshirt and wiping the sleep from my eyes. It was early afternoon on a Saturday, but I'd slept late, waking up to my mother bellowing at the bottom of the stairs, "Ellie, are you up? I need you to go to the store for me. Ellie, are you hearing me? Christ. It's noon!"

As I drew closer to Jenny we both did this half-wave-half-smile thing, no hugs. She slurped her coffee and looked me up and down, her eyes finally resting on my rat's nest of hair. "Ellie Frites," she said. "I haven't seen you in for*ever*."

"It's been a while," I said.

She squinted. "I know when I saw you last. You were at the Clam Shack, waitressing."

"Oh. Well, college then."

"I remember because I was home from my internship. In the city." I could just hear the capital "C" in her voice. I could also hear the condescension when she asked, "Do you still waitress?"

"No," I said, a little too loud. "I live in Boston now."

"Boston," she scrunched up her nose. "Boston's okay but it's just like, so *small* compared to Manhattan."

I knew she lived in Manhattan. I screen-grabbed half of her Facebook posts and sent them to Sarah to scrutinize. I cocked my head though and said, "Wow. You live in *Manhattan*?"

As Jenny Cummings prattled on about her fantastic commute to NBC, her networking group, and her lawyer boyfriend, I couldn't help but stew over the fact that she *looked* perfect, too. The slumped shoulders, the victimhood, the bacne—it was all gone, replaced with an arched spine, a jutting, confident chin, and a spray tan. The good kind of spray tan, the kind where they grind up cocoa beans and vegan ingredients and you're left with a Jennifer Lopez dew. I got a spray tan once, and it smelled like they were smearing compost all over me.

I nodded along to Jenny's life story, aware that this tell-all rendezvous was her sweet, sweet revenge. I deserve it, I thought with a wave of shame. In middle school, Lauren, Maxine, and I used to—

Suddenly, a shiver shot down my spine and I felt as if my temples might burst. I blinked; dancing in front of my eyes were yellow and gray dots, like faint, faraway stars.

A few seconds (or maybe minutes) passed, and by the time Jenny moved on to discussing her recent raise, my vision had almost returned to normal. But there was still a slight thumping in both temples and my stomach was in knots. I steadied myself on Jenny's luxury sedan, noting the New York plates, picturing it parked in a covered garage. I thought of where in the city I parked my car, on side streets far, far away from my apartment. There, my little shit box was subjected to side mirror swipes and ticket after ticket after ticket since it was impossible for me to remember on what side of the street I parked half the time for street cleaning.

"So, Jenny," I said, cutting her off—I think she was onto her volunteer work with legless orphans at this point—"it's been real nice to see you, but I need to get going."

"Oh! Wait, before you go…" Soon her finger was swiping up, up, up on her iPhone. "I wanted to show you a couple pictures of me and Vince V—"

"Sorry, I really gotta get to the pharmacy," I said, pointing. Out of the corner of my mouth I added, "UTI."

The stinging vagina thing was a lie, but it did the trick. With a shake of her empty iced coffee and the *bleep beep* unlocking of her $60,000 car, Jenny was out.

Aside from all the jealousy she'd successfully extracted from my cold, dark, underemployed soul, there was something odd about Jenny Cummings. Maybe not about her, per se, but about what she represented from my past—middle school pettiness, adolescent self-doubt, and something more, something I couldn't put my finger on. Whatever the case, she gave the creeps.

***

"Repeat your last name?" The pharmacist was dark-haired, low pony-tailed, skeptical. Her nametag said *Val*.

"Frites. With an *eff*," I said. Then quieter, "Ortho-*low*."

Val sighed, turned, and squatted down to riffle through the F-L pile once more. I turned and made eye contact with the craggy woman behind me who wore a small gold cross around her neck. I wanted to explain to her, and the other foot-shifters in line, that I didn't even need this birth control. In fact, I should just stop taking the pill altogether. It was a jinx for all I was concerned.

I turned to pick at the magazine rack: soap opera rags, *Us Weekly*, celebrity deaths. I glanced at *Seventeen*, thinking the last time I'd read that I was probably around twelve in Lauren's bedroom, where we all used to gossip and trash people like Jenny Cummings. My sixth grade "BFFs" trashed me too, of course. As soon I'd leave the room. One time, I overheard Maxine say that I—

Suddenly, my temples were once again throbbing, a pall of white dots appearing before my eyes. Then…and there's no other way to explain this, but I was no longer inside the pharmacy. I was no longer in 2009.

I was standing in the twilit woods of the Hollow, shivering. At my back was the faint whirring of cars, and facing me was a tree split into a V, like a Barbie doll's upended legs. I reached into the crotch of the tree and pulled out two limp cigarettes.

A voice rang out behind me, strident, disgusted, "We can't use those."

I pawed at the cigarettes, rotating them. "I think they're okay."

"Too wet." A long sigh. "They'll never light. You're such a loser."

I turned to face Maxine, ready to tell her I was not *a loser; it was Lauren's idea to put the cigarettes in the tree and I had* told *her it was going to rain. But as my eyes adjusted to the dim light, I gasped. Leaves and mud and muck and something else—dark, thick, red—sullied Max's white-blonde hair. And her face…*

"What?" *she asked, sneering at me.*

My eyes jumped from the shiner circling her left eye to the bloody gash across the right. "Max, your…"

"What?" *She touched her cheek absently, smearing the red muck across to her ear.*

My lips were moving, but no sound escaped.

Maxine wagged her blood-caked palms in the air. "What, Ellie? What?"

The yellow dots returned, intermingled with faint dots of red. There was so much blood. Blood on Max's bare arm, blood in her hair, blood on her cheek…

"Ex*cuse* me!"

I jumped. Val, the pharmacist, was shoving the paper bag into a plastic bag, glaring at me. "Could you pay attention? We've got a line here."

***

I drove back to my mother's house in a fog. I was unable to put my finger on exactly what was bothering me, what I'd seen while waiting in line at the pharmacy. Something about the Hollow, the creepy woods in the center of town? Something about…Jenny Cummings? No. *Maxine Lang.* But the images were fading, quickly, and by the time I walked up to the mudroom of my childhood home the odd vision, or hallucination, had all but disappeared.

My mother was sitting at the kitchen table working on her laptop, peering out the bottom of her glasses at the screen. Her bifocals were never right, pair after pair purchased cheaply at the pharmacy I'd just left.

I slipped a gallon of milk in the fridge, and when she still didn't look up, I stuck my birth control in the front pocket of my purse. It wasn't that my mother didn't know I was on birth control, it was just if she saw the little package she might get something into her head, and I'd have to rattle off my excuses: I was too busy; it was impossible to meet anyone worthwhile; Boston guys were short, and for some reason, very sweaty—

"Busy, Ellie?" she'd balk. "What do you do, exactly, that makes you too *busy* to meet anyone?"

And there I'd be cornered into her trap. Always her last damning inquiry: "Well, could it be your drinking, Ellie? Spending all your time at *bars* that precludes you going with anyone?"

Luckily, my mother was too absorbed in her work to notice me squirreling away my birth control. She barely acknowledged my presence as I skirted around her chair in the tight space of the kitchen, knocking around the cabinets in search of crackers or chips or cookies—food I refused to keep in my own apartment because I'd eat it in one sitting.

Finally, she sighed. "Could you stop slamming?"

"Sorry." I chomped on a granola bar and peeked over her shoulder. "Heroin? Who?"

She shut her laptop and looked up at me, this time over her bifocals. "As if I would share that information with you, Ellie." She shook her head at me, adding, "What are you, insane?"

She loved saying that: "What are you, insane?" You'd think she wouldn't throw the around the word "insane" like candy at a parade, being a social worker. Though, maybe after over twenty years, and after all she saw on this peninsula, she was desensitized.

"Did you pick up the milk?" she asked.

"I forgot."

"Ellie, I mean, can you be more self-absorbed? What were you doing all this time?"

"Mom, are you blind?" I opened the fridge door and

pointed. "I was kidding. I put it in here right in front of your face. You work too hard. Take a break."

I shut the fridge and leaned against the counter, picking through my mother's mail with mild interest, getting crumbs everywhere. "You know who is self-absorbed?" I murmured. "Jenny Cummings."

But thinking of Jenny made me think of the parking lot, which made me think of Max. The images, though faint at first, conjured to clarity: Max, smeared in blood and leaves and muck, curling her lip at me, calling me a loser.

"Did you hear me?" my mother asked.

"Sorry, what?"

"Who is Jenny Cummings? Name sounds familiar."

I sighed. "No one."

She took her glasses off and rubbed her eyes. "You're a regular raconteur, Ellie. When do you go back to Boston?"

"Raconteuse. Tonight. I'll try to beat traffic at the bridge and leave late."

"Good idea."

And looking at her like that—her rail-thin frame, her hunched back, her cheap bifocals—suddenly made me sad. I'd leave her alone to write up reports about local moms with opiate addictions, or moms with daughters my age who'd never left the Cape. Women she'd have to pretend not to see at the supermarket. Tonight, she'd slip into her leggings and curl up in the easy chair and talk to her best friend, Shelly, on the phone about God knew what—me and my younger brother, Jack, probably—and she'd watch TV and go to bed. Alone.

"I can take the day off tomorrow, Mom, if you want. We can, like, hang out. Go to lunch."

"Don't be silly," she said, waving her hand at me. "I've got so much work. And you, too, I'm sure."

Trifling, boondoggling, idiotic "work" assigned by my moron of a boss, I wanted to say. But I didn't. I could see where that conversation would go, too: "It's 2009, Ellie, you're lucky you *have* a job in this economy."

I rounded the corner to the living room, where I sat on the couch and looked around at the ratty furniture and old, unread newspapers littering the coffee table. *What to do*, I wondered. Sitting in traffic was out of the question. Though it wasn't summer yet they'd closed one lane of the Sagamore Bridge, keeping all traffic on and off the peninsula to a crawl.

"If you need something to pass the time, you can clean out your closets!" my mother called from the kitchen.

"You like having my stuff here," I called back.

"False." She appeared in the doorway, hands on her hip, her glasses holding back curly grayed sideburns. "Those closets are filled to the brim with junk. You're twenty-four years old. You don't live here anymore."

"I don't really feel like it right now."

"Take a garbage bag."

***

My mother had left my bedroom largely untouched all these years. Posters of Fiona Apple and Alanis Morissette grimaced at me between curled, faded corners. Fiona looked like she just climbed out of a rat hole, famished and pale. Alanis at least had a little glimmer in her eye.

There were two closets and I knew which one I'd tackle first: it had the older junk in it, while the other closet still housed prom dresses and my graduation robe and exercise balls I'd never used.

Upon opening the closet door, an object loosened from its precarious perch on the shelf, landing with a big thump at my feet. It was a photo album, dusty and stuffed with photos from front to back. The inside cover read *Ellie Frites. Marshside Middle School 1995-1998. KEEP OUT JACK!!!!*

Slid beneath the first few transparent sleeves were pictures of me and my longtime best friend, Sarah. Photo booth strips from the Cape Cod Mall, each of us sporting thick bangs and braces. I took out my phone and snapped a photo of a photo, meaning to send it to Sarah over email; we still talked daily. But as I looked for more pictures of the two of us I found that beyond those first couple of pages, there were fewer pictures of Sarah and me. It must have been around the time she'd been shipped off to boarding school.

That would explain why, in the following pages, there was a greater number of pictures of me with a waifish, rat-faced girl named Lauren Vine. Lauren had been my "school best friend," though I hadn't seen or thought of her in years.

I pored over the pictures of Lauren and me getting ready for the fifth-grade dance, Lauren and me on a field trip to the cranberry bog, knee deep in waders, stomping around in red muck...

I kept flipping, squinting my eyes at each photo. Lauren, Lauren, and more Lauren. But as I reached the middle of the album, I noticed our twosome had expanded. The pictures of Lauren and me started to include Maxine Lang.

My hand clutched my thumping chest as I stopped at one photo: Lauren, Max, and I were at the beach, on a field trip. I could tell it was a field trip because we were fully clothed, and because a bunch of awkward middle school kids were in the background, kicking sand, flinging seaweed. I could even spot pale, pre-spray tan Jenny Cummings with her shoulders slumped, glaring in our direction. Max, with her pin-straight white-blond hair and flared jeans, wound her arm tight around Lauren's shoulders. I stood slightly off to the side, one hand awkwardly holding a conch shell, my eyes shifted down. My jeans looked like Mom jeans, likely from Bradlees.

I slid the photo from the sleeve and flipped to the back: *January 1996.* That put us in the sixth grade. I feverishly flipped through the rest of the album, looking for more clues about Max. But by the time I'd reached the end of sixth grade and on to the summer, Sarah was back into my life, and Lauren and Max were nowhere to be found. There were pictures of Sarah and me taken at Barr Beach with our underwater disposable camera, snorkeling and splashing and wearing seaweed hair. There were pictures of Sarah and me at tennis camp, zinc oxide slathered on our noses.

I closed the album with a *thwap* and returned it to the shelf, then sat on my twin bed, dazed. Beyond sixth grade, I couldn't for the life of me remember what became of Maxine Lang. Or, come to think of it, Lauren Vine. Did they move? Switch schools?

I halfheartedly tossed some moth-eaten clothes into the garbage bag so I could show my mother I threw something away, and on my way out, I glanced again at Alanis and her scraggly hair, remembering how Sarah and I would giggle as we sang along to, "…blow jobs in a theatahhh!"

After saying goodbye to my mother, I threw my duffel bag in the car and headed to the highway. While in bumper-to-bumper traffic on Route 6, Max crept back into my mind. But this time I settled on a certainty: I would never have been alone with Max in the Hollow. I would never have been retrieving cigarettes for her, just the two of us. We were always a threesome, Lauren, Max, and me. And I never witnessed Max with a bruise and a gash on her face like that…it was just too violent, too brutal to be real.

By the time I returned to my apartment, I considered it settled. The visions, or hallucinations, or whatever you wanted to call them, meant nothing. God, Maxine Lang, I almost laughed to myself. Bleeding out her eyeholes. I *certainly* would have remembered something like that.

2

The Clasp

There was a law in Boston harkening back to Prohibition that disallowed drink specials from being called "happy hours." Regardless, our "Symbicorean Night Out" was just that, an open bar paid for by our overlord—excuse me, CEO—for "teambuilding." Teambuilding, to me, meant cloistering myself off in the far corner with the only co-worker I could stand, my friend Mel, a petite Latina with wild hair like a lion's mane and a trucker mouth worse than mine.

By the second hour Mel and I had triple-fisted at least four Red Bull vodkas and downed at least two tequila shots. Time escaped me, but I did remember the bartender shouting over Ke$ha, "Company tab's finished. You're on your own." Mel and I scrounged for our cards. I found mine first, and as I handed it over to the bartender I prayed I had enough in my account for at least a few more drinks, plus the cab fare home.

Shortly after, Mel was gone. A text from her said, *Mexican exit, sorry, girl!*

I looked around a bit dizzily and steadied myself by leaning against a stool. Things get hazy here, but my next memory was this: I'd struck the fancy of some freakishly tall male specimen named Bryan, or maybe he said Ryan. Who knows what we were chatting about. He was boring, and the more my eyes could focus on his unibrow and distended lower lip, unattractive. No matter, I was getting attention, and all was right with the world.

"You look fly!" Bryan/Ryan suddenly shouted. Brown spittle dribbled down his chin. His dip cup was beside him and he was forgetting to use it. It looked like poop. Poop mouth.

I smiled. "Thank you."

I drew the back of my hand to my chin, trying to give this goon a hint. His lower lip looked like it was stuffed with a Portabella.

Finally, he shook his head and bent down to shout in my ear, "Do you not hear me? I said you look like you're about to *cry*. Are you all right?"

"I'm fine," I said, and for the eight millionth time I denounced the dour look that so easily found its way to my countenance and attempted to smile. I caught my face in the mirror behind the bar. I looked pained.

The bell above the bar rang out. Last call. The music shut off and the lights flashed on, blinding me for a second. I covered my eyes with my hand and pressed my thumb against my temple, cursing a hangover that had somehow already started.

Except, when I opened my eyes, I was no longer in the bar.

I was crouched down low, on a soft carpet. Someone was standing over me. His heavy breath was uneven and I could smell a putrid whiff of something…like the stench from a bottle my father used to keep in the top left cabinet, up where Jack and I couldn't reach.

"Please," I said, my voice high-pitched and small. As I hugged my arms around myself, I realized I was small.

I looked up at him; he was tall and wearing a red baseball hat, the bill obscuring his face. He fumbled with his pants, getting tripped up by the buckle. He swayed as he attempted to undo the clasp with his large, hairy fingers.

"*Please*," I said, my sobs growing heavy in my chest. As I scooted backward my shirt slid up and my skin burned against the rug. I was halted when I struck a hard corner of something. Pain shot up my spine. I knew then what was behind me. A bed.

I heard a clink and a click. One end of the belt now hung down, limp, and the man's thick fingers pinched the zipper. A beam of light caught the belt buckle, a shift in the sun through a window, and I was blinded. I strained to see but all I could sense above my forehead was the heaving hot breath, and that rancid smell.

"*Please—*"

"Seriously, are you okay, Melanie?"

God, I thought, as my vision cleared and saw the giant tobacco-dipper was craning his neck down towards me in concern, his gigantic hand cupping my shoulder, *I'm* wasted.

I bumbled around the other patrons, girls in too-high heels clearly in pain and guys in suits clearly trying to take them home. The girls were checking their phones, whispering to one another, deciding who was going home with whom. The guys fiddled with their loosened ties, wiping away the sweat from their faded sideburns, tossing side-glances at their friends.

I had almost reached the bathroom when suddenly a solid mass, an arm, barred me from moving any further. I tottered backwards. My heart jumped. This man looked familiar too. I stopped in my tracks and stared at him, my heart caught in my throat.

Pointing to the exit he grumbled, "Everybody out."

"But—" I said.

This time he shouted it. "Everybody out!"

My eyes stung. I now remembered this was the same bouncer who yelled at Mel and me, "No shots after eleven!" like we were a couple of *savages*.

***

I woke up, alone, in my apartment. I stared at a brown spot on the ceiling for a few seconds, my eyes puffy and swollen, and then looked around my bedroom. My wristlet was on the ground by my open door, cash and my license spilling out of it. I could see all the way out through the hallway to the kitchen, to the trash, where a pizza box was jammed into the top. I must have been unaware last night that a large square box did not fit into a small, oblong opening. My tongue ringed around my bottom teeth, catching small bits of pepperoni.

My phone alarm was buzzing. It was somewhere in the bed, in the mess of sheets, but as I felt around me, my arms and hands grazing the sheets like a snow angel—Hershey's wrapper, a sock—I felt no phone. The cool plastic of my Blackberry rubbed against the side of my foot. I kicked it up to my hand and read the time.

"Shit!"

A shower was out of the question—quick rinse, maybe, but no hair wash. I knew my hair probably smelled like alcohol, and told myself to Google if it could seep into the follicles.

"Ricki?" I called out, spritzing dry shampoo as I fumbled for my work bag.

Silence.

I pulled on jeans from my semi-clean pile, then a top from the clean pile. I padded barefoot down the hall and peeked into her room. Her bed was unmade but untouched for days. Maybe weeks. Ricki spent every waking moment at her boyfriend's apartment, a surprisingly nice, quiet finance major with whom we'd gone to college but had never met during our time there. One night grinding at White Horse Tavern in her hooker boots was all it took, and Ricki and Tyler had been inseparable ever since. Some people had all the goddamn luck.

I checked the time on my phone again. "Shit."

On this morning, I was not thinking of the man in the

red hat, or the coruscating gleam of his belt buckle, or the terror coursing through my young body. I'd tucked that away, along with other moments from the night before, like how I managed to hail a cab downtown at one of the busiest times, or how I managed to rustle my keys out of my purse to get into my building, or how many texts I'd sent, then deleted, to my college boyfriend Pete, who lived a convenient two miles away but when drinking *in*conveniently tended to wet the bed.

No, I wasn't accessing any of that. Instead, I was thinking of the trundling cesspool of the Green Line train that would bumble me across Boston to my miserable job, and to my weekly check-in with my boss, Buster. Buster the Buffoon.

3

Symbicore

Symbicore Technologies rented out a high-rise set back from the main road in Cambridge and was fronted by a lush, green courtyard ringed with metal tables nailed to the concrete. Next to the tables were metal chairs stacked high and locked up after five o'clock. Apparently, chair thieves lurked in Kendall Square, and you could never be too safe.

It was late April, still chilly, but I was sweating by the time I cut across the grass and reached the entrance. After the elevator shot me up to my floor, I realized I'd forgotten my key card again. I knocked on the glass doors of the office and motioned to an attractive redhead in a nearby cubicle. He looked up at me, took his headset off slowly, and ambled over to the glass door. He pushed it open with one hand as he strode past, heading in the direction of the communal kitchen. I slipped through and thanked the back of his head. He nodded without turning around.

The door suctioned shut behind me like a hissing fart, and I rounded the corner to my personal hell: the Symbicore Technologies Customer Service cubicles. I was smacked with the deafening sound of frantic keyboard taps, ringing phones, and the A/C's dull hum.

I plopped into my rolling chair and booted up my laptop, peeking through the glass of our shared cube wall and over the curly head of Susan Ellmore, a sourpuss who loved heating leftover fish in the communal microwave as well as nosing into other people's business.

I caught the eye of Mel, who was settling back into her chair. She must have just returned from her check-in with Buster. Buster called Mel's weekly meetings "check-ins." He called our meetings "tune-ups" because he said I wasn't living up to my potential. This was in between him staring at my boobs and me staring at his pit stains, which were large, dark, and usually resembled the size and shape of California.

Mel put a finger to her temple and mouthed, "Boom."

***

Buster Flaherty had been Team Lead, Manager-in-Training of the Symbicore Customer Service group for six months. At an unknown juncture, he adopted this pet name for us, his subordinates. He started calling us "ninjas", and every time I heard that term I considered throwing myself out the eighth story window. Unfortunately, there was no window in the small meeting room where we now sat—only a glass table, a white board, and my pounding headache.

Buster was wearing his uniform: a baggy and wrinkled blue button-down and jeans that gripped his thick thighs. I tried not looking directly at him, and I tried to tell myself that he was not eyeing my hairline, specifically the grease forming at my widow's peak. *Are my highlights brown right now?* I wondered. *Do I need a new brand of dry shampoo? Does it smell? God*, I seethed. *Stop looking at it.*

Mercifully, he stopped staring at me and sprung up from his chair, spending the next twenty minutes jotting nonsense on the white board.

"Now," he huffed, scrawling letters on the board. "The company tagline for the month is R.A.V.E.! and we'll be quizzed on this, so listen up. R.A.V.E.! stands for Responsive, Adventuresome, Valued, and Enterprising!"

He slapped the dry erase marker onto the sill and finally sat back down, steepling his hands on either side of his nose. He appeared to be holding his breath.

Oh God. *Here we go.*

Out came Buster's serious manager tone, his nasally, condescending honk voice. Budget cuts, hiring freezes. No raises this quarter. I'd heard it all before. I said nothing, of course, just smiled, and nodded my dumb head.

"It is 2009, right?" he honked. "And in this economy, we're lucky to have jobs at all, right?"

He waited for me to say something, but I could only shrug. I didn't feel lucky. I felt like an idling nothing every day, tapping away at my computer for clients who were less than nice, and salespeople who were flat out impatient and lazy.

As he spoke, his eyes dropped to my chest again. I covered my left nipple with my upper arm, aware that it was beaming like a bullet out of my V-neck. The office was always so fucking freezing—I swore it was so slobs like Buster wouldn't sweat all the way through their shirts. For those of us who didn't weigh three hundred pounds? Well, it got a little *nippy*.

"Anything on your end, Ellie?" He started packing up the laptop he'd never opened.

I smiled. "Nope. Everything's good."

***

I met Mel outside at one of the metal tables for lunch. She and I were hired around the same time, and we bonded over how many times the recruiter lied to us about what we'd be doing on a daily basis. "Market research" had somehow manifested in setting up sales calls and scheduling meetings.

"Burger two days in a row?" Mel asked.

"I'm hungover—I get a pass," I said, peering into my bag. "Dammit, I forgot ketchup."

"How'd your meeting go?"

"Same as always. Buster regurgitating the company Kool Aid he's been chugging for five years…"

"Oh, I'm sure he was raving about the new client tagline."

I snorted. "You betcha."

I looked to the other side of the courtyard, closer to the street. A man in a red hat, a collared white shirt, and jeans was sitting at one of the circular tables reading a newspaper. As he turned a page, his face came into view and I met his eyes. My breath caught in my throat. I blinked; there were those white dots again. The vision from the night before came flooding back—the belt buckle, the blinding clasp, the thick fingers gripping the zipper…and now the certainty. *I know this man.*

"Ellie?" Mel cocked her head to the side. "Are you okay?"

I tore my eyes from Mel and looked back at the table across the quad. The man with the newspaper was gone.

"Sorry," I shook my head. "I just—"

"Just what?"

"Feel dizzy."

"Are you eating enough bananas?"

Before I could answer, Mel nodded. "You're not getting enough potassium."

I nodded back. "That must be it."

My teeth chattered. I hugged my arms to my chest, looking back once more as my mind raced. Was that man ever even there?

Mel was staring at me.

"What were we talking about?" I asked.

"You were telling me what makes you sick about this place."

"Oh," I said. I felt my heartbeat almost return to normal and went on my daily rant about how our customers were thankless turds and how Buster was a sweaty pissant. Mel giggled and nodded as she listened.

I finished by saying, "Can you believe my thumb is still twitching?" I held up my right hand, willing it to twitch.

Mel examined my thumb and shrugged. "Maybe you have carpal tunnel?"

"It starts happening when my hand is resting on the mouse. For hours on end. This place is literally giving me a disability."

"Have you looked at other jobs lately?"

"I scour job boards, LinkedIn. I hope this place doesn't track what sites we're on like they did with our SymbiChats. I'm a dead giveaway."

"And? Find anything?" Mel asked.

"No," I said. "It doesn't help that I don't know what exactly I want to do. And when I do see something interesting and send my resume out, it's like I'm sending it right up someone's fat ass, never to be seen again."

We sat in silence for a moment and then, as if on cue, we said in droll, low tones, "Well, in this economy…"

We cackled and gathered our things to go back inside. Mel strode on ahead of me, hopping up the steps to the revolving door. I hesitated at the bottom of the stairs, glancing back across the quad at the vacant table.

I tried to think back to the vision at the bar again; I tried wiping away the blurriness, the intoxication, like condensation on a mirror. I tried to connect the man with the red hat to seeing Max in the woods, bloodied. But I couldn't make sense of any of it.

"You coming, you weirdo?" Mel called as she propelled herself through another cycle of the revolving doors. "I'm getting dizzy."

I snapped out of my reverie. "Yeah, sorry. Coming."

***

Later that night, with tweezers from my dresser, I pinched and plucked a stray black hair under my eyebrow arch, then one from my chin.

My cell phone was on speaker mode, lying on top of the dresser beside bobby pins and eyeliner pencils and a Post-it note where I'd scrawled, *make dentist appt. before u quit in fit of rage & lose your dental ins!!!*

"You never listen to my voicemails," my mother was saying. "Why do I even bother leaving them. It's ridiculous!"

I plucked a piece of skin instead of a strand of black hair from my eyebrow and winced. "Mom. You know I don't know my voicemail password. What's up?"

She sighed. "Not too much...I'm just checking in. Anything going on? How's work?"

I grunted. "Sucks."

"Still? Why?"

"It just does, Mom. I feel like I'm utilizing a very small percentage of my brain."

Mom laughed. "I'm sure it's not that bad."

"It's bad, Maureen."

"First, don't call me Maureen. You know I hate that."

"Sorry."

"Isn't there anything you're drawn to, El? Why don't you focus your search—"

"Because I don't know what I like to *do*, Mom!" I yelled.

"Alright, calm down, Ellie. I'm just saying you could stick it out working at Symcore—"

"Symbicore," I corrected with an exaggerated sigh.

"Symbicore, right, sorry. Can you simply enjoy your weekends? Try to enjoy life outside of work?"

I rolled my eyes in the mirror and plucked a long hair from my neck. How many days was that there? I wondered, aghast.

Then she said, "You're lucky to have a job at all in this economy."

"Oh, for the love of God, Mom," I said through gritted teeth, "Is it too much to want to go to work in the morning and not want to gouge my eye out with a coffee straw?"

"You're so overdramatic." She laughed. "You've at least made friends there, right?"

"Yup. There's Mel. She's my work wife. She hates it, too."

"Misery loves company…" She trailed off and then cleared her throat. "I'm glad you at least have a social life there. You're good at making friends.

Silence.

"So…what else is new?" she asked. "Anything?"

"Nope, my life is boring."

"Any…dates? Are you going with anyone?"

I started to get huffy again, but then stopped. I couldn't tell her about my latest "dating" prospect, an enormous tobacco-dipping giant who prompted that strange vision at the bar. Or about how I'd come home that night only to eat a whole pizza on the kitchen floor, dunking the crusts in Ranch dressing while fighting the spins. She'd pluck the least important piece of information out of the whole story, anyway: my drinking.

"No, Mom," I said softly. "I'm not *going* with anyone. Still."

"Well, could you join some clubs, or a softball team? You never know, it's always when you're not looking."

I rolled my eyes at myself in the mirror again. "Wouldn't joining a club or a team to that aim be 'looking'?"

"I'm saying don't focus so much on it," Maureen said. "What about Sarah, does she have a boyfriend?"

"No," I said.

"Why not?"

"What do you mean why not, she just doesn't! Just like how I don't!"

"Stop yelling!" my mom yelled.

I picked the phone up off the bureau and shook it in the air violently. Then I took a deep breath, disabled the speakerphone, and said calmly into the mouthpiece, "Mom, I don't want to talk about this anymore."

Silence.

Suddenly, I felt guilty. "Wait. Sorry. I didn't ask anything about you. What's new with you?"

"Not too much going on with me," she snorted. "Twiddling my thumbs, thinking about my daughter. The center of my universe."

She thought she was being very funny. I cut off her cackling. "And Jack? How's he doing?"

"He's fine, grades are decent. Living off-campus, seems to be doing well. You should call your own brother once in a while."

"I'll call him more when he's a real person. College kids aren't real people. They're in fantasy camp. Wait till he realizes."

My mom laughed. "Oh God, Ellie, realizes what?"

"That corporate life is a never-ending vortex of suckiness peppered with a few vacation days."

"Now you're being glib."

"I'm just kidding. Sort of."

I waited for her to say something else, but she didn't. Instead she asked in a small voice, "You know what day it is, Ellie?"

"Know what day what is?"

"Daddy's, uh, anniversary."

"Your anniversary? Why would—oh. Of his…death."

My mom sighed. "Thirteen years. Not, you know, a real milestone year, but, do you want to…do anything for it?"

My mom never asked this, hence why none of the remaining Frites clan—Jack and my mom and me—ever fell in the habit of commemorating the actual day. "Ahm, not really, do you?"

"No, no," she said quickly. "Just seeing if you did. Okay, hon, I have to get going."

"Okay, goodb—"

"Yes," she said. I thought I heard her voice crack, just slightly. "Goodbye." *Click.*

I stared at my phone. Then, as if swallowing a tornado,

sudden and swift, I was overcome with grief. I looked at my face in the mirror, red, wet, and swollen, the tweezers midair, still pinched between my thumb and index finger.

4

Therapy

The next afternoon I opened a blank email, and instead of tending to the needy clients and client-coddling salespeople, I crafted a message to my best friend Sarah. I had much to tell her, starting with the visions, but every time I started typing up the story I dragged my cursor over the words and deleted them. I sounded like a crazy person, hallucinating about bloodied little girls and rapey old guys. I decided to start out with the basics. It had been a few days.

From: ellie_frites@symbicore.com.
To: Muppet <sarah_mupetta@email.com>
Subject: Life Updates

Hi Muppet!

Have a nice weekend? Haven't talked to you in so long! (5 days??) How's the job, how's life, how was the DATE? Spill it, sisterfriend.

I'll start with myself. Category: Memory Lane: Ran into Jenny Cummings on the Cape this weekend. She looks amazing and bragged out loud about everything she already posts on Facebook. Wanted to vom.

Category: Living: I officially have an absentee roommate. Ricki is NEVER home. If she ever makes an appearance, it's to grab her stuff. She darts in and out of the apartment like a mouse. (Oh, PS, we actually have mice. It's so disgusting. The Hershey's wrappers I leave all over my bedroom floor don't help the cause.) Point of the story: I'm lonely, and I miss my best friend.

PS: How is that PALEO diet of yours? Sounds like misery to me…but maybe I need something like that? My muffin top is getting out of control.

Love you my Muppet friend.

–ELF
Ellie Frites, Customer Service NINJA
Symbicore Technologies
Clients R.A.V.E.! about us! x5624
Please save the environment. Do not print this email.

From: Muppet <sarah_mupetta@email.com>
To: ellie_frites@symbicore.com
Subject: RE: Life Updates

Sorry to email you back so late. I was running around all day. A patient peed on my hand. Catheters…what can you do?

On Memory Lane: Grrrr. Jenny Cummings hit me with a field hockey ball in the shin sophomore year and I'm pretty sure it was on purpose. Then there was that time she told Coach Fowler that I'd been drinking at homecoming and it was a total lie. F Jenny Cummings.

On Living: I'm sorry Ricki sucks and that she's attached to Tyler's balls. I wish we lived in the same city. I'm still searching for a nursing position in Boston, but it's so competitive at the hospitals there…especially in THIS ECONOMY (thought you'd like that one).

My latest life updates.

Category: Dating: Date. Went. Terrible. First of all, I have NO idea how on earth my coworker Paula thought we were compatible when she set us up. He wasn't bad looking, but he was blond. You know my aversion towards blonds. And he was like a BLEACH blond. What a wannabe-surfer-dude-bro is doing in Burlington, Vermont is beyond me. Dirty hippies, yes, but borderline-Albino surfer dudes? Second of all, he's a lawyer, and he's really busy, and he made sure to tell me that several times. He kept looking at his phone, up at the TV, anywhere but at me. It was humiliating. Even the waitress was uncomfortable. We only had one drink. He paid. I wanted to say, "Thanks for the three dollar Bud Lite, you cheap fuck," but I refrained. All in all, dude was a DUD.

PS: How did that happy hour thing go the other night? Meet anyone? (I despise getting that question from anyone else. Only you and I are allowed to ask each other. That's it.)

PPS: Paleo lasted a day. Impossible. I wanted cheese.

PPPS: I still can't believe you use your company email for personal stuff, by the way. After what you went through with the inter-office chat software? When you found out they were monitoring all your shit? (Should I be saying "sh$%?") You're nuts.

Love,
SAR

Sent from my iPhone

From: ellie_frites@symbicore.com
To: Muppet <sarah_mupetta@email.com>
Subject: RE: Life Updates

If the SymbiFucks are trawling my emails—great. Fire me.
Okay, actually, please don't fire me. My credit card balance is
up the wazoo.

RE: happy hour: Ugh. I didn't want to tell you about this
because it's a little unbelievable but…something weird
happened. In the middle of talking to some freakishly tall loser,
I got dizzy and my sight went out and for a second and I
saw these white flashes, kind of like lightning bugs. I felt
this gripping terror. What I saw next is hard to describe. (A
memory? A drunken vision? A hologram?!) Some tall dude
was standing over me, his hand over the crotch area of his
pants. It felt menacing. And familiar. A few seconds passed and
I snapped out of it, thankfully. Then I realized how drunk I
was and shame-spiraled into one of my crying sprees in the
bathroom, before the bouncer kicked me out.

It gets worse. I had another vision, sober, in the courtyard
while I was having lunch with Mel. I'm looking around,
nursing my staring problem, and spot a guy who has on a red
hat sitting at a nearby table, reading the paper. Normal, right?
Well, next thing I know I'm all dizzy, feeling the exact same
way I felt after seeing that guy in that vision at the bar. The
only way I could recover in front of Mel, without her thinking
I was crazy, was pretending I haven't been eating enough
bananas. I don't know what to think about all of this. But I do
know lately I've been feeling, I dunno, gloomy and lost. I hate
my job, dating is hopeless, I'm drinking too much…plus it's
around the time of year that my dad died. Every spring I get
a little mournful for no apparent reason. Do you think it's all
related? Please tell me I'm not crazy.

Love,
ELF

From: Muppet <sarah_mupetta@email.com>
To: ellie_frites@symbicore.com
Subject: RE RE RE: Life Updates

Oh, my little ELF, those crying sprees are still happening? In college we always chalked it up to the booze. I have no idea what those episodes mean, but have you thought about seeing someone? A therapist? Maybe it would help you…I really miss you, and I'm worried about you. I'm checking what time off I have for a visit. We'll get to the bottom of this. Oh! And say hi to your mumma Maureen for me.

-SAR

Sent from my iPhone

***

Sarah's gentle push towards therapy was nothing new; I'd been thinking of seeing someone for years. And I would never tell my mother this, but I knew I drank too much. I spent too much money on it, at the very least, money I didn't have. Plus, Sarah was right about how long it had been going on. My crying episodes weren't new. Maybe I was just a sad drunk. But I knew I shouldn't make a habit of opening weeping at McGreevey's on a Thursday night in front of coworkers. It was embarrassing.

So, I booked an appointment. And when the day of the appointment arrived, I came close to cancelling about eight times. I told myself I didn't need it. I had Sarah to vent to, I had Mel to complain about work to…I had friends. I wasn't some freak who needed psychological help. In the end, though, I kept the appointment. *You are kind of a freak.*

The train ride home from work seemed interminable, and so did the walk to my car, parked eight blocks away. For once I'd left enough of a buffer, so despite hitting traffic I made it to the therapist's office on time. I pulled onto a residential street, squinting at house numbers that matched the listing of the practice online. I'd chosen Dr. Rollins almost blindly through a database search. First making sure it was covered by insurance and close to my apartment, and before I lost my nerve, I clicked the red button: *Book Appointment*.

I parked up the steep driveway, yanked the emergency brake, and not for the first time in the last few weeks, I caught a strong sense of déjà vu.

The paint-cracked steps of the triple-decker creaked beneath my weight. Residences on either side closely sandwiched the building; I could see and hear shrieking children and the spray of a hose in an adjacent backyard. When I reached the door at the top of the steps I pushed the button next to a small, simple nameplate: *Dr. Elizabeth Rollins, Mental Health Counseling*. I was buzzed in.

Inside, standing at the top of the stairs, was a squat, frizzy-haired woman in her mid-fifties, thick spectacles atop her head. She wore cranberry-colored corduroy jeans and a linen shirt. She was beaming, and I smiled back, disarmed.

I climbed the steps and shook her hand. She led me to a small room and gestured towards a futon. For a moment, I stood over it: should I lie down on it like in the movies? It was so short, lengthwise, that I'd have to lay in the fetal position to fit.

Dr. Rollins observed my hesitation and chuckled. "You can just sit, for now."

I nodded, sat, and silenced my phone, placing it in my purse. I peeked inside one last time to make sure the cash co-pay was tucked in an accessible outer pocket in case I had to make a run for it. Dr. Rollins, who insisted I call her Liz, sat in a wicker chair across from me with a yellow notepad in her lap.

A few seconds of silence passed. I wrung my hands and tried to look fascinated by the generic nature pictures hanging on the wall. There was a bookcase, too, and I silently read the spines: *Dealing with Grief, Loss and the Human Brain, Coming Out: How to cope with intolerant family members*, and *Lucid Dreams: Psychophysiological studies of consciousness.*

It was Liz who finally spoke. "So."

"So," I said.

"I think you are my first client who skipped the phone screen and communicated only via email," she said, not unkindly.

"I got nervous. I almost canceled."

"That wouldn't have been a first. What brings you here?"

Hearing the question, I felt foolish. Was my life that bad?

I cleared my throat. "Well, I've been unhappy at work, and lonely. I feel so unsettled and out of sorts. I wish I could just be happy. I'm also starting to think I'm socially inept? Maybe it's anxiety. But, like, you could tell me that, of course."

I couldn't stop rambling. "And, uh, this happened a long time ago, and I'm not sure if it's affecting me now, after all these years, like, compounding my problems or something? But my dad died. When I was eleven, almost twelve. I've never really talked about it to anyone. My mom was so scared of losing my brother and me after he died that she was hyper vigilant, overprotective. We didn't have the best relationship, especially when I was a teenager. We're, like, fine now? But I feel so bad about how I treated her. And how, sometimes, I still treat her."

I paused. I was getting too far ahead of myself. "Well, also. The weird thing is, I can't recall many memories the year my dad died. It was a pretty rough year..." Tears were now streaming down my face and my stomach hurt. It wasn't a stomach pain due to nausea, but more a strain in my insides, like a pocket that would come unzipped if I let it.

I sighed and reached for a tissue on the side table, which quickly became drenched. Then I reached for two more.

Liz smiled. "Well! I would say that's a good start."

I laughed through more hiccups and sniffles. "I…I felt kind of stupid for coming here…like I'm blaming things on my dad when it happened so long ago."

Liz cocked her head. "Why, exactly, do you feel stupid?"

"Because my problems are trivial, I guess." I put air quotes around "problems."

Liz wrote down a note. She paused and then spoke slowly. "I would say the death of a parent at a young age is anything but trivial. You suffered a deep loss, a void in your life. Work is a central part of your identity. Longing for a partner and wanting love is a basic human need. So, altogether, feeling overwhelmed with these holes in your life, especially at your age, is not only common, but it can also feel particularly traumatizing. A quarter-life crisis, if you will."

"That's really a thing?"

"Yes."

"Oh, I just thought that was the type of thing websites use as click-bait for articles."

She cocked her head. "I don't know what 'click-bait' is, but I assure you, I have many patients of a similar age who are going through it. Is this the first time you've tried therapy?"

I shook my head.

"When was the last time?"

I glanced at the clock. Half an hour. "Just seeing if we have time for me to tell you about it."

Liz smiled. "We have time. Go on."

I told her the whole story. A couple months before my father's cancer spread like wildfire from his pancreas to his liver to his bones and finally to his brain, his oncologist suggested we all see a family therapist. My dad was reluctant about the whole thing, and at the time, I thought he was being a jerk. As an adult, I understood that the final, terminal chunk of his life accelerated so fast, so painfully, that his mind was likely unable to catch up, to process it all. But, unfortunately, that man—reticent, overwhelmed—was who Jack and I remembered most vividly.

The therapist had thinning dark hair and glasses. We sat in a semi-circle: my mother and father on the couch with Jack in between and me in a lone chair opposite them. I kicked my feet and kept my head down. I couldn't look my father in the face. But when I raised my head slightly, cocked to the side, I used my peripheral vision to look at him. He wore a Red Sox cap. Sparse gray tufts of hair dotted the base of his scalp. My dad had refused, thus far, to shave his head.

After what felt like an hour of silence, the therapist pointed the first question at me in a low, steady voice.

"Ellie, what are you feeling?"

I couldn't look at the therapist. I couldn't look at my parents either, or Jack, so I looked down. And then in the silence of the room, swift and without warning, I burst into tears. I couldn't form words—my throat thickened with mucus, worry, pain. It was always my stomach that hurt most. It was if my organs—my lungs and my heart—weighed too much. I could feel them sinking into my intestines like the middle of two couch cushions. Sobs came heaving out of my chest. My mom began crying, which just made me cry harder. Then Jack started in. What a mess.

"For cryin' out loud…." my father said under his breath, his face pained. He looked down at the floor.

The therapist cut through our mewling with a scratchy, throaty drawl. "There's an outpouring here—it seems you've all been holding your emotions inside. Would you agree, Ellie?"

I looked desperately at my parents. Did I agree? I sensed nodding would make things worse, for everyone. I shrugged my shoulders. I couldn't tell them I had no one to talk to; Sarah was at boarding school and could only talk on the phone limited hours of the week, and my "best friends" at school had perfect lives. Lauren had a mom and a dad, healthy, and she was rich. Rich compared to my family at least. And Maxine, her parents were divorced, but she was rich too. Her mom had a BMW! I tried my best to fit in with them, not ruffle their feathers, invite any comments about my sick dad. But they saw him, all skinny and gray. They saw him, and one time I even heard them snickering about him.

I said none of this, of course. I looked up at my mother, who appeared frightened and overwhelmed, which made no sense to me. As a social worker, she'd been trained in matters of dire psychological trauma and hardship, but was somehow inept at communicating her feelings with her own family.

"No one talks," she said suddenly, sniffling and stroking her fingers through Jack's blond curls. "Jon doesn't talk to the kids. Ellie doesn't ask me any questions—though I suspect she listens in on the line when I'm giving updates to friends, to family." She sneaked a look at me. I quickly looked down.

"And then," she hiccupped, "all Jack does is ask questions. And I have no answers, just dwindling hope. And he doesn't understand." Her thumb, jutting out from her tight fist resting in her lap, pointed at my dad.

The therapist cleared his throat. "Well, this is a start, Maureen."

He looked at my father. But he was still looking blankly at the floor.

So, he turned to my brother. "And, Jack, how do you feel about this?"

Jack looked up at my mother expectantly.

"He's seven. I mean, c'mon." My father's voice was almost

whiny, petulant. He turned to my mother, shifting his body, closing his shoulders off even more to the therapist. "Are we really subjecting him to this, Maureen? Are we?"

Silence.

Dad shifted in his seat. His jeans were loose, his throat swollen. He looked pudgy from the neck up, from the meds, and malnourished from the neck down.

My mother was silent; her face stone. Finally, she turned to face my dad, pushing her shoulders back, jutting out her chin. "Subjecting him to what, Jon? *Talking?*"

"Stop," I said, my words muffled through my hands.

"Speak up, Ellie. What you would like them to stop?" asked the therapist.

I lowered my wrists and looked up. I wished my father would talk to me. Tell me what he was thinking. Confide in me. Tell me his favorite song, his favorite number. What he liked about my mom. What he liked about me.

With the therapist, my mother, and my younger brother watching intently—I choked.

"It's okay, Ellie," the therapist said. He looked at my brother. "Jack? What are you feeling?"

The boy, the tiny boy in his Superman t-shirt, looked at me now.

His lips trembled. "I…"

"Yes, Jack," my mother pressed. Nodding, prodding.

"I…just don't want Daddy to die." And with that he started wailing and shaking. I didn't know he knew was dying was. Maybe he didn't. He buried his head in my mother's chest.

Now my father was crying, my mother was crying, and my sobs felt like they would collapse my lungs, not just my stomach. The only person in the room who seemed pleased was the therapist.

"Happy now?" my father growled at my mother. He got up, uneasily, and limped out. The door slammed behind him.

"I'm sorry," my mom said to the therapist as she gathered her purse. It looked as if she was going to say something else, then thought against it. "I think it's time we go."

My mother hustled us out into the waiting room. While she filled out some paperwork and spoke in whispers to the nurses at the front desk, my brother and I read some *Highlights* magazines until she told us to follow her out to the car.

It was a beautiful sunny day, unseasonably warm for February. When we reached the parking lot, my father wasn't in the car. My mother told Jack and I to hop in anyway, and we watched through the semi-tinted windows as she walked helplessly around the lot, and then back in and out of the cancer wing of the hospital. She came back outside and cased the lot a second time, like she expected to find him squatting in between two cars, or possibly squatting *in* a car. Even Jack knew not to rile my mother any further, so when she returned to the car we avoided asking the obvious and sat tight in the back.

After fifteen minutes driving around and searching for my father, I couldn't stand the silence and asked, "Do you think he's okay? Did he get hit by a car? Does he hate us? Does he not want to come back?" The inquiries spurted out of my mouth. Through the rearview mirror my mother's expression remained stoic, and she didn't answer me.

We circled cul-de-sacs and shopping mall parking lots. We were stunted at dead-end roads. Just when I was convinced my father threw himself in front of a car somewhere my mother said, "Ah. I know." She whipped around in a three-point turn and the centrifugal force propelled me against the window and Jack against my arm.

We found my father at one of the docks off a small side street. He sat with his shoes beside him and his feet dangling just above the water. He'd always complained of his ankles being swollen; maybe he was cooling them off. He was staring out at the moored boats, which ranged from seventy-two-foot yachts to Boston Whalers to little dinghies.

My mother pulled into an empty dirt lot behind the dock and she hissed at us to stay inside. We watched out the window as she walked up and stood behind him. She kneeled on the ground and put one hand on his shoulder. He didn't move, and they just stayed like that, not speaking. We watched, rapt, with our noses squished against the glass window. After a few minutes, he got up and walked to the passenger side of the car. My mom followed and got back into the driver's side, her cheeks ruddy. He stared out the window the whole ride home. Not a word to Jack or me.

I sat behind him, staring at the back of his cap, reading the cursive *Red Sox* over and over. I wanted so much to reach around the seat and hug him or put my own hand on his shoulder. I sat very still, though. He seemed so distant that it scared me. Like he'd given up.

***

Liz interrupted my story here, her eye on the clock. "That was the only time you tried therapy?"

"I fought with my mother months later, after he died, about going to therapy again. She said it would help me. I said it wouldn't. Things escalated, and we ended up screeching at each other for a half hour, exchanging horrible insults. I denounced her parenting skills, her cooking. I told her I wished Dad had lived instead of her."

I'd never forget what she said next. "Sometimes," she said through gritted teeth, "I wish you weren't my daughter. That I hadn't given birth to such a wretch."

I ran, sliding in my socks on the hardwood, hopping the

steps to my room, crying and crying and crying until I had to gasp big wheezing gulps of air. How dare she say such a thing, I thought. How dare she.

A few minutes later, there was a knock at my door. I sat up cross-legged on my bed.

"What?" I spat.

The door opened with a small creak, and Jack's blond curls appeared level with the doorknob. His huge brown eyes looked up at me, the saddest I had ever seen them.

He held what looked like a piece of paper. He lingered at the door.

"You can come in."

He stepped in and closed the door, looking around in wonder at my room. It was so messy it looked like a bomb went off. He wouldn't know which end was up anyway, because he was never allowed in.

"What's that?" I asked, eyeing the paper in his hand.

He walked closer, shy. He held it out.

"It's…it's a picture. Of Dad."

It was Dad holding Jack, when he was about three or four, in his lap on a swing set. The swing set he had built for us.

"That's very nice, Jack." I was on the verge of tears. I handed it back. "Where'd you get it?"

"Mom put all the rest of the old pictures in the basement. I found it when I was playing down there."

"She just wants to forget him."

"I think…I think they just make her sad."

"Well, they make all of us sad. That's no excuse." I hated my mother then, for not keeping our father's memory alive, for not forcing us to talk about him as a family. She wanted a therapist to do all the work.

"I can show you where, if you want." He didn't meet my eyes, probably scared I'd say something cruel.

I wanted to squeeze him into a big bear hug. I nodded. "Good work, brother. Yeah, maybe you can show me when she's in the shower or something."

"Okay." He smiled and looked at my bookshelf with the board games stacked unevenly. Then we heard my mother rustling downstairs, the clicking of light switches. He lowered his voice as he tiptoed towards the door. "Wanna play UNO with me tomorrow?"

"No…ugh. Fine. Just one game."

He smiled and booked it towards his room at the sound of my mother's light steps on the stairs. I switched off my light and tried to sleep.

***

By the time I finished, I'd cried myself tired. I was relieved when Liz glanced at the clock and said, "Thank you for sharing that with me. We're out of time, but I wanted to say before you go that I could see that as you spoke about that day, you seemed to open up and really share the emotions from that time. It gave me a great window into you."

I didn't have much to say to that, so I just smiled.

"Shall we schedule another appointment?" she asked.

I nodded. I handed her my co-pay and then walked out to my car. Sitting in the driver's seat, I took stock of how I felt, aside from the exhaustion. A single visit was by no means a panacea, but I did feel a little better. I purposely hadn't mentioned anything about the visions of the strange man. I figured I'd dumped enough on the table to start with. I'd ease into the weird stuff.

I drove home with the radio off, stealing quick glances in the rearview at my swollen face and bloodshot eyes. I pictured my likely empty apartment, Ricki gone, the hum of the fridge, the city noise, the utter lonesomeness of the place. I drove around a little while longer before going home.

5

The Blind Date

From: ellie_frites@symbicore.com
To: Muppet <sarah_mupetta@email.com>
Subject: The rapist I mean therapist

You'll be proud of me, Sar. I didn't chicken out of my appointment. It went pretty well. I cried a ton, laid it all out there. I went through a half a box of tissues. I'm still processing everything, but, overall, it was a positive experience. Plus, no weird visions since. I didn't tell her about them yet though…I'll keep you posted on when I go next.

PS: Is that creep Caleb from the bar still texting you dick pics? You haven't sent him a booby pic back or anything, have you?!?! Please say no my SMART nurse friend Sarah. And if the answer is yes, for the love of God you'd better have cropped out your noggin.

–ELF

From: Muppet <sarah_muppeta@email.com>
To: ellie_frites@symbicore.com
Subject: RE: The rapist I mean therapist

My sweet Ellie!!!! I'm so happy for you. I'm glad you went through with it. Maybe you have, like, a bank of tears, and you have to spend the currency and invest in yourself, like you're a stock or something, versus more frivolous stuff like shirts from Forever21. You know? Oh, I know. I'm terrible at metaphors. That doesn't make any sense. I'm a nurse...LAY OFF ME! I'M STARVING! (Chris Farley voice).

PS: Awesome news: There's a job opening at Mass General Hospital! I applied, and I have an interview! I was thinking: Since Ricki is never home anyway, maybe she would want to sublet to me, and move in with her boyfriend? Or maybe she could just move out early. A couple months before the lease is up isn't a huge deal. Half her shit is at Tyler's place already, right?

RE: Caleb. No head shots. No comment beyond that...

–S

Sent from my iPhone

From: ellie_frites@symbicore.com
To: Ricki Bordane <pretty_ricki@email.com>
Subject: Can we talk?

Hey Ricki,

Let me know when you'll be home next. I have a proposition.

–E

From: melania_fernandez@symbicore.com
To: ellie_frites@symbicore.com
Subject: This message has no subject.

SOMEONE'S BEEN ASKING ABOUT YOU...

Melania Fernandez, Customer Service NINJA
Symbicore Software
Clients R.A.V.E.! (TM) about us! x5624

Please save the environment. Do not print this email.

***

Mel bounced up and down in her chair beside me. "His name's Tim, and word has it...he's into you."

"What does he look like?" I asked.

"Dunno."

"Dunno?"

"Dunno."

"What department does he work in?"

"Um..." Mel touched the tip of her nose. "Marketing?"

"Marketing...as in Direct Mail? Web Marketing? Customer Insights? Database Marketing?"

Mel shrugged. "A little birdy told me he was asking what your name was. Then he contacted me over SymbiChat. We're getting the ball rolling. You don't have to lift a finger." She looked down at my legs and scrunched her nose. "Just don't wear those pants."

I threw up my hands.

We were sitting in a conference room at a long oval table as far away possible from Buster, who was attempting to get his PowerPoint to work so that our colleagues from Amsterdam could join the WebEx. We had important "talking points" to discuss. According to Buster's bulleted list in the calendar invite, our customer surveys indicated that we were not conducting ourselves as R.A.V.E.!-worthy employees.

A red dot darted across the ceiling, the table, and then the wall—it was Buster's laser pointer. Annie, a forty-year old

Dutch woman who had been inexplicably slogging away in Customer Service at Symbicore for seven years, appeared at the top right corner of the enlarged screen. Buster cleared his throat and asked, "You hear me, Annie?"

Mel finished tapping a message on her phone and then slipped it between her legs. She then scooted her chair closer to me, leaned into my shoulder, and whispered out of the side of her mouth, "Double date. Tonight. Seven. I'll pick you up."

"Double? Who are you dating?" I hissed back.

"You'll see."

"Flavor of the month?"

She smirked. "No—"

"Girls!" said the honk voice.

"Sorry," we chirped, straightening our notepads and erecting our spines against the back of our chairs.

For the rest of the meeting, I panicked about the blind date that was mere hours away. How terrible would it be to see this person around the office if he didn't end up liking me? Or worse—he liked me at first, but then he'd dump me unceremoniously over SymbiChat and our romance would come full circle? We'd have to see each other on the elevator, staring placidly ahead as if he didn't know what my vagina hole looked like. Or like I didn't know he washed his sheets once every five weeks. I would have to get a new job.

Then I perked up. Maybe the mortifying failure of a workplace romance would be a good thing. Maybe it would impel to me get the hell out of here.

I looked up at Buster, who was waving his arms around wildly, and saw that today the outline of his pit stains resembled a Basset Hound.

I looked at the clock again. Three and a half hours to go. And by the time I got home from work on the train, I wouldn't even have time to shower or throw an outfit on my credit card. As softly as I could, without moving my lips, I said, "Mel, I'm gonna kill you."

***

When Mel and I walked in the door of the restaurant a fashionable fifteen minutes late, my intended was leaning against the bar. I recognized him before he even turned around. And how could I not, with that red hair? My personal Keymaster, who let me into the Customer Service wing on days I forgot my badge, was, evidently, my blind date.

Standing next to Tim the Redhead was Savannah Carlson, a bodacious bombshell from sales. They were smiling at one another, and she put her hand on his shoulder. I took one look at her long gazelle legs, toothpick waist, and shiny black hair. A stab of jealousy pierced my chest. What was *she* doing here?

Then my underarms started to sweat. Did Mel misconstrue the SymbiChats from her "little birdy"? Was Tim on the double date with *Savannah*? Did he even know I was in the equation? Maybe wires got crossed, and he abbreviated D.D., as in "designated driver, not "double date," thinking the greasy-haired girl was a little slow, since she forgot her key card so much…

I tried grabbing Mel's arm, but she was already marching up to the both of them. "Hey, guys!"

They turned. Savannah shot Mel a side smile and put her hand on Mel's back as she kissed her cheek. That was when it dawned on me. Mel's date was Savannah Carlson.

My surprise wasn't over Mel dating a woman. She had told me weeks ago, after two Red Bull Vodkas, that she was a "big ol' lesbo."

I was surprised because first, Savannah Carlson was a big ol' lesbo, too, and second, while Mel was cute, she wasn't nearly as glamorous as Savannah.

As the three of them greeted one another, I stood

awkwardly outside their little semicircle. Finally, Mel noticed me mousing around and shoved me towards Tim.

"Tim, Ellie, Ellie, Tim."

We shook hands.

I thought back to the way he would push open the door, flash a smile, and saunter back to his desk in one fluid motion. All in all, he'd let me in three, maybe four times. I'd found his breezy, confident manner attractive, but he'd barely nodded in my direction. He was the last person I'd have guessed was interested in me.

A hostess led us to a rounded corner booth. I slipped in first and landed in the middle, and already my bladder ached in apprehension. I'd have to disrupt everyone's meals to get out. I could see it already: me slithering across the seat like a legless sea lion, the vinyl cushion making fart noises in my wake.

It was darker inside the restaurant than it was outside. I drew the menu close to my face to read it.

"Do you wear glasses?" Tim asked. He'd slid in to my left.

"No, it's just dark in here. And the font is baby-sized."

Tim picked up a menu, peered at it closely, and nodded. "Yup. Infant-sized."

To my right was Mel, and Savannah sat with her thigh so close to Mel's it was almost imbricated. Savannah's head bent back as she laughed and squeezed Mel's arm. One more surprise: Mel hadn't seemed the PDA type.

I turned back to the menu, pondering what to drink. Something weak, like a light beer. I didn't want to want to ruin anything.

"So, you like Symbicore?" Tim asked. His left arm was draped across the back of the booth, and if I sat back his fingers might have grazed the nape of my neck. I stayed leaned forward with my boobs crushed against the table.

I paused and wondered how to respond. Should I be

honest, or politely chipper? I chose something in the middle. "I don't really like Symbicore. But I'm trying to."

He nodded and laughed.

I relaxed a bit; I always appreciated an easy laugher. "It's been over two years," I continued. "I'm looking for a way out of customer service, because clearly it's the worst job to have there, but…yeah. Still figuring it out." I sighed. "Do you like it?"

He shrugged. "It's okay. I've only been there, let's see…eight months? The honeymoon period is over." He paused. "Those Interface meetings are kind of absurd. I thought Oliver was pretty cool from what I'd read about him as this, like, forward-thinking CEO, but man…I think the guy just likes to talk. And embarrass people."

Oliver Windig, our Napolean-syndromed CEO, did indeed embarrass people. A lot. Our company meetings were not called "meetings," for one. We were to call them "Interfaces." If Oliver heard anyone refer to an Interface as a "meeting," he shoved a microphone in his or her face and barked at them for five minutes in front of the whole Cambridge office, plus all the employees from Amsterdam, London, Paris, and Sydney, their floating heads smiling dumbly on monitors along the perimeter of the room. Oliver usually ended his tirades by forcing a poor sap to recite the monthly company tagline. I cringed, reminding myself grudgingly to study the R.A.V.E.! acronym lest he called on me in front of everyone.

I sighed. "Those company Interfaces make me question where my life is going."

Tim laughed again and asked, "Where do you sit at those things?"

"The way, way back," I said, pleased as he laughed again. "We have to hide from our manager, Buster, who sits in the front row."

Savannah leaned in and put her hand to her mouth. "Sorry to interrupt. But, Buster? Buster Flaherty?"

I nodded.

"He's still at Symbicore?"

"You know him?" Mel asked.

"Yes, I know him," Savannah said. "We were in the same orientation class. We were junior sales people, back in the day. He was terrible at his job, and he kept trying to get a promotion, and finally our boss, Terry, essentially demoted him to customer service." She paused. "Oh. Sorry, guys." She smiled at Mel and me. "No offense."

"None taken," I said quickly, admiring both Savannah's smooth skin and self-control; she hadn't touched the bread in the basket. I'd already sent two down my gullet, date-shmate.

"Please go on about Buster," I said. "This is too good."

"Well, that's it." Savannah shrugged. "Buster got moved over to C.S., and that was five years ago. I didn't know he still worked at Symbicore, honestly."

"He's still only a Manager-in-Training after five years?" I asked, incredulous. "No wonder he's such a dickwad."

There was a comfortable lull in conversation after the waitress delivered our food and we ate. I tried my best to not let the meat juice from my ill-chosen burger drip down my chin. As I was mid-bite, Tim asked if I'd been to any of Symbicore's happy hours.

I put up my pointer finger as I chewed for an interminable amount of time and swallowed the too-big bite so hard it hurt. *Could you be more gross?* I scolded myself.

Finally, with a mouth free of red meat, I said, "I've been to a few." Understatement of the year. "You?"

"Not too many," he said. "The thought of spending extracurricular time with work people doesn't appeal to me." He winced. "Well, plus I had a girlfriend until kind of recently. I heard those things are hookup fests. I stayed away for that reason too, I guess."

The more Tim talked, leaning back in a nonchalant slouch, sighing occasionally, stretching his legs, making easy jokes, the more I felt my insides leap. I liked Tim's red hair. It was less Conan O'Brien and more the dude from Dexter, who you could barely tell was a redhead. Tim's face was tanned and symmetrical, and his eyes were a beautiful hazel-brown.

He caught me staring and grinned. "Like what you see?"

Flustered, I said, "I'm, um, no…"

"No?"

"Yes! Yes. I guess. I don't know. I don't know yet."

"I'm just joking. But I'll tell ya something. You seem like a swell chick."

"Who says swell?"

He shrugged. "Me."

"A person who says that word is the equivalent of someone who winks," I said.

"Winks?"

"Yeah it's, like, corny and old fashioned, and if anyone did it to me I would say, 'Who winks?'"

"That's fair," he said, smiling.

Mel's head swung around; she'd caught the end of our conversation. She kicked me under the table with her little elfin boot, hard.

I kicked her back without breaking eye contact with Tim. I had to admit. He was pretty swell.

***

It was a little over a week later and I now sat in my cubicle, cursing the very day Mel set me up with Tim. At the top of my email inbox was a message from him that I'd read and over and over, wanting to die each time. *Ellie, are you okay?*

The rest of the date had gone wonderfully. We even agreed to a second date, and he *actually* called. But because I am the biggest self-sabotaging idiot on the planet, that first date euphoria proved to be short-lived.

The second date with Tim kicked off with a nice dinner in the South End. There were jokes. There was laughter and steady conversation with few awkward silences. I was over the moon.

Then we decided to get a couple more drinks at the bar next door after dinner. It was busy inside, and dark, and we kept getting bumped. Conversation still flowed, though, and at one point he asked me about my parents, which naturally necessitated mention of my dead dad, an exchange I got through without growing emotional. I offered a perfunctory, "He died a long time ago. I was so young."

Tim let it drop and changed the subject to something else. I was a little tipsy by this point, and now couldn't recall what else we started talking about. But I did remember what happened next.

His eyes drifted to a skinny blonde sitting with her friend at a nearby table, and I became overwhelmed by how attractive she was. I imagined his hand in the curve of the girl's hip—an inward curve, not an outward curve like mine—and wondered what he was doing out with me when there was someone like that in the same room. There were women like that everywhere I looked, thinner, or more buxom, probably funnier, or much smarter, driven, or already more successful, not a loser customer service rep whose boss put her on a performance plan because she can't control her attitude.

Suddenly, boom—the floodgates opened. I turned away, my arms stiff in front of me, clearing the mass of bodies in my path so I could get to the door and run outside. Through a sheet of tears I hailed a cab, which came quickly, and I jumped in without looking back. I didn't even know if Tim saw what direction I'd raced off to, but I did know I left him stranded there with no explanation.

The problem now, as I bent my computer screen so my inbox was visible again, was if I wanted to sop up that mortifying trail of tears with an explanation and somehow salvage this two-date relationship, I'd have to actually have an explanation. My meltdown made not one iota of sense, not even to me.

I marked his email unread, then stared at the subject line of the message above it.

Confirmation: Dr. Elizabeth Rollins 6:00 p.m.

I debated whether to drag it into the trash bin. My first session had gone so well, but I'd held back. I didn't even discuss what had been bothering me, the visions. And now, with the added stress of Tim, I felt overwhelmed. I wouldn't know where to start. While my palm lingered on the mouse, a breathy heat tickled the nape of my neck. I whirled around.

Mel was hunched over my right shoulder, pretending to read my inbox with exaggerated interest. She did this often, usually to recite irate client emails in a snobbish British accent. Today, though, she was peering at something wholly personal, something I was not prepared to share. I bent the laptop screen down and tried to smile. "Snoop."

"Someone's jumpy. Whatcha lookin' at?"

I had no choice but to tell the truth. "It's…it's an appointment to see a therapist. To go back, actually. I've seen her once already."

Mel backed away and put her hands up. "Oh. Sorry, dude. I didn't mean to pry—"

I shook my head. "It's fine. I don't care if you see it. I just don't know if I'm going to go again. I'm torn."

"I didn't know you were having problems." Mel motioned around her with her hands. "I mean, aside from this."

I left out the part about the visions, but said, "I've been thinking about my childhood, particularly my dad's death. I barely remember the year it happened."

Mel bit her lip. "Your dad passed? You never told me that."

I lowered my voice. Through the glass cubicle wall—why glass, why even have a wall? I wondered once again—I caught Susan Ellmore's beady eyes staring at us, her curly head leaned all the way forward.

I bugged my eyes at her and she looked down.

I cringed. "To be honest with you, it's not just my dad. That's a part of it, but more immediately, like, now, is what happened with Tim the other night. It was a disaster. I sabotaged the whole night by acting like a jealous freak. God," I said, burying my face in my hand again. "He probably thinks I'm such a psycho."

Mel bit her lip. "Whatever happened, Ellie, I'm sure is not a huge deal. Everyone has their own issues, their own crap." Mel narrowed her eyes, her voice grave, and repeated, "Everyone. No shame in that."

I smiled. "I should just talk to you instead of a therapist."

"Well, I think you're brave for seeking help. If you need anything, you let me know. I'm a good listener." Then she said something in Spanish I didn't understand, but I nodded anyway. It sounded like something nice.

She smiled at me. "That means, 'You're a good friend to me, so I hate to see you so sad.'"

A lump formed in my throat. "Thanks, Mel, that means a lot."

She patted me on the shoulder and returned to her cubicle just as Buster came waddling back from the kitchen, slurping on a Diet Coke. I turned back to my computer before he could make eye contact with me and minimized my inbox.

6

Wake me up in Dreamland

This morning, I woke up in my childhood bed. Swinging my shortened legs to the floor, I almost fell down. The soft pads of my feet crunched a pile of CDs and hair clips. Alanis watched over me from the wall, her brown eyes following me out the door.

I limped to the bathroom to pee and almost plopped right onto my little brother's piss. "Jack!" I screamed, "Stop peeing all over the toilet seat you mor-on!"

At the sink I picked up my pink toothbrush and brushed my teeth until my eyes went wide in the mirror, the foam from the toothpaste spilling out the sides of my mouth. I pulled my hair until it hurt. I slapped my face. There was something so familiar and routine about every move I was making, yet here was something…off. I felt detached, outside my body, except I also felt every prickle on my skin, every speck of sand underneath my bare feet on the wood floor. *Ah.* As I padded out of the bathroom I whispered to myself, *You're dreaming.*

I walked downstairs, letting my stumpy legs lead the way. I poured cereal, packed my backpack, checked the time, and caught the bus.

And now here I sit in Mrs. Ford's sixth grade science class, listening to her prattle on about cumulonimbus clouds at the chalkboard. The date printed in big block letters on the top right corner of the board: April 15, 1996.

My left forearm and wrist curl towards my chest as I write in the diary splayed between the spirals of my notebook. I show no one this diary. I use it to record my dreams, especially my Dad Dream. The one I have over and over. The one where he's not sick.

Across the desk cluster is Maxine. One time, she told everyone a cover artist discovered her in Sally Beauty Supply and asked if she'd model for the Sweet Valley High series. Everyone fell over themselves about that, but do you think she made the cover of *Tall, Dark and Deadly* or *Kiss Me at Midnight*? Of course not.

Max catches me gawking at her. I smile; maybe I can get her good graces today. She curls her lip in disgust and rolls her eyes.

She whispers to Lauren, who sits beside her, using a chunk of her hair as a wall. My stomach drops at this. Ever since my dad got sick earlier in the year, Lauren and I had been drifting. I was fast losing her to Max. Plus, I'm pretty sure it was Max who convinced her not to go to my dad's funeral by spreading the false rumor that it was an open casket. That it would be too "creepy." God, I look up at the date. He died last week.

Max looks down at my legs. "Where'd you get those cords?"

My impulse is to draw my legs in quickly under the desk so she can't see them. After a slight pause, I tell Max I got the cords from a catalog, praying she'd stop there.

"Not from Delia's," she says. She ticks a list in the air with her pointer finger. "Not from Alloy…"

My tongue clings to the roof of my mouth and I stare at her razor-straight bangs like a dolt.

"Which one, Ellie? I didn't hear you."

"I…I can't remember." I look down.

"Bradlees," she shout-whispers to Lauren, who, I notice with a sinking heart, does not stick up for me. Max makes an L shape with her hand on her forehead. Loser.

Suddenly, I jolt upright. My heart starts pounding and I stare at Max and cock my head. Loser. A rush of unease, then stronger—a hot panic—floods through my chest. White dots interfere with my vision…and then it clears.

I am in the dark woods of the Hollow, running, chasing something, someone. I see a red dot that's receding into the dim night and into the thick forestation. I'm panting, hard. I stop to catch my breath and rest my hands on my knees. I call out, "Max!"

I blink, and I'm no longer in the woods. But I'm not back in the classroom, in Mrs. Ford's science class; I'm back in my childhood bedroom, sitting cross-legged on my bed. My stuffed animals are kicked to the carpet and my bookcase is propped against the door. My mother bangs on the wood with her open palm, calling out, "Ellie? Honey? Ellie, open this door!"

I don't budge. After a pause, she bursts through, shoulder first, but the door opens only a crack. Hunched forward like a linebacker, she slides the bookcase out of her path with her shoulder, slowly, until the entryway widens. A few of my Nancy Drew hardcovers tumble off the shelf like dominoes.

She steps over them and rushes to me, repeating, "Honey, I'm sorry, I'm so sorry." But my head is thumping, and her words are drowned out. I reach to feel the back of my head and my fingers graze a painful lump. I look beside me. An ice pack melts on my pillow. Thumbprints of blood stain the sheets. My mind races, and of all things, of all people, I can only think about Maxine.

My mother sits on the edge of my bed and tries to hug me. I slap at her, kick at her, try to push her off of me. To get away from her, I dig my heels into the mattress and try to heave my body backwards, until my skull whaps against the headboard. After a millisecond, I'm seized with a shock of pain that radiates from the behind my ears to my temples.

My mother's mouth is open—she's talking, but I hear nothing. A blood-curdling scream echoes through the room. I jerk up and look around. Is that my brother? Is he okay? Then I realize, as my mother grips my tiny hands in hers, begging, "Ellie, please stop," that the scream is coming from me.

***

I looked up. Dr. Rollins, or Liz, as she kept insisting I call her, was jotting down the last of her notes. "What year did it say it was in the dream?" she asked.

"It said April 15, 1996 on the board," I said. "He died just a week before."

"And you were…"

"Eleven. I'd turn twelve that summer."

"You remember seemingly every detail about this dream," Liz mused.

I smoothed the pages of my diary, still open to the entry. "I wrote everything down when I woke up. I haven't remembered my dreams in forever. Not since I was little."

"About how long ago did you have these types of lucid, memorable dreams? Do you know?"

"Um, I think…I think maybe around the same age I was in this dream. The year following my dad's death. I recorded those dreams in a diary then, too. It was like, meta. I had that dream diary open in the dream. Just like this one." I pointed to it.

"These dreams around the time your father died, were they disturbing?"

I shrugged and said, "I don't think so. They weren't disturbing so much as frustrating. I had this one dream over and over. My dad was standing across from me, far off in this grassy field. It was dusk. He was calling to me, telling me to come to him. He was young, healthy. He wasn't all puffy from the chemo; his pants weren't falling down..." I trailed off; I was beginning to get choked up.

"And you'd record those?"

I nodded.

Liz said it for me. "You wanted to remember him that way."

I nodded again. "I was so afraid I'd forget what he looked like. Healthy, I mean."

"How would those dreams end?"

"I could never reach him. I tripped in holes, ran into landmines, boulders—he kept getting further and further away. I never caught up to him before I woke up. As a habit, I've always kept a journal beside my bed, even now, because part of me always hopes to have that dream again. And to finally catch up to him."

"So, this dream you had last night. I think it's great that you wrote everything down immediately when you woke up. Did you happen to include any lingering feelings, any more emotional responses to the dream, aside from what you saw?"

I nodded.

"Do you mind sharing that with me?"

I skimmed to the end of the entry. "Feel sick. Scared. Déjà vu."

Liz was about to say something, but I cut her off. "Um, I also recorded the waking visions I was telling you about, the one from the bar and from the courtyard. The tall guy wearing the red hat."

Liz stared at me intently. "Are you positive this man you're conjuring, this man in the red hat, is not your father?"

"I'm positive," I said, re-crossing my legs. "I told you, my father wasn't tall. He was maybe...five-foot-nine. And even before he got sick, he had a very slender build. Nothing like this guy I keep seeing. Plus, in the dream, if it's around the same time as I was in the classroom, my dad had already passed away."

"But in these visions, and in the dream, you can't see this man's face," Liz pressed.

I shook my head. "No. It's...blurry. Or actually, it's not really there."

"The events in this dream, your classroom, waking up in your bedroom. Can you say with any certainty that these were events, conversations, that happened all those years ago? In other words, are they actual memories?" she asked.

"Yes and no. Obviously, I can't remember exactly what I talked about with my friends when I was eleven. But the gist of it rings true: the way Max would talk down to me, the insecurity, all that. Except..."

"Except?" Liz pressed.

"Well, that weird stuff with the bloody sheets, the lump on my head—I don't remember that ever happening. Or chasing someone through the woods."

Liz dragged her middle finger down her page of notes, not realizing she was flipping me the bird. She stopped on a line towards the end of the page. "Tell me about your relationship with this Max."

I shrugged. "She was a twelve-year-old who looked like a sixteen-year-old. She got boobs before everyone else, she got her braces off before everyone else, she was, like, perfect looking," I paused, "and she was a horrible little bitch."

Liz chuckled. "Okay, and when was the last you saw her?"

I struggled to remember. "Honestly? I don't know."

"Middle school, high school?"

I shook my head. "I...seriously, Liz. I have no idea. I can't even remember the rest of that year. I remember high school...I remember eighth grade graduation...well, kind of. Who I had for teachers and whatnot. But Max..." I was sincerely at a loss.

"What about this…" Liz consulted her notes again, "…Lauren Vine person. Do you remember anything else about her?"

I shifted my position on the futon and said, "It's funny, when I started having these vision things, and I went home and looked at some photo albums, I realized I hadn't thought about either Lauren or Max in forever. I don't remember how we stopped being friends, what became of either of them, anything."

Liz raised her eyebrows. "Alright. How about—" she stopped and glanced at the clock "—oh, this hour flew, didn't it?"

I nodded and started gathering my things. I plucked a check out my purse and reached out to hand it to her.

"I want to try something new next time," Liz said, gingerly taking the check. She repositioned her glasses to better hold her hair back and rocked back in her chair. "It will require your written consent; it's a form of hypnotherapy. It's experimental. I'll send you some materials over email. I think you're a perfect candidate, with your ability to dream so lucidly. Not many people can do that."

I stood up. "Well, I could dream like that this one time…but I haven't for years," I reminded her.

"Exactly. Something, I think, is just itching to emerge from your consciousness. A memory you may be repressing."

I didn't like the sound of that.

"We'll talk more next week," Liz said, her smile overtaking her face, her eyes dancing. She stood up, and as she walked me to the door she slipped the check into her pocket. She followed me and leaned against the banister as I descended the stairs to the exit. She called after me. "We'll get to the bottom of this. It may not be the most traditional route to get there, but we'll find out."

I couldn't muster the same enthusiasm. "Uh, okay," I finally said over my shoulder, wishing she'd just let me go. My stomach started garbling. I didn't know if I was ravenous or just sick from nerves.

"All right, bye, Ellie," she said.

"Bye, Dr. Rollins."

"Remember, call me Liz!" She waved at me from the top of the stairs.

It wasn't until I walked out to my car that stopped in my tracks, and thought, Do I even *want* to find out?

***

When I got home I slumped down on the couch, my mind reeling. On top of all the eerie shit drummed up in therapy, problems from my present life were looming larger. Ricki still hadn't been home to talk about moving out early. I had two voicemails, and an email, from an understandably antsy Sarah, who had officially been offered a job at Mass General and needed to make living arrangements. "I can't wait much longer, ELF," she said in her last voicemail. "Can't you get a simple yes or a no from Ricki?"

Then there was the unresolved debacle with Tim from earlier. The law of Seeing People You Never Saw Before, But When You Don't Want to See Them, You See Them Everywhere was in effect. I saw him on the way to the train even though I'd never been let out at the same time as him; his manager usually let his team leave early if they went in early. He was walking impossibly slow, and despite my best efforts at lollygagging a safe distance behind, I was threatening to catch up.

He stopped at a crosswalk at one point, turned around, and locked eyes with me. I panicked and darted into the street to walk on the opposite side. Right at that moment, an MBTA bus whizzed by, almost barreling me into high heaven. It missed me by inches but honked so loud it drew attention from other Symbicoreans walking to the train, many of whom stopped to ask—loudly—if I was okay. Tim was staring at me. I dipped into a nearby coffee shop just so I wouldn't cross paths with him at the train station.

I closed my eyes and tried to block that mortifying scene from my headspace. The easiest dilemma of all seemed to be dealing with Ricki first. I dialed her number and it went straight to voicemail. Her mailbox was full. I texted her again. *Can we please talk? Trying to get hold of u.*

I wasn't hungry, and I barely had any energy to get off the couch to make anything. All I had was boxed pasta and canned soup, anyway.

I picked at the couch cushion, my thoughts wandering back to what we discussed in therapy. Should I take a dream seriously? Should I at least ask my mom about that bloody scene of me and her in my bedroom? Liz strongly suggested I should, but I felt silly asking someone about a dream.

I was just too exhausted to do so right now anyway. I wouldn't be able to handle all my mother's follow-up questions. I knew what she would focus on—me going to therapy after all these years. I wondered what she'd say about the hypnotherapy suggestion; my mother was also in the mental health field. I was afraid she'd call Dr. Rollins a quack. I'd avoid that can of worms for now, I thought, at least for tonight.

Since I didn't want to return Sarah's calls, only to let her know I still hadn't gotten hold of Ricki, I was forced to face my next dilemma: Tim. I needed to explain myself, and apologize for the scene I caused on our second date. Oh, and explain why I threw myself in front of a bus so I wouldn't have to run into him today. I stared at my phone. My first inclination was to just let the thing die. Why would Tim want me? I was obviously acting like a crazy person. But…he'd emailed me. He genuinely wanted to know if I was all right.

Arrested there on the couch in the fetal position, I heard

a light scratching on the hardwood over by the hallway near Ricki's room, and when I lifted my head, I saw the mouse skittering along the sideboards in plain sight. I suddenly felt itchy.

Suddenly, my phone rang. My heart pounded hard as I held up the ringing phone, sheathed in its hot pink case. It was Tim. I let it go to voicemail. I was unaccustomed to a member of the male sex calling me on the phone. Where were the flippant, typo-riddled text messages? The late-night, Neanderthal booty calls?

I punched in the wrong voicemail password three times before I was able to listen to his message.

"Hey, Ellie," Tim began, his voice deep, his tone pleasant, "just, uh, you know, seeing if you got my email. From yesterday? Or two days ago. Can't get the days straight, hah. Anyway, uh, I hate how we left things at the bar—I feel like I said something to upset you. If I did, I wanted to apologize. In person, of course. We were having a good time. I thought…" He trailed off.

I pulled the phone from my ear and stared at it in shock. Then listened more.

He was still going. "I thought maybe we could get together again, and maybe start over? I saw you today, uh, almost get hit by a bus. God, I wanted to run up to you but you didn't really…anyway, if you didn't want to talk about the other night, I mean, it's not a huge deal. Uh…oh man. I'm just rambling up a storm here. Just, um, if you want to call me back, that would be great. If not, totally fine too… Okay, uh, yeah. Bye, Ellie."

I extracted the phone from my ear again and peered at the screen in amazement. He was being so normal. And nice.

With sweaty palms and the urge to throw up, I called him back. First we danced around the incident; we small talked about the new lime green Adirondack chairs in the quad—think they'll chain those to the cement too? Hardy har har.

After a couple awkward silences, I bucked up and apologized. I told him I had a hard time talking about my dad, I got upset, I panicked, and I left. Such a shameful copout that was, blaming my insecurities and neuroses on my dead dad, but I couldn't admit the truth. And what was the truth? I still didn't know what was wrong with me, why I was so easily reduced to a blubbering mess, why I ditched a guy at a bar I really liked, why I was hallucinating.

Unbelievably, Tim said he was relieved he hadn't done something to upset me. We scheduled another date: the movies in a couple of days. He'd pick me up. He was looking forward to it. He was glad we talked.

After we hung up, I put the phone down on the coffee table and slipped off my sneakers and curled up on the couch like a cat, a gigantic smile plastered across my face. I even heard the mouse again and found I didn't really care. Fine! Live here, little mouse.

After everything was patched up with Tim, my other problems didn't seem so bad after all. I went to sleep that night, fast and deep. I dreamed of nothing.

7

The Barbie Crotch Tree

My mom, Jack, and I are downstairs watching *Star Trek*. I don't admit to anyone I like *Star Trek*, so when the landline rings and my mom says it's Lauren I bolt up off my beanbag chair and tell her I'll take it upstairs. I pray Lauren can't hear Patrick Stewart's booming voice in the background, "To boldly go where no man has gone before…"

I'm not allowed to have a phone in my room, so I'm either tethered to the downstairs handset in earshot of my mother, or tethered to the neon green phone with the tight coils in the common area upstairs, at the mercy of my mother picking up when the mood struck. I pick up the green handset. "Hello?"

My mother waits an extra beat before hanging up.

"Mom," I say through gritted teeth. "I got it."

Pause. Click.

I speak low. "What's up?"

Lauren's heaving breaths blare through my earpiece. "Maxine made out with TJ, but you *can't* tell anyone. She'll *kill* me if she finds out I told you."

"Ew. TJ?" I asked. "How'd *that* happen?" TJ, a zit-ridden kid from the town over, wears baggy t-shirts and Vans. All I know of him is that he knocked Chris Schwartz's front teeth out in a soccer match last year. He's not really Max's type.

"They were in the Hollow smoking cigarettes after school," Lauren said, then paused, knowing she was buttering

69

me up. She breathed into the phone and continued. "And then he, like, *felt her boobs* for, like, an hour. And then he, like…I dunno, *she* says he told her he liked her, but…" she paused again, "…and then, bam, they're going *out*."

We chortle and gossip and speculate over whether TJ's zits would pop if they rubbed their cheeks and lips together too hard. It was just like the old days, well, six months or so ago, before Max took such a liking to Lauren and Lauren started following her around like a puppy dog.

Then Lauren gets real porno on me and starts talking about maybe TJ is good at *finger banging*, and my blood pressure spikes as I cut in to remind her that my mom could pick up at any moment. Lauren is lightyears ahead of me when it comes to talking about sex. She goes on and on about blowjobs and orgasms and she is the first person I have ever heard use and expound on the term cunnilingus. Max must have gotten her into it. The two of them are like two little Jenna Jamesons in training. Maybe that's part of why they started bonding—leaving my prude ass in the dust.

"Ellie!" My mother screams up the stairs. She says the first syllable hard and fast. "Time's up! Get down here for dinner. *Now*."

I sigh. "Gotta go, Lauren, sorry."

"God. Your mom is such a bitch."

My face reddens. I can call my Mom a bitch, but no one else can. I want to tell her my mom is not a bitch—she's stressed and money-strapped and sad.

Instead, I betray the womb in which I incubated for nine whole months and say in a low voice, "I know. She's crazy."

"Wait," Lauren says, as I'm about to say goodbye.

"Yeah?"

"Come to the Hollow with us after school tomorrow. Max is bringing TJ. I don't want to be stuck with them alone."

I think I hear breathing on the line. "Mom?" I ask tentatively.

I don't hear a click, or breathing anymore, so I let it go. "I'll come," I say. "But...what should I tell my mom?"

Lauren clucks her tongue. "Um, the truth? That you're coming to my house after school? Tell her my parents will be there."

Trying to hide my thrill—they've been "forgetting" to invite me places after school lately—I say casually, "Cool. See you there."

I hear breathing again and the whir of a machine. It sounds like...a blow-dryer? Then, "Max!" It sounds like someone is screeching from far away.

"Bye," Lauren says hurriedly, then hangs up.

My stomach churns as I stare down at the handset. Three-way. I try desperately to play back what I said about Max. They'd each done this to me before—one sits silently on the line while the other goads me into gossiping about the other. Shit, shit, shit.

My mom hollers up from the bottom of the stairs. "*Ellie! Do you not want to eat?*"

***

The next day, Lauren, Max, and I walk to the Hollow after school to play manhunt with TJ. As we trudge up the street, there is no mention of the three-way call from the night before. I cling to the hope that I was being paranoid, that Max wasn't lurking on the line, and that they really aren't horrid little she-demons.

Soon we come upon the edge of the Hollow, the edge that starts along the road from which we walked, Route 38. From there only the tops of trees are visible; it's not evident just how deep the Hollow is. A brittle fence separates the road from the precipitous drop-off. On the other side—the safer, more open side—is the Rec Center.

My mother doesn't know I'm here. She'd kill me, and not just because we're unsupervised. Every week in the paper there's something about streakers and flashers and weirdos passing through the Hollow, but we pay no mind. It's the perfect spot for a game of hide-and-seek, and it's closest to Lauren's house, where we can grab snacks first.

Lauren's black-shuttered Colonial sits at the end of a cul-de-sac atop a steep grassy hill. It has a nightmarish, almost ninety-degree angled driveway that's great for sledding, but a nightmare for my mother's '88 Subaru. Our emergency brake is iffy, so instead of risking a roll down the hill to our deaths, my mother usually parks at the bottom, walks me up to the door, and requests to speak with Lauren's parents. They smile at her, nod—but it's obvious they're patronizing her. My mom usually deals with Lauren's mother, Claire Vine, a night nurse who only works three days a week. Instead of "supervising" us, she leaves us alone while she gardens or watches soaps recorded on blank VHS tapes that are splayed in collapsed piles on the floor of the living room. Lauren's father rarely emerges from his home office, or else he works late at the law firm. If the three of us were ever in a police lineup, he would have no idea who I was, despite meeting me numerous times. I must have that kind of face. Plain, unmemorable. Teachers take at least a full month to get my name right. Max, on the other hand? Seconds.

We arrive at the mouth of the Hollow, which is marked by an arch of tree branches wilting over two decrepit, weatherworn benches. TJ is already there with his hands stuffed in his pockets, standing next to his bike resting against the trunk of a tree with two slim limbs that remind me of upside down Barbie doll legs. The little nook is where Max hides cigarettes.

"Ellie, grab me a butt," she orders.

I got to the tree and peel back a rock. My heart is in my

throat as I realize they're wet. It was Lauren who stored them there last week, insisting they'd stay dry. I tried telling her…

"They're wet," she says, over my shoulder.

I turn around. She stares at me with her arms crossed. I wonder if she can hear my heart pounding.

She rolls her eyes at me and walks over to TJ, who'd begun to walk off, leaving Lauren and me behind. Within three minutes the two of us are treated to the Max and TJ Show.

We watch as Max woops in delight as TJ chases her around trees, running just fast enough to graze her back with his hand. She shrieks as he lets her get a little farther ahead. They run around in continuous loops while Lauren and I look on, bored and jealous, leaning side-by-side against a tree.

Lauren has been copping a major attitude today, not only towards me, but also towards Max—whom she normally deifies. Max, so far, has failed to notice. After fifteen minutes of Max's flirtatious yelps she bounds towards us, sneaking looks at TJ behind her with her mouth in an "O." We wait with our arms crossed as she nears.

Max takes no notice of Lauren's scowling face and walks right up to her. She's almost a foot taller than Lauren, who is exceptionally slight for our age, and although I'm average height, Max is still a whole head taller than me. And her boobs are huge. Alyssa Milano huge.

TJ slows his run to a walk and trudges up behind Max. "I'm sick of being the hunter. Max, you be It." Then he nods his head sideways at Lauren and me. "We'll all hide."

It's the first time TJ has made eye contact with Lauren or me, and it's the closest I have ever come to him. On closer examination his pimply face covers a strong jaw; he's actually quite attractive. Plus, he is taller than most of the boys in sixth grade. He looks like an eighth grader, maybe even a high schooler.

I smile shyly at him, and say in a small voice, "We'll hide.

Give us two minutes. Lauren, we'll hide together?" I stick my elbow out. Lauren pushes her back off against the tree like a catapult and hooks my arm.

We head towards the far left side of the Hollow, the safer side, where eventually the trees break and you come upon a gazebo, tennis courts, and the playground of the Rec Center. It's still a great hiding area, enough thick shrubbery shrouds you from view.

Lauren and I stomp along aimlessly, unable to decide on a hiding place. I suggest we climb a tree, but she balks. She hates heights. My suggestion of the thicket by the brook is "stupid, she'll see us." Finally—at Lauren's suggestion, of course—we decide on a low bush and lay behind it on our stomachs.

After a few minutes, we hear Max's giggles. She gets close; through the bush I see her shaved legs—I'm roiling with envy—but she doesn't see us. Instead, she veers past and heads deeper into the back of the woods. She calls out TJ's name. I notice she does not call out "Lauren!" or, God forbid, "Ellie!" Her voice fades, and after a couple minutes we no longer hear her at all. Lying there, we become giddy. We can't suppress our laughter, our thrill. We wait about a minute more. Lauren itches her arm, adjusts her position. An ant carrying another ant scurries in front of my nose, making me sit up with a jolt. I feel itchy and scratch myself all over.

"I don't hear her anymore, do you?" I ask.

"No. She's probably making out with TJ. Maybe he's fingering her."

"Ew."

We stay down for another couple of minutes.

Finally, Lauren stands up, stretches her legs, and wipes dirt off the bottom of her wide-legged jeans. She walks authoritatively in the direction from which we came. I follow. I always follow.

We make our way back to the benches. As minutes pass

in silence I kick the dirt, wondering what time it is. I start worrying about my mom. Clearly Lauren's parents are unaware of the streakers in the Hollow. Had they not received the letters from the School Committee? Then I think of the mail pile in the Vines' kitchen, the unopened envelopes and countless catalogues strewn across the table. Lauren had just casually shouted to her parents that we were walking to the Hollow. Her mother had just called back, "Be safe!" Why can't my mother be like her parents?

If my mom knew what I was up to, it would be the last straw. I'd likely only be allowed to invite Lauren to *my* house, which was a total drag because my mom watched us like a hawk. And I would never invite *Max* to my house. That little snot would stick up her nose at our paint-chipped house with the scratched-up floors and yard sale furniture; she'd snort in knee-bending laughter at my father's decrepit old work truck at the corner of the driveway, weeds growing up the tires. Lauren would probably laugh along with her.

Lauren is scribbling her initials in a notebook: LUV. Block letters, bubble letters, cursive, circled in hearts. I eye her L.L. Bean monogrammed backpack beside her on the ground, and for the eightieth time that day I'm overtaken by envy. My mother had scoffed at me when asked for one for Christmas. "A sixty-dollar backpack? Are you insane?"

"But, Mom!"

"First of all, they are too expensive. Second of all, they'll give you scoliosis. You see all those kids practically dragged down to the pavement? For Christ's sake."

Lauren got a new bag every year, *LUV* etched in white over the top pocket. If my mother suffered amnesia or won the lottery and allowed me to have one, mine would just say *Ellie*. My initials, ELF, would be a recipe for disaster; my ears stick out a little.

I sigh and ask Lauren, "Where are they? Should we go look for them?"

She rolls her eyes. "I don't know, Ellie. God." But she looks back into the depths of the Hollow with her eyes narrowed.

We hear someone coming, running, breathing hard. Our heads whip in that direction. It's TJ. He stops short in front of us and puts his hands on his knees, gasping. "I don't know where she is," he says. "Something's wrong."

My heart leaps. "What happened?"

"Max never found me. After a while, I thought I heard her, and I even said, 'I give up, I'll just come out.' I yelled it a bunch of times. But she didn't come out. You guys didn't see her either?"

"Nope," Lauren says, then she shrugs, looking bored. "She'll be back."

TJ rubs his hands along his chin, and I wince, wondering if any of his acne, a painful rash of red bumps along his jaw, would pop and start to bleed.

"I don't want to scare you," he says, "but I saw this dude in the woods before you guys got here. He was far away, closer to the road, and seemed to watch me for a minute. He walked towards the deep part, sort of where Max went looking for me. Maybe he's just a bum, but I think we should go try to look for her. Just in case."

"What'd he look like?" I ask. I struggle to remember the description of the streaker in the police log. My mom had read it aloud to me from the paper and ended it with, "Don't you *dare* go in there."

"I couldn't make out his face really, but he had on a red hat. He was old. He was holding a bag."

"Red hat," I say slowly. One of my mother's nervous diatribes comes back to me. I speak faster. "There was a guy described in the paper who was loitering by the school. He was wearing a red hat." For as much as I try to ignore my mother, her apprehensions permeate.

"He had a bag?" Lauren asks, her lip curling. "Like a backpack?"

"No, like a black garbage bag."

Lauren huffs loudly. "Yeah, TJ, some man is going to put Max's body in a garbage bag," she says, her voice awash with sarcasm. "She's probably trying to get our attention. She does this *all* the time at my house. She runs off in to the woods and we have to go looking for her." She shrugs and glares at me. "I don't have time for this. I'm going home. Ellie, you can come with me or not."

"Well, we can't leave *without* her." I step a little closer to TJ. "Can't we just do one more search for her?" I plead. "Before we go?"

TJ's eyes flick over us. He hadn't signed up to hang out with us undeveloped trolls. But he sure seems to like Max, and now he shifts his feet and bites his lip in concern.

A rush of panic courses through me, and suddenly I am convinced something is wrong. I feel it from my dry throat down to my tingling toes. I touch Lauren's arm and say urgently, "We have to search for her, just once. Please."

Lauren slams her notebook shut and slings her backpack dramatically over her shoulder, almost whaling me in the face. "*Fine,*" she says. "God, Ellie, you're being so annoying."

Trudging through the Hollow, we see nothing and say nothing. We walk all the way to the left, and reach the row of trees that dot the playground. Nothing. We look nervously at one another, knowing we have no choice but to head towards the center, towards unknown territory where the woods go far, far back.

We hop over a small brook. It's getting colder and darker. After we walk for ten minutes, calling her name to no avail,

TJ crams his hands in his jeans and says hopefully, "Maybe her mom picked her up?"

"Her mom's working," Lauren says. "My parents are supposed to drive her home tonight."

We hear a stick crack, and we all swivel our heads toward the sound. I strain to see. TJ's eyes are wide, and now even Lauren looks rattled. We listen for more.

Nothing.

I step towards the sound, shushing Lauren before she could say anything dissuasive or bitchy.

Another crack.

I start running, and I start to feel a lightness; a fearlessness. I'm untouchable. Who cares what happens to me? I'm playing manhunt with an acne-riddled freak who barely knows my name. I have awful friends who would never care enough to search for me in the dark woods. Maybe my mother would be better off without me leeching off her meager social worker paycheck. Maybe she could adopt a kinder sister for Jack, one who doesn't scream bloody murder at him for breathing too loud at dinner. Maybe I could be with my father, in whatever world waits for me beyond this one. There, we could finally form a bond.

I walk faster, emboldened, until past a thick oak tree I see something. A flash of red. A man. My blood runs cold again. Just as quickly, I'm back to a rush of good old-fashioned fear.

Then I hear a high-pitched, faint squeal.

"Max!" I turn back, but realize Lauren and TJ are no longer in tow. I've hustled too far away from them. I hear more rustling. I squint, but can see little ahead of me. Clouds are rolling in, and the trees blot whatever waning sunlight remains.

Despite every rational thought telling me not to, I rush toward the sound, deeper into the Hollow. "Max?" I yell.

I see movement. The back of a grey hoodie and a red

hat…far off, though, and he seems to be getting further and further away. There are too many trees in the way to see him in a continuous motion. I wait a few more beats behind a tree then walk carefully forward.

Max is lying on the ground in the fetal position, wedged between thick, spindly tree roots. Her hair is splayed out like a fan, the white-blonde streaks sullied with chunks of dirt and twigs, and red streaks. An oversize black garbage bag is beside her, flattened, unused, as if pulled directly from the Hefty box.

"Max?"

She doesn't answer. She doesn't move.

"Help!" I scream, looking around me, realizing with terror how dark it's gotten, how lost we are in here. I can't even hear road sounds anymore. I can't see the lights outside the Rec Center. "*Help!*"

I kneel down and pull Max's shoulder gently towards me, to get a look at her face. She doesn't budge, but I see she has a purple bruise on her cheek and that she's bleeding from somewhere, the source of the gash or cut blended with all the discolorations of her face. Her eyes are wide open. She blinks, but doesn't turn her head to look at me or react to me touching her. I look down at her pants. They are unbuttoned and zipped only halfway.

I hear footsteps behind me. My stomach drops and I look back. It's Lauren and TJ. Lauren's hand slowly covers her mouth as she gets closer to us. She peers down at Max.

"Is she dead?" Lauren whispers. She cranes her neck around me but does not dare come any closer. Her hands are shaking.

TJ rushes over to Max and kneels beside her. He gently shakes her shoulder. "Max?" His voice cracks. He stands up and puts the palm of his hand on his forehead, the way my mother does when the health insurance company calls with bad news and she has to think hard, as if to say, "What the fuck do I do now?"

Again, I try to roll her over so she'll lay supine. I clutch her small shoulder and gently nudge. She resists and eventually I drop my hand.

"Are you okay?" I whisper, feeling foolish. Of course she isn't okay.

She whispers back, "Is he gone?"

I nod and stroke her hair.

8

Pandora's Box

I opened my eyes. Bookcase. Nature pictures. Lumpy futon. I looked to my right, at Dr. Rollins smiling at me.

"Well," she said. "Looks like it worked!"

"Whoa," I said.

"Tell me how you feel."

"Like I just woke up from a dream."

"Would you say what you saw was a dream, or a memory recall?"

"Both?"

Liz wrote down more notes on her yellow pad. "This incident in the Hollow, is this a memory you've thought about before? As an adult?"

I shook my head.

"You've never recalled anything about the Hollow, even?"

I shook my head. "We went into the Hollow all the time...maybe just vague memories of typical after-school hangouts in there."

"Well, now is your memory jogged at all? Has it opened anything up? Or does this still feel foreign?"

"No..." I trailed off. "No. It's not totally foreign. It jogged my memory somewhat, I guess."

"Somewhat?"

"Yeah, but it's like looking down into a well. I've got

this opening scene, and then when I try to delve into what happened after it, I've got nothing. Dark."

"You're saying you're not sure if they ever found the culprit?"

"Right."

"You don't remember the aftermath at all? School, or how the community reacted to this?"

I thought for a moment. "Maxine, I think, was known as a liar, kind of…"

"Is there anyone you can ask about this?"

"I can ask my mom. I mean, she picked me up from the police station and all that."

"Think. The police must have been involved."

I shut my eyes.

"Do you want me to start the music again?"

"Sure," I murmured.

The music rang out softly, but all I could focus on was the sound of Liz's pants, the corduroy, rubbing together as she crossed and re-crossed her legs.

I opened my eyes. "It's not the same. I can't do it."

Liz wrote something down. "Okay, I say we try this again tomorrow."

"Tomorrow?" Our meetings had started out two weeks apart, then one week. Now every day?

"I don't want too much time to elapse between this last session, which I believe produced very vibrant and informative memories, and the next, which I'm hoping you can do the same."

"So why can't I now?"

Liz shrugged. "Too much pressure. Too much stress from what you just witnessed."

I got up and handed her the co-pay. "I guess I'll see you tomorrow."

***

My mother and I are in the car driving home from the police station. Despite the initial fury over me playing in the Hollow with a boy and not safely in the home of Lauren's parents, my mom is eerily calm. She asks simple questions, her eyes not leaving the road.

"How close did you get to the man, in feet?"

"I'm bad at measuring, I don't know. Like, from our swing set to, like, the bird bath."

"Okay. Had you ever seen this man before?"

"I didn't even see him. Just saw a red hat. A hoodie. I told you all of this."

"I know. I just...I just can't believe this." She shakes her head. "This is the Cape. It's supposed to be safe here."

I glance over at her, and notice then that she is very thin, thinner than even when Dad died. Wasting away.

I press my cheek against the cold glass. Jack's in the backseat, sleeping. I feel the pull of sleep myself; it's nearly ten o'clock.

"Are you feeling okay? You look pale." She puts the back of her cool hand to my forehead. Someone stops short in front of us and she slams the breaks so her hand kind of whacks me. I can feel her ring—the wedding ring she still wears for some reason, but on her right hand.

"Sorry," she says. Then she repeats, "So, are you feeling okay?"

"I'm okay," I say. "Just tired."

Officer Davies questioned me for forty-five minutes, and for the duration I was blasted with his grotesque coffee-and-cigarette breath. I kept leaning further and further back in the chair until my head hit the concrete wall behind me.

He asked me a lot of weird questions. Some were about Max, what she was like, how long she had known TJ. He said that TJ was currently out on a three-day suspension for lighting a trashcan on fire in the gym at Seaview Middle

School, was I aware of that? I shook my head. He then asked me, "Does Max lie a lot?"

I asked, "What does that have to do with it? There was a man, I *saw* him." Then he asked me to help with a police sketch, but I was at a loss. "Red hat" and "grey hoodie" and "old" aren't too helpful.

"Old, like around thirty? Or, like, around sixty?"

What was the real difference, I thought.

Max wasn't at the station to defend herself or give her side of the story. Lauren and I had stayed with her in the Hollow while TJ ran to a pay phone at the 7-Eleven to call the cops. A few minutes later, we saw the lights of a squad car flashing; it had pulled up to the Rec Center parking lot along with an ambulance and a fire truck. They came in and retrieved us from the woods, using directions provided by TJ. Lauren and I walked shoulder-to-shoulder back to the parking lot; a large blanket had been placed around the both of us by an officer who walked closely behind. Max, still almost catatonic, was placed on a stretcher and was rushed up ahead. I noticed she'd zipped up her pants.

Once we got back to the parking lot, Max was still there on the stretcher. As we approached, she sat up and looked around, bewildered. "I don't remember," she kept saying to the EMT, over and over. An electric blue BMW screeched into the parking lot—Max's mother, Mrs. Lang. She got out, slammed her car door, and started yelling at the cops, yelling at the EMTs, yelling at *Max,* who I know is awful, but c'mon! The girl just got attacked. Mrs. Lang ranted about insurance "bullshit," not trusting the police, not trusting doctors, not trusting "instruments of the government."

Mrs. Lang's movements were stilted and her behavior manic. Her eyes were darting from one person to another, one object to another. The odd thing was how the cops seemed familiar with her; it was like they knew her. They called her by her first name, Larissa, and treated her like a petulant child. But she made such a fuss and wouldn't shut up, so finally they told her she could just take Max home and they would follow up the next day. She didn't hug Max or console her or anything. She told her simply, "Get in." It was odd.

I'd only met Mrs. Lang a few times. On the rare occasions Lauren and I went to Max's house, Mrs. Lang would come to the door, peering first through the chain-locked crack. She looks like she might have been attractive when she was younger, in the '80s: passé feathered bangs; over-processed high hair; rough, tan skin; lines around her mouth from smoking; a sandpaper voice.

My mom will always beam at her, but Mrs. Lang sneers back. It's awkward between them—a strangeness hangs in the air. Sometimes I think my mom believes she'll bond with Mrs. Lang over being a fellow single mother. But divorcehood and widowhood are two different animals, especially when the former calls for alimony payments from Max's dad that pay for that blue BMW, when we can't afford to fix our emergency brake. For whatever reason, Max's mother, like her daughter, shows little interest in the members of the partially orphaned and widowed Frites clan.

I notice, though, that Mrs. Lang puts on a show for all the other parents, especially when Max holds her infamous coed birthday parties. Mrs. Lang speaks sternly to Max and tells the rest of us we all need to behave. She acts like she cares where we put our coats. But once the last parent drops their kid off? The lady changes into a different person. She pours herself a clear drink and chain-smokes and shoos us all down to the basement, where we play the kissing game Seven Minutes in Heaven.

Seven Minutes in Heaven is best played in closets, or at least in a room with a door. But since Max's basement lacks closets, the crafty hornball drapes sheets from the ceiling beams and affixes the edges with thumbtacks. In effect, we have ourselves our very own see-through make out kiosks.

I use the plural "we" lightly. My turn often gets skipped while Max reaps, on average, about twenty-eight minutes swapping spit with multiple partners. This doesn't upset me really. Sharing saliva with an audience makes me want to fasten Sony headphones over my ears. I don't have to hear the wet lip smacking and slimy prodding tongues of classmates I'll see the following Monday. If I did participate, what would I say to my paramour at school? "Hey, Chris, remember when the tiny crumbs of funfetti that were stuck in my gums made their way into your braces?"

If my turn isn't skipped, I have a backup plan. My Romeo and I stand behind the sheet and it's understood: "Let's just pretend we did it." We count down with our heads close together so the audience outside the diaphanous sheets thinks we were sucking face.

The good news is I'm not the most undesirable person in the room—Lauren is. When the spout of the IBC Root Beer bottle swirls and stops at Lauren, the boys are blatant in their disappointment. Chris Schwartz grabbed the bottle once and simply spun again. John Eldredge sucked in his breath and said, "No."

Part of the problem, I'm sure, is due to her appearance. She's frail, pale, and if I was considered flat-chested, she is positively concave. But more than anything, Lauren's pettish attitude is the turn-off. Her lip is in a permanent upwards half sneer, and when she gets fired up about something—which is often—she breaks into a full-blown Cujo snarl. I think she believes combativeness is a form of flirtation. Whatever the case, Lauren and I don't get dudes. Max is primed and bred to get dudes. And her mother practically lays out a red carpet for them.

But the Mrs. Lang I saw today in the parking lot was acting

stranger than usual. She spent twenty minutes excoriating the officers who just rescued her own daughter from the dark woods and, no big deal, an attacker. When Mrs. Lang and Max drove off, the rest of us were gently placed in squad cars and taken to the police station to wait for our parents and to, ostensibly, give our statements.

TJ lasted only five minutes at the station. His mother flew in the front door and insisted on getting a lawyer.

"Lady," Officer Davies said, a steaming Styrofoam cup of coffee in his hand, "this isn't some crime show. We just want to get an ID and get these kids' stories straight. I mean, come on."

But his mother wouldn't have it, and she marched out the door, pushing her son with a stiff arm to the back.

Lauren lasted ten minutes. Mr. Vine, an attorney, marched in with his tie loosened, his white dress shirt wrinkled, red-faced, and carted Lauren out of the station after speaking heatedly to another officer. I couldn't hear what they were saying, but I agreed with Officer Davies. We didn't do anything wrong—why won't these parents let their kids cooperate?

That left me and my testimony alone. My mom was on her way, but on the phone she said to tell them nothing but the truth. I couldn't help but be thrilled by the whole scene. I hoped a news crew was waiting for us outside—it wasn't. I imagined being a newswoman myself, reading the news. I dictated newspaper articles to my stuffed animals a lot, trying to get the voice down: the dips in octaves, the forced tonal changes, the over-emphasized words.

My mom now pulls into our driveway and turns to me. I just finished telling her about Mrs. Lang and how she hadn't even given Max a chance to explain or give her side of the story. How TJ's mother had pulled him from the station, too.

To my shock my mother says, "You know what, honey?

I've heard that TJ is a troublemaker. Who knows what those two were up to. I know Max was hurt today. But…I don't know if I would believe that little girl either."

***

I sat up, my head ringing. "This is exhausting."

"I know, Ellie, but you're doing so well. We're achieving some continuity here. You're producing answers."

"Well, all I have is questions," I said, trying to keep the irritation out of my voice. "Like, why would my mom not believe Max after all of that? That's crazy."

"Well," Liz looked down. "I have a note here that you said Max was known as a serial liar."

"But I wasn't a liar. Why didn't she trust me?"

"Why don't you ask her?"

I sighed. "She…she doesn't even know I started therapy again."

"Are you afraid to tell her?"

"Sort of."

"Why?"

I shrugged. "I'm not really sure. Every conversation with her leads to some sort of argument. She constantly finds things wrong with what I do, what I say, how I approach life, basically."

Liz waited for me to say more. When I didn't, she asked, "Is there anyone else you can consult with over these events? Another friend you'd have spoken to about it?"

"My best friend, Sarah. I talked to her about everything back then. She went to boarding school though; she didn't know Max or Lauren personally."

I looked at the clock. Five minutes left. Five minutes too long.

"Liz, I'm done for today."

She straightened her back. "I understand. I don't want to place undue stress on you."

I fought the urge to roll my eyes. All of this was producing stress. I got up.

"Do you feel closer to the answer, at least, after today?" Liz asked.

I thought of Max, lying on the ground with her bruised face and pants partially unzipped. I looked at Liz. "I feel like I've opened up Pandora's Box."

She raised her eyebrows. "You may have."

9

Maureen

My mom sat beside me on the beach blanket, her long peasant skirt tucked beneath her knees, and unloaded the cooler: two water bottles, grapes, Triscuits, a block of Muenster cheese, and a knife. Strands of dark brown hair, frizzed and gray at the temples, escaped her low, messy bun. She tried absently to curl them around her ear, but a constant wind prevented their taming. She smoothed her skirt, over and over, with her hands.

My mother had always been slim and nervy. Even before Dad died, she was always fussing and worrying and fretting about something. When he was sick she was a wreck, understandably a wreck. In the thirteen years since, I'd have thought she'd calm down some, but with age, she may have gotten worse. When you've lived alone so long, your neuroses can go unchecked.

I sat cross-legged beside her, sipping my iced coffee and flicking clear-bodied sand bugs off the blanket. I smoothed the surface with my hand. A seagull hovered overhead, occasionally dipping low then floating back up again, coming closer each time. I popped a cracker in my mouth, waving it away. "Shoo, bird!" I've had sandwiches snatched right out of my hands by brazen gulls at this beach, even in the spring.

"It's those moron tourists who feed them," my mother said

as she struggled with a jar of jam. "Now they'll come within an inch of your face."

I took the jar from her, opened it, and said nothing. I'd seen my fair share of locals feeding the birds, but I didn't feel like debating my mother, a staunchly protective lifelong local, about the feckless tourists.

Instead, I said, "So, Mom. What did I have to drive all the way down here for? You made me nervous."

She narrowed her eyes. "Well, for one, you don't need to be nervous. I mostly just wanted to see you. It's not summer. You're not gallivanting around with your girlfriends treating my house like a hotel. I miss you, believe it or not." She chuckled, but she wasn't smiling.

"I miss you, too," I said, although I did believe some space benefited our relationship. Those summer days my mom spoke of so fondly were not always peachy. By August her patience was thin.

I narrowed my eyes at her. "So, what couldn't you tell me over the phone when I asked about Maxine Lang?"

She winced. "I didn't mean to alarm you. I just thought your questions came out of left field. It was what, twelve, thirteen years ago? I was mostly just curious as to why now."

"Ugh, Mom, you're killing me." So this was just a ploy to get me to come see her, apparently, and here I was freaking out for a whole day about some haunting childhood crime I may or may not have witnessed. She'd been so strange on the phone when I'd brought it up. I said now, "The truth is, I went to see a therapist. I thought maybe I should, you know, work out any lingering issues from losing Dad. I know it's dumb after all this time, but...it's actually helped."

Her face brightened. "It's not dumb. I'd hoped you'd go on your own one day. I was afraid you'd never go back after that awful family session with your father. I never wanted to push it."

"So you're happy I went?" I asked.

"Yes, of course!"

"Oh, I just thought—"

"Thought what?"

"Like you never wanted to talk about Dad. Like it was too painful."

"Ellie, I tried to talk to you kids…I mean, yes, of course, the year it happened was very hard. Maybe I kept a little too much inside. But I always encouraged you to come with me to his grave, to visit with his brothers out in Pennsylvania. Don't you remember?" She looked at me hopefully.

Softly, I said, "I guess…yeah. I do remember. I guess that year…had a big impact. Kind of stayed with me a little stronger than the years afterward."

My mother nodded sadly and picked lint off the blanket. Oh man, I thought. This wasn't what this trip was supposed to be about. I didn't want to make my mother to cry. I cleared my throat. "So we talked a little about Dad. The lady, Dr. Rollins, or I call her Liz, wanted to explore why I get into random crying fits. She believed there was some sort of trigger."

My mother looked at me sharply. "Ahem, would it have anything to do with how much you girls drink?"

I rolled my eyes.

"Don't roll your eyes, alcoholism runs in the family!"

"Who?"

"Your great-uncle, for one, he was a fall-down drunk, and your cousin Marnie on your father's side."

"Anyone born after 1950?"

"That's not the point."

"May I continue my story, Maureen?"

She gritted her teeth. "Fine."

"Okay. Long story short, Liz talked me into trying hypnotherapy."

Now she rolled her eyes at me.

I held my hand up. "I was leery at first, too, Mom, but it worked. She coupled it with lucid dream therapy after she discovered I can have vivid dreams. I guess that's rare in people—"

"None of this has been proven whatsoever," she said sharply.

"Excuse me, I'm talking," I snapped. *Here we go again.*

"Okay, fine. Finish."

"Well, she had me lay down, and got me in a really relaxed state, and I started witnessing…scenes. From sixth grade." I looked at my mom, my fists clenched in my lap.

Maureen sighed. "Let's start from the beginning so I can get this straight. You remembered something about Max Lang and your old friend Lauren Vine. About being abducted. That's what you told me on the phone."

I nodded and recounted the incident in the Hollow and what I saw during hypnosis. When I finished, I stared at her. "So? Did that happen?"

My mom hesitated. "Well, yes. But you certainly didn't talk to me about any of it. We weren't on the best terms in those days, you and I, being so soon after Dad died. We were all out of sorts. But I can tell you that evening in the Hollow haunted me."

I sat up straighter. "Tell me what you remember."

"Max was attacked in the woods. You were shaken up by it. And I was furious with you. You were supposed to be at Lauren's house, for God's sake. Her parents let you girls run amok. I never trusted them." She stopped and strained sand in between her fingers.

I pulled my knees to my chest. "Wow. So I did block it out." A gust of wind rustled a small pile of napkins, and I had to stamp the water bottle on them to prevent them from blowing away. I shook my head and huffed.

"What?" she asked.

"Well," I said impatiently. "What next? Did they ever catch the guy?"

"Catch what guy?" My mother cocked her head and looked alarmed.

"The guy who attacked Maxine in the woods."

She relaxed. "Oh." She waved her hand dismissively. "No one attacked her, Ellie, she made it up."

"No, she didn't, I saw him."

"You thought you saw someone," she said, looking out at the water.

"Um, I definitely saw someone. And flashing back to it during therapy proves I did."

My mother waved it off again. "You probably saw a homeless person or something. Nothing ever came of any of it. What is Maxine Lang up to these days, anyway? I see her mother around town from time to time. She said Max is doing well, said she lives in New York, or New Jersey?"

My mind was all jumbled now because Max, by some standards, was indeed alive and well. I'd looked her up on Facebook when I got home from therapy. She was a makeup artist in Queens, and all her public pictures featured one of three things: either her small rat dog dressed up in various costumes, still shots of Patron bottles on ice in club after club after club, or her boobs. Big, surgically enhanced to at least double-D sized boobs squeezed into tiny shirts revealing miles of cleavage. In 2009, Max Lang was alive and, by her own deranged mother's standards, "doing well."

My mother absorbed my silence, took a sip of water, and said nothing.

Frustrated, I said, "I can't remember, like, anything else about that year though, don't you find that strange?"

She shrugged and said softly, "It was a tough year. When

Sarah came back to public school things got better for you."
She patted me gently on the back.

I was silent for a moment, then said, "I wouldn't think a
memory like that would just go *poof* out of my consciousness.
The brain is crazy."

Maureen laughed. "Yes, the brain is crazy. Did you
remember anything else, or was that it?"

I thought hard. I saw a flash of the police station—me
sitting in a cold metal chair next to a detective's desk. I had
looked around in wonder, having driven by the station
countless times, watching out the window of the Subaru. I'd
expected to see handcuffed convicts, dramatic interrogations,
rooms with two-way mirrors. Instead, there were unkempt
desks, ringing phones, and men hunched over piles of paper at
their desks. And Officer Davies, jotting down notes, sipping
his coffee.

"They thought we were doing it for attention," I muttered.
"It didn't help that Max went silent and barely cooperated after
her mom freaked out and took her home. Her crazy mom
didn't let her even speak to the cops and give her side of the
story!"

My mother opened her mouth, then shut it again.

"That's crazy, right?" I said again.

"Sorry, honey, nothing came of that incident, I don't know
what to tell you."

I felt immensely dissatisfied. "I just thought…there was
more to this. I blocked it out of my memory. I thought…I
remembered this stuff for a reason."

My mother sat up straighter. "Well, just be careful, Ellie.
With hypnosis, sometimes the power of suggestion outweighs
reality. As a social worker, I've seen it a lot, with kids
especially. A health professional goads them into remembering
a potential past trauma, and then there's really no way of
knowing if it's their imagination or not."

"I'm not a kid, Mom. And you're disproving your presumption that hypnotherapy doesn't work. So far my memories during hypnosis, now that I know they are memories, are matching up with your account. So, it works great, actually. Hell, there could be more crazy stuff for me to remember."

Maureen started packing up, wrapping the cheese back in its plastic, sweeping the crumbs off the blanket. The gulls had given up, but a couple plovers loitered nearby, tottering on their stick figure legs, racing down shore.

When all was shrink-wrapped and zipped away, my mother and I fell silent for a couple moments. Finally, she said, "I should have—I could have been a better mother to you back then. Things were just hard."

I touched her shoulder. "Stop, Mom. You did your best." The comment sounded trite, but I meant it.

She turned to me. "Ellie, are you unhappy?"

I bristled and dropped my hand. "What's happy?"

"What do you mean, what's happy?"

I shrugged.

"Do you ever think about switching up your routine? Try new things? Meet new people?"

"We've harped on this enough, Mom. I don't need new friends. That's the one department I'm happy in."

"But what do you do? Just...drink?"

"Well," I stuttered, "I-I see them for dinner or drinks, yeah, and that's all fine. We commiserate over our jobs sucking, and punish ourselves on Facebook stalking everyone's accomplishments and happy relationships." I took a breath. "But for the most part, I just take everything in stride. Wake up, rinse, repeat."

"That's it?"

"What, you want details? If it's a weeknight, I try to go for a run if it's nice out. If not, I eat dinner and watch TV and go to bed. Weekdays, I go to work. Where I'm far from satisfied or happy."

"Your generation has this me-me-me thing going on," my mom said. "Do you think all the generations before you were skipping happily to work, always motivated, always satisfied? It's work! It pays the bills."

I opened my mouth to respond, then shut it. How could I explain the conundrum of working for a technology company in 2009 to a fifty-five-year-old woman? Her career path was so linear—attaining a degree in social work, training in the field, then, ultimately, changing the lives of those less fortunate. Sure, it paid terribly, but she was impacting other people's lives. She was contributing to society.

How could I explain what I did every day? "Work" that wasn't tactile, tangible, or altruistic. If I wrote up a report on enterprise architecture, if I spent hours on a cloud computing document, if I "brainstormed" on a video conference for ninety minutes about "raising client expectations," what could I show for it? The charts, emails, instant messages, they shoot off into the ether, into a web of invisible fibers connecting nothing and everything.

I pictured myself at fifty-five, looking back at my illustrious, scintillating professional career replete with free candy jars and cardboard cutouts and diversity training and R.A.V.E.! memorizations. What would I have to show for it? What would there be to look back on but a life staring at a computer screen?

"Mom," I said. "I don't want to get into it."

"I worry about you. You can't just drink and go to work. That's just sad."

I opened my mouth to tell her I was doing fine, actually—I'd met someone. Tim and I had gone to the movies the other night and it was fun and breezy and I'd managed not to cry like a deranged woman-baby again. But I stopped. Too soon. I didn't want to jinx it.

I offered a different angle. "I went to therapy," I said quietly. I drew in the sand with a stick, swirling it. "That should count for something. I thought you'd be proud of me, especially considering your line of work."

She sat back on the blanket, placing her hands behind her to hold her up. With her chest thrust forward towards the sun and her eyes closed she said, "Yes, I am happy you went. I just...I wish she hadn't forced hypnotherapy down your throat."

I shrugged.

"It feels...forced to me." She opened her eyes and turned to her me. "Just promise me you'll take it all with a grain of salt. If something revealed is upsetting, or implicates someone we know, you remember something unseemly...please tell me. Immediately. And don't jump to conclusions. Promise me."

"I promise," I said, but so many things were still bugging me. What happened after that day? The rest of that year? At some unknown juncture, my friendship with Maxine and Lauren ceased. I broke off friendships with grade school friends all the time, certainly, and I couldn't remember each and every one of them, either.

But there was a definite hole. It wasn't as if the whole remaining two years of middle school were forgotten. I thought back. There was the seventh grade dance where I had my first kiss with Chris Schwartz. I'd been wearing a powder blue sequined one-shoulder dress with five-inch platform shoes. The kiss was wet and long, and I had to stoop over and lean on the handicap bar along the wall to steady myself as I came in line with his lips.

"What are you thinking about now?" Maureen asked, rolling up the blanket and hefting the soft cooler bag over her shoulder.

I got up from the ground and stretched, looking out at the water. "Nothing."

That dance. Seventh grade. I'd gone with Erin and Selma and Betsy, girls I'd been friends with in elementary school. Not Lauren or Max. I was almost certain an old corkboard littered with multicolored thumbtacks holding up boarding school portraits of Sarah, and pictures of Jack and me gawking at actors in colonial garb at Plimouth Plantation, still sat in my childhood bedroom closet, pinned behind an abandoned trumpet case. I didn't see it the last time I looked, but I knew it was in there somewhere. I had to root around more.

"You're in your own little world," my mom commented as we climbed into the car.

"Just thinking."

She didn't ask about what this time.

***

When we got back to the house, I rushed upstairs. I went straight to my closet and wrestled against the heavy hindrances trapping the corkboard and yanked it free. I sat on the floor and examined the assortment of pictures: more peeling, faded photo booth shots of Sarah and me; the photo from Plimouth Plantation just as I'd remembered it, Jack's blond curls falling into his eyes, my arm in a rare half hug around his shoulders.

Then, behind a school picture of Sarah—on the back was *Hi Elf, it's Muppet. I miss you. I hate it here*—was the photo of the seventh grade dance, just as I'd remembered it. A few friends from homeroom, Betsy, Erin, and Selma, leaned against Erin's mother's sedan, making peace signs and flashing braces and curled-under bangs. This must have been less than a year from the incident in the Hollow. No Lauren. No Max.

I went back to the closet and dug deeper into the pile of junk. I spotted a lime green cover and reached in. It was another photo album, different from the first that included the first half of sixth grade: Lauren and me, then inclusive of Max, and then the following summer, with Sarah. Inside, slipped behind flimsy plastic coverings, were more pictures of the same dance. My mother had taken several. I flipped through, marveling at the passage of time. I struggled to apply names to faces I hadn't seen in over a decade. But still no Lauren or Max outside the auditorium. No Lauren or Max among the sequined powder blue and hot pink dresses, posing with their arms around each other, their stomachs full of butterflies wondering who they would dance with, begging each other, "Don't leave me standing alone…"

I set down the album. There was a reason I blocked out the day I found Max in the woods in the Hollow, splayed out on the ground, wide-eyed and mute. The hairs on the back of my neck rose whenever I thought of the man dashing through the woods, the speck of his red hat receding in the dark.

I sat down on my creaky old twin bed and sighed. Despite my mother assuring me there was nothing else of importance to recall—just drop it, it was so long ago—I knew there was more to unearth. More than my mother had ever known, or imaged, would happen to a child from the safe Cape Cod town of Marshside.

Still, while I recognized a visceral need to fill in these crucial holes of my past, I was becoming increasingly frightened to find out.

10

Field Trip

"So what the hell were you expecting me to do?" I was standing at my kitchen counter with my arms crossed.

Ricki leaned against the opposite wall with her arms crossed as well, sporting sweatpants and unwashed hair. For a few seconds it was a stare down. Finally, she shrugged. "I figured you'd just work it out."

"Are you kidding me, Ricki?" I knew my face was beet red, and I couldn't help my arms from wagging around in the air in disbelief. "What if I hadn't asked you about renewing the lease just now? When were you planning on telling me? What, you'd have just moved out next week, leaving me with the rent for two months?"

Ricki rolled her eyes. "Well, you've been a little distracted lately. It's not like you were around to talk about it with me."

"Are you kidding me? You're never here. You're at Tyler's ninety-nine percent of the time."

Ricki sniffed. "I've been home more lately, and you haven't even noticed. You're always off at 'appointments.'" She made air quotes, pouted, and said, "You barely talk to me."

"This is insane. You've been MIA for months. Months."

She shrugged. "I'm in a relationship. Get over it."

"So you'd have screwed me on the rent without thinking twice?" My voice rose.

"I'm not screwing you on the rent. Sounds like you've had

a plan to boot me from the apartment so your friend Sally or whoever can move in."

"Oh please, Ricki. You know who Sarah is, stop pretending. She went to college with us. Remember? Back when you weren't obsessed with your boyfriend? Before you lost your damn mind?"

"You can't blame me for having a boyfriend who I love. Sorry you're single. Sorry I'm not sorry."

"Oh, shut up Ricki," I spat. My anger was almost blinding. "You've barely come up for air. You think I'm jealous of that? Don't act all high and mighty with me. Don't even try."

Ricki shrugged. Her slack, unexpressive face infuriated me even more.

"Well, here's my notice," she said, and spoke the next words deliberately slow and robotic, like I was some sort of dolt. "I'm…moving…out…early…next…week."

I threw up my hands. "Jesus!"

I knew I could celebrate her moving out and everything would fall into place later on, but right then, I was livid. If there wasn't the opportunity for Sarah to move in early, Ricki was planning on sticking me with two months' rent to pay for myself. Taking her to court over a couple thousand dollars wouldn't have been worth it, and she knew that. I only happened to catch her in this botched plan by accident, when I brought up the possibility of Sarah subletting.

"I'm sure Sally will love living with your moody ass." Ricki smirked.

My mouth hung open in disbelief. If she was referring to what I thought she was referring to, it was months ago, when she butted into a conversation I was having with Sarah on the phone. I'd asked her, politely, to let me have privacy. There could have been an edge to my tone, but was that enough to justify ditching out on the rent?

"Ricki, that was not even a big deal. I got annoyed with

you for two seconds, two months ago. Deal with it. Are you so dissociated from the real world from speaking only to one person that you think this is all normal behavior?"

God, I sounded like Liz.

She laughed. "Ha! Again, just jealous. No one wants you, and you're mad about it."

My hands curled into fists and I started feeling lightheaded, like I was going to faint. I gripped the side of the counter so I wouldn't lunge at her and do something I would regret. I was so mad I could cry, but I willed the tears to stay in their eye sockets with all my might. *This is not the time to show weakness*, I told myself.

"I'm dating someone, Ricki, if you must know. Fuck off. You're never here when he comes over."

She snorted. "Sure, how convenient."

"Oh shut up," I snapped. "I don't see him every waking moment like an obsessed psycho, unlike someone I know."

Ricki turned away and started opening up the cabinets one by one. She stood on her tiptoes and grasped soup cans and cracker boxes and chip bags and stuffed them into a canvas sack. I stayed to be sure she didn't pilfer any of my food.

Then she took out her phone, dialed, and said, "Hey, babe." She stole a glance at me. "Yeah, I just told her." Pause. "Yup, she was a huge bitch about it, just like we thought."

"Who are you?" I shouted as I stomped out of the kitchen and into my bedroom and slammed the door. Did that girl have any self-awareness? I stopped. Maybe I wasn't as aware of my own "moodiness" as I would have liked to think. I guess I had snapped at her a couple times over the last few months. I was annoyed, though, I protested silently. She kept ditching me!

I tried not to stew too long and plugged ear buds in my ears to drown out her stomping around the apartment while talking shit about me to Tyler on the phone. I took out my favorite A.M. Homes novel and read for a while, determining that Ricki would make a great character in that particular satire about suburban strife. In five years, I thought with loathing, Ricki will be a frumpy, disgruntled housewife with no life.

Hours later, when I no longer heard Ricki riffling through the kitchen, I poked my head out. She'd left. Only then did I allow myself to celebrate the fact that now, if Sarah's Craigslist appointment went horrifyingly bad—I hoped it would—she could move in as soon as three weeks. My heart leapt. I took out her phone and texted my best friend since age eight, Sarah "Muppet" Muppeta, that my apartment would soon have a vacancy.

***

I arrived at therapy two days later, brimming with excitement. "I can't wait to tell you what happened last night."

Liz sat down and got her notepad out and smiled beatifically at me. "Did you have a breakthrough? Another lucid dream? Start slow."

"No, no," I said, brushing her off, slightly annoyed. "Tim. Tim—the kid who I cried and made a fool of myself in front of, and then we talked, and everything was cool again?"

"Oh, okay." Liz's disappointment was written all over her face but she made a valiant attempt at recovering. "Tell me about Tim, then."

I launched into my last date with Tim. How perfect he was. How courteous, gentlemanly. I left out the sex stuff, not that we got that far in the car, just a ten-minute make-out and some thigh stroking. Liz didn't need to know that kind of stuff, anyway.

After we finished sucking face that night, we made plans for him to pick me up for dinner the following Friday. I didn't care where, I said, along as it wasn't Indian food. He said he didn't care either, as long as it wasn't sushi. He would fill me in on which restaurant once he made the reservation. Before he changed his mind, I quickly said I had to go and exercised a lot of restraint and didn't invite him up. He even called me later that night just to say goodnight, and I threw the phone down like a burning hot stone and bent into my pillow and shrieked. There was a lightness in my chest I hadn't felt in a long time.

Liz waited me out, smiled, told me this was great, how nice for me, and well, anything else?

"No dreams," I said proudly. "And after the trip to see my mom, it's pretty clear nothing ever happened to Max. Just that weird incident in the woods. I mean, I swear I saw that man, but who knows? Maybe my imagination got the best of me. Maybe I was just really stressed about work or whatever, and I thought I was seeing things, and I really wasn't. You said yourself that first day that I was going through that crisis-thing or whatever."

She winced. "Well, Ellie, that's before you mentioned—"

"I know but…" I wanted to talk more about Tim.

Liz did not. Instead, she asked me to really reach back and tell her what else I could remember from sixth grade. "Who is Lauren?" she pressed. "Who is Max? Why are they so significant to you?"

"They're not," I said.

"They must be, on some level."

I shrugged.

She pushed her glasses up the bridge of her nose. "Describe one day. One day with the two of them, your sixth grade year, if you can conjure it. See where it takes you. See where it leads."

I rested my hands in my lap and closed my eyes. "Okay."

"You can lie down."

I crunched myself into the length of the futon, and soon, the words started to flow.

***

It's not summer, barely spring, but we're on a field trip at the beach down the road from the middle school. I wrinkle my nose at the fishy stench of low tide, at the creepy-crawly hermit crabs underneath the packed sand that nip my toes and scratch my heels. "Ew," we all keep saying as we hop along, holding our sneakers with our socks stuffed inside, squandering the unique opportunity to grow up in a beautiful seaside town. But to us, at age twelve, a lame hometown is a lame hometown.

A hippie conservationist from Truro named Eli leads the beach walk, his dark brown dreads swishing from shoulder blade to shoulder blade, stiff, like a pendulum. Mrs. Ford, our feathered-banged science teacher with a screechy voice, stays back with the bus, citing a headache. We're left to listen to Eli yammer on about erosion and protecting the endangered piping plover nests, little birds whose protection years later would render my two hundred and fifty dollar off-road beach sticker null and void. He turns around every so often to shush us. "Alright, alright, alright, chillll."

It's too cold to do more than stick our feet in, but I put my sneakers back on and stay on the packed sand just beyond the water line. Eric Eldredge and Chris Schwartz fling dried black seaweed and dead horseshoe crab shells at the backs of Jenny Cummings and Sheryl Berg, two slump-shouldered, greasy-haired perpetual victims. Eli doesn't notice and drones on.

I get elbowed out to one side of the walking cluster consisting of Lauren, Max, and John. As I trail the group, I suddenly feel trapped and lonely and disappointed—so heart-wrenchingly disappointed. I wish I lived in a place where kids ride bikes on vanilla streets until dusk, where life is easy and "normal." What I am picturing is, essentially, the opening credits to *The Wonder Years*, me as Winnie Cooper in her nerd glasses waving to button-nosed Kevin Arnold.

What I really want is a life with parents who are whole

and unencumbered and there is no death or sickness or stress. A place where every summer, local adults won't bemoan the clueless tourists and clogged streets and cloistered lines at their favorite restaurants filled with screaming kids. A place where our parents don't bitterly envy the money that fuels second homes and gas-guzzling Suburbans.

I look around and realize no one has spoken to me, or acknowledged me, in almost a half an hour. I walk into the water, shoes and all. Maybe I can drown myself.

Jenny Cummings, having hung back to avoid seaweed rockets, turns around and gapes at me, eyes wide. "Ellie?" she whispers, looking back and forth at Eli, far ahead, and me, wet up to my knees in the freezing water.

The shock wears off and all I feel is the arresting cold. With much effort I run with high knees out of the water, trying not to make loud splashes. I put my finger to my lips. "Don't tell anyone I did that," I say, shivering, regretting almost embarrassing myself, then regretting the decision to live. I should have drowned myself.

"What, don't tell anyone you waded in the water with your shoes on?"

"Yeah, I spaced out."

Jenny, whom I'd always found repulsive, gives me a repulsed look of her own. "It's not like anyone would care," she says, rolling her eyes.

I give her a wide berth and walk ahead of her.

No one does care. My drenched shoes and socks squelch together as I return to Lauren and Max's cluster, as welcome as a hangnail.

Later when I get home, Maureen Frites, social worker, widow, and part incisive bloodhound, is on to me as soon as I walk in the door. "Why are you wet?"

Though hours have passed, you can still see the briny, damp ends of my jeans and the spray of salt powdering my shoes and pant legs. I look behind me. I've also left clusters of sand in my wake.

"I'm not wet."

She marches up to me, bends down, and pinches my pant leg. "I repeat—why are you wet?"

"Why do you care?"

"That's not an answer. Why are you wet?"

I've still got my Bradlees backpack slung on one shoulder. I'm tired, I'm hungry, I just want to smash some Gushers or Kudo bars, and I want my mom to leave me alone. I try to brush past her.

"You're not answering me. Answer me!"

"I got wet at a field trip! The water crashed on my feet, okay? Why are you mad? Why are you always mad?"

I am browsing through the kitchen drawers and opening up cabinets, loud and fast, trying to hoard some snacks in case we get into one of our ever-brewing arguments and she sends me to my room.

"You had a field trip today? I don't remember signing a permission slip."

That's because she didn't. I had forgotten to give it to her in time and I forged it.

"Yes, you did, Mom. You just don't remember."

"I think I would remember a field trip to the beach."

I shrug, not meeting her eye. I shove a ginger snap in my mouth to stall. It's stale. It doesn't snap so much as melt.

"You're lying, Eleanor Frites."

Yup. Just like I lie about stealing dollar bills out of her coat pockets. I lie about this stuff…drumroll…because I'm eleven.

We squabble back and forth like this for five more minutes and then she banishes me to my room. Thankfully, I manage to pound two granola bars, a hunk of Monterey Jack cheese, and another cookie. As I sit here in my room, an unwelcome, lingering question remains, like a slow-moving fly trapped inside a windowsill. What if I drowned? What if I did die? Would I not hurt any longer? Would I not feel anything?

***

Liz interrupted me. "Ellie, did you used to think about suicide a lot?"

I stretched my cramped legs and sat up, feeling slightly dizzy. After a moment, I looked at her and said truthfully, "No, I don't think so. If I did, I wasn't serious. Just typical, like, I wanna die type stuff. I mean, when you're young, you get all dramatic like that."

Liz looked unconvinced. "Your relationship with your mother sounds rife with contention back then. Is it still that way?"

"No, we're a lot better. She was just so overprotective back then. She was, like, crazy. Nervous nelly."

Liz nodded. "Okay, Ellie, it's almost time to finish up. But can I ask one favor, and you can decline of course."

"Sure."

"Would you allow me to try one more full-on hypnotherapy session? This is helpful, you getting into a semi-relaxed state and verbalizing your memories. It's fantastic. But…we need to go deeper. We need to get at more difficult memories."

"If there are more difficult memories," I reminded her.

"Of course."

I shrugged. "Okay. But for the record, I'm, like, a lot happier these days. Due to Tim, obviously."

Then Ricki entered my thoughts like an intruder. Ricki, whose world revolved around Tyler and nothing else. I frowned. I did not want to become like her.

"Well," I conceded, "I guess having a dude can't solve all my problems…"

Liz smiled and waited.

I sighed. "Okay, one more session, we'll see how that goes."

"Terrific."

***

From: Maureen Frites <Maureen_Frites@child-family-services.gov>
To: Ellie Frites <ellie_frites@symbicore.com>
Date: Tuesday, 3:30PM

Hon,

Doing some research on hypnosis, and I really want you to take what you're "remembering" at face value. I know I've said this before, but I wish your "doctor" would take the proper steps to set boundaries and gain your trust before using such extreme, unproven measures. Has she even discussed the limitations? The false memories that can be, and I'm not saying she would do this necessarily, suggested to you? At the very least, confabulation can occur. Do some research.

I hope you're telling me the truth when you say you've stopped this nonsense for the time being. I can refer you to more reputable therapists. Where did you find this woman, anyway?

Oh, Jack is coming home from school this weekend, if you're interested in going out to dinner on Saturday.

Love,
Mom

From: ellie_frites@symbicore.com
To: Maureen_Frites@child-family-services.gov
Date: Sunday, 12:30PM

Sorry I left the house in such a huff. But you need to get off my back about therapy and the methods Dr. Rollins thinks work best for me. You're being really annoying. It's all you talk about. You're, like, obsessed. Maybe focus instead on the fact that your son was high as a kite the ENTIRE WEEKEND?

Love,
Ellie

11

Group Project

Eric Eldredge, sitting in the desk to my right, is scribbling *Kurt Cobain* in his notebook over and over, digging his pen down hard, next to the words *Nevermind* and *Smells like Teen FARTS*. Cobain died two years ago, but popular music takes a while longer to reach our tiny town on the Cape. I can't stop staring at the grease that collects at his widow's peak, or how he keeps itching his shoulder with his chin, where his flannel shirt is frayed at the collar. He adds a vertical, *OЯN!!!* to the *K*, like he's playing Scrabble. Then he looks up at me staring at him, scowls, and curls his arm tighter around the paper, blocking my view.

I lean back in my chair and sigh. Lauren is out sick today, and I'm supposed to be partnered with Max for a group project. But Max slid her chair over to John's table and I'm left to do all the work alone. Max and I haven't really spoken since I "saved" her in the Hollow. Anytime anyone asks her about the incident, her favorite response is, "I can't talk about the case without my lawyer present."

To many twelve-year-olds, that statement may sound valid, but to me, it's a total crock of shit. Lauren thinks so, too, and even called her out the other day as we walked to the bus.

"Why don't I ask your mom about this 'lawyer' of yours, Max?" Lauren turned to her and asked.

"Do it," Max challenged.

"Or how about I ask my dad, Max? Who is a lawyer?"

"Fine," Max said quickly. "I don't have a lawyer. Just drop it."

"No, you drop it. And shut up." Lauren readjusted her backpack, so big and unwieldy it looked like it was holding a couple cement blocks, and she turned toward the bus. She stomped up the stairs and walked all the way to the back, selecting the seat with the wheel hump. She scooted to the aisle and placed her backpack beside her. No *sitsies*.

While I'm not thrilled to be ignored by Max today in class, I have to admit it's kind of nice not having Lauren around. A couple weeks ago, when Lauren complained to me about Max hanging out with TJ so often, I reveled in the gossip. I felt included. I felt that maybe I could win after all, that maybe Lauren would finally tire of Max and we could resume being normal sixth graders who played in the backyard filming fake horror movies with her dad's old camcorder. That's what we used to do, before Max decided Lauren would be a sufficient minion: she was far less attractive, she had lenient parents, and she was a serial suck-up.

But after incident in the Hollow, Lauren's jealous gossip morphed into something darker, something even I couldn't glom on to, no matter how poorly Max treated me in the past. Yesterday, for instance, Lauren and I were alone in the locker room, having arrived early. As we changed out of our training bras by wriggling the straps through our shirtsleeves, Lauren said, "You know what, Ellie?"

"What?" I said, my words muffled by my shirt.

"Max acted like a total, retarded mute in the Hollow that night."

My face reddened as I pulled my shirt down and looked quickly around the locker room. I really hoped Ginny Potts wasn't nearby, who had special needs. "What?" I asked. "Why was Max...a mute?"

"Like, how she didn't say anything about who did it? She just laid there? She's probably lying about the whole thing. She probably fucking fell on her face and felt dumb, so she concocted the whole thing."

Pigs were flying and I found myself sticking up for Max. "You're wrong, Lauren," I insisted. "She wasn't making it up. I saw him!"

"Bull," Lauren muttered. She slammed the locker door shut and didn't speak to me for the rest of the day. When I got home from school that afternoon, I noticed a thumb-sized hole in my back jeans pocket, and while I had no proof, I wouldn't have put it past Lauren to have sneaked back into the locker room and cut it out of spite. She did it to Jenny Cummings once before with scissors stolen from the art room, and Jenny had blamed it on me.

Lauren being out sick today is a relief. But watching Max lap up all the boys' attention at the next table is not much better.

A bold thought arises: maybe I shouldn't sit back in defeat today. I scooch over to their table and ask, "John, where did you get that pen?"

He doesn't look up. I clear my throat and say louder, "John—"

Max leans forward, blocking my view of him. "John, look over there."

He looks out the window, in the direction she is pointing. Max grabs the pen out of his grasp.

"Hey!" He laughs. She giggles and they chase each other around the table. My forced smile starts to pain my cheeks, and I grow dizzy from turning my head back and forth as they pivot and pause, pivot and pause.

Suddenly, I stop caring about whether it appears as if I am in on the goddamn fun. My smile cracks and falls, and all I feel is ugly and small and hairy and poor. I think of all the insults Max hurls at me in veiled questions such as, "So, is that a secondhand car? Or third hand…I thought I saw it in the junk yard by 7-Eleven a few months ago." Forget her. I don't need any of this today. I slide my chair back to my desk.

It's clear Mrs. Ford miscalculated the time needed for our group assignment, so we still have forty minutes left of our long period. She shuffles her papers at the front of the room, eyes the clock, and surprises us all by saying, "You know what? Since it's such a nice spring day, we should all go outside and enjoy it!"

We all look at her like she's an alien, but when it's evident she's not joking, we jump up from our desks in a whirl of excitement and start filing out the door. Once outside, Mrs. Ford instructs us to stay within the bounds of the track behind the school, but Max immediately prances off with the boys to the furthest corner of school property possible. Mrs. Ford calls after them weakly, and tells them to stay on the property.

With Lauren out sick and Max slutting it up with Chris and John, I'm left alone. I glance over at the next tier of girls in my class who are sitting on the bleachers. Their clothes resemble my own, their smiles are genuine, and their laughs aren't dripping with ugliness. They probably assume I'm just as much of a bitch as Lauren and Max, not because I behave as awfully, but by association. At some turning point, maybe as we entered middle school, I had two options: join Lauren and Max's coterie and be the punching bag—but semi-popular nonetheless—or stay behind with the less popular girls. I unwisely chose to subject myself to the churlish duo of doom.

I watch the male athletes of the class race one another around the track, then look again at the girls sitting on the bleachers. Betsy Mills is sharing headphones with Selma Watson, and Erin Bleakman, sitting to their right, catches my eye. She waves me over and offers a friendly smile. Erin and

I were friends in Mr. Belfort's homeroom years back. We've drifted. In any case, she is being nice. Thank God.

I walk over to the girls, smiling. Max's venomous comments echo through my head in a familiar scene: Max sprawled out on Lauren's canopy bed thumbing through *Seventeen*, and me in my relegated position—cross-legged on the carpeted floor.

"Betsy Mills has a huge butt," Max would sneer. Lauren would laugh too hard. I would wince, but smile. Max would go on. "Selma Watson is poor and her dad is *trash*." "Erin Bleakman wears the same pair of pants four days in a row. I counted."

Looking at the sweet girls before me, I am ashamed that even at nearly twelve years old I want to associate myself with someone like Max who is cruel but pretty, stupid but admired. And Lauren? She's getting to be worse than Max.

I accept Betsy's offer of some Goldfish and recline on the second-to-last stair of the bleachers. Free of Max and Lauren, I am completely relaxed. I look towards the farthest edge of the track, where Max is laying on her back in the grass in between Chris and John. Her sweatshirt is on the ground beneath her, like a towel, her shirt lifted above her navel. Chris shimmies on his elbows to get closer to her.

There is movement in the line of trees behind them. I squint. It's a figure—a man. I can't make out the face. My heart starts to race and as I sit up, the tinny bleachers rattle. "Do you see that guy, over there in the woods?" I point. "Behind Max?"

The girls strain their eyes, shielding their foreheads from the sun with their hands.

"Look! A little to the left, behind John," Erin says, perking up.

The man is now pacing along the edge of the woods. Max, Chris, and John are oblivious, facing the opposite way. I try to remember what the man looked like from the Hollow, from the crappy police sketch that had resulted from my fragmented memory.

I think out loud. "Well, at least he's not wearing a red hat."

"Yeah," Selma agrees. "I heard Max said the guy attacked her wore a red hat."

"Well, technically it was *my* description to the police." I say. "Max never made a statement. But I was there, I saw him. Well," I pause, "the back of him."

"You were there?" Erin asks. She looks at Betsy, who also looks skeptical.

I gaze at them with my mouth open. "What do people think happened? I saved Max."

"You saved her?" Betsy cocks her head the way my dog does when I start belting out Mariah Carey in my room. "I thought Lauren did."

"Yeah, right," I scoff. "Lauren and TJ were hanging back like pansies while I ran towards the guy and screamed. He ran off, and then I rushed to Max. TJ called the cops after that."

The girls look at each other and smirk.

"I did!" I say. "If I could get a copy of the police report, I'd show you. Lauren and Max might have pretended like I wasn't there, like always, but I was. Not that Max would ever admit it."

The girls smile. Now I am talking their language.

"Maxine is such a bitch," Erin hisses. "And Lauren is a poser."

Betsy and Selma nod hard.

"Don't you think I know?" I say.

Selma stands up with her hands on her hips. "Um…shouldn't we tell Mrs. Ford there's some creep in the woods watching our class?"

We all start heading toward Mrs. Ford, who is reading a book and looking up periodically through her feathered bangs. She's wearing the same wool skirt she always wears, and an ill-fitting vest that makes her look ten years older. She can't be more than thirty, but she looks my mom's age.

Mrs. Ford sees us and gives us a stiff arm, holding up her hand in the universal sign for "stop."

"Girls, we have ten more minutes. Then we go inside. You can go to the bathroom then."

"Um, Mrs. Ford, there's a man in the woods." Betsy points.

"Where?"

"He was…he was behind that tree, we saw him."

Our arms waver in the air, pointing, trying to locate the same spot. He's no longer there.

Mrs. Ford stands up slowly and her bones crack. She peers into each of our eyes, as if weighing the truth of our claim. It must sink in that we are four sensible girls, not troublemakers, because she whips a whistle out of her vest pocket and blows hard. We jump.

"Class!" she yells. About forty percent of the kids look up, while the rest pretend not to hear. No one wants their rare outside time cut short. "This is an emergency!" she bellows. "I need a roll call, right now!"

Our classmates reluctantly walk towards us, ambling along in deliberate zigzags. She tweets the whistle again. "Now!" she roars. She is actually facing the class as she yells, for once, unlike when she puts her back to us at the chalkboard and speaks low and stern. She thinks the rejection approach is more effective, but it's not, it just gets her blasted with more spitballs.

I turn and see Chris and John running towards us. Max is not with them. "Where's Max?" I ask. Everyone starts murmuring among themselves.

The blood draws out of Mrs. Ford's face and her forehead is sweating. Her voice grows shriller. "Chris, Jon, where is Max?"

Chris's face is white. "I don't know."

"What do you m—" Mrs. Ford whirls around and her crazed eyes land on me. "Ellie, go inside and report Max missing to the office and have them call the police. Please run. I'm walking the rest of the kids inside with me."

"You want me to 'run'—by myself—while some man might be lurking around?" I look at her with my hands on my hips. What is wrong with this woman? It's almost a tenth of a mile back to the nearest school building, and the path is surrounded by trees, the same trees that could be hiding the strange man.

She presses her fingers to her temples and breathes out. "Ellie, you're right. Um, Erin. Please go with her. Buddy system."

Erin shoots to my side. At Marshside Middle School, nothing is ever this exciting. Especially not in the off-season, which means any time from September to May, when all the tourists go back to their own boring suburban towns.

Erin grabs my hand, but I resist and look back at John and Chris, who are slinking away from the increasingly irate Mrs. Ford. Erin drags me towards the back entrance, but not before I hear Chris: "She wanted to play manhunt."

John: "She didn't come back…"

Mrs. Ford, again: "What do you mean?"

Erin tugs my arm now, but I don't budge. I look again at the wide path back to the school, flanked by a sizable chunk of trees on either side. What if the man is in there? I give one last beseeching look to Mrs. Ford.

She looks back at me. "Girls, we'll all be right behind you. But run."

Erin drags me along in haste. I speed up just to get through to the clearing. We make it to the back steps, and we're panting. My heart feels like it could rise up and eject up and out of my throat any minute. I start to have trouble breathing. I'm dizzy. The back door is propped open with a small wooden triangle.

"C'mon!" Erin urges as she puts her body between the door and the door jam, waiting for me to go.

I try to form words, but everything is spinning. I eke out, "I can't, wait…" Tears stream down my face as I gasp for breath. I crumple, kneeling on the concrete step with my head down. I feel like I am going to be sick. Erin's voice suddenly sounds far, far away.

"Ellie?"

12

Muppet Recall

I opened my eyes. Dr. Rollins was hovering over the futon, her notepad clenched in her hand by her side. "Ellie, are you alright?"

My heart was racing and sweat was trickling between my breasts. My bra felt tight. I was laying on my back, my legs folded to fit on the futon. A small cylindrical pillow supported my neck.

I sat up and looked around the room, at the pictures on the wall, at the clock, and instinctively pulled out my phone. "What...?"

"It's alright, keep calm. Do you know where you are?"

"At—at therapy."

"Yes. And what year is it?"

I paused. "2009."

"Yes, 2009. Can you tell me what you remember? Starting from the beginning of this visit?"

My mind was so cloudy. I looked at the floor and concentrated.

"We thought we would try hypnosis once more," Liz offered softly.

I nodded, and my head started to clear. "Yes. I remember."

"Tell me exactly what you remember."

"I remember coming here, from work. I was late."

Liz nodded. "We started talking about…" She waited for me to fill it in.

"Tim again. You weren't that interested in that, though, and wanted to get down to business."

She bristled. "I did not—okay. And then?"

"You got me to lie down. Then—wait, can you just tell me if I was unconscious? Sleeping?"

"You started in a sort of trance, yes. You would speak occasionally, even answer my questions. Eventually, you fell deeper. Tell me, was it different from the other times we've tried this?"

I nodded. "Yeah. More realistic. All the details, all the conversations. They were more pronounced. I felt like I was there."

"You didn't feel like you 'there' in the last hypnosis sessions?"

I faltered as I attempted to explain. "I did…this just felt…more immediate. Like…I was moving towards something. Something big."

I offered a shortened account of what I saw, due to time and sheer exhaustion. Liz nodded along and didn't seem surprised by anything I said. I asked why.

"You were giving a kind of play-by-play, kind of muttering dialogue, what you saw. And it was quite detailed."

"So why'd you ask what I was experiencing?"

"To see if you remembered once you snapped out of it."

"Oh."

"I suspected that since it took more effort to wake you that you were in kind of a fugue state. Less aware of your surroundings."

Fugue. Sounded ugly.

When it came time to leave, I agreed to another session, and Liz was beaming again, sending me off with that sparkle in her eye, like I was her star pupil heading off to Yale on a full ride. I, on the other hand, was frustrated. What I'd witnessed during hypnosis so far hadn't answered any of my questions. It had only formed more.

I walked down the creaking steps to my car and rummaged through my purse for the keys, shivering. I thought back to that year, 1996. Sixth grade. Marshside Middle School. I thought of Lauren and Max; how close the short-lived friendship had taken place to the loss of my father. I always knew on some level that my memory was spotty the year he died. I just had no idea I'd block out whole days, whole events.

I needed someone else's perspective, someone who knew me at that time. Someone other than my mother who could help corroborate the events of that year. There was only one person: Sarah.

I pulled out of the driveway and called her, but got voicemail. I pulled over to text her. I was being a safe driver, but to be honest, I was shaking too hard to text with one hand on the wheel. I wrote in all caps: *CALL ASAP.*

As I drove, I racked my brain. Who else could I ask? I was no longer friends with Betsy, Erin, or Selma, though I supposed I could look them up. But they weren't there that original day at the Hollow. I couldn't contact Max—what would I even say? How would I explain that I didn't remember the demise of our friendship? That I was dredging up nonsense from years ago, even though it probably meant nothing now?

When I got back to my empty apartment, cardboard boxes lined the hallway and Ricki's jackets lay in heaps on the closet floor. She would officially move out next week but had been staying at Tyler's ever since our argument. As if she was making any sort of statement. She'd have been staying at his place anyway. I kicked a pair of her shoes out of the way as I made my way to my bedroom and felt a flutter in my chest over Sarah moving in. I couldn't wait.

I slipped into some sweatpants and a sweater and retrieved my iPad. I settled into the couch and conducted a quick Internet search of newspaper archives from the *Marshside Chronicle*. Nothing turned up about Max or Lauren in the last few years, though as for back in 1996 there was a dearth of any information whatsoever, because Cape publications were behind the times in digitizing old content. Interestingly, I found police reports involving Max's mother, Larissa Lang, from the early 2000s: one domestic disturbance, and one possession of a Class D Controlled Substance. An image of Max's mother chain smoking in the kitchen came to mind, along with her erratic behavior when she picked up Max from the Hollow. Of course she was a druggy, I thought meanly. Just because you had a BMW didn't mean you were particularly high class or better than everyone else. I wished I knew that at age eleven.

I rubbed my temple, frustrated, and jumped when my phone rang, which was wedged beneath my thigh on the couch. It was Sarah. I picked up, itching to talk about the past. But Sarah was fixated on the present. She wanted to know the amount of our average heating bill, and what channels we got—did we have HBO? Because we should totally have HBO, she said, and she would pay extra because she knew how much I made and that I hadn't had a raise in over two years because of stupid Buster, but she'd be making decent money at MGH, and she really didn't mind paying more for cable! I answered her questions, half-listening, my heart a steady thump in my chest, until finally she asked, "What's up with you?"

And that gave me the opening to launch into the calamity that was my life at the moment, and the opportunity to ask about sixth grade.

But as soon as I started delving into therapy—I'd only briefly mentioned it up until that point over our abridged

"Life Updates" emails—she started in on the importance of mental health to a person's well-being, and how she also went to a therapist once in a while and it helped so, so much.

I had to cut her off. "Wait, Sarah? We can talk about all that later. Sorry to be so blunt, but this is important."

"Oh, sorry," she said. "I'll shut up."

"Long story short, I had a few sessions, normal ones, I guess, of just talking. Well, of me trying to talk. You know how much I cry when I drink? Well, you can imagine how much I cry when I'm in a so-called 'safe place'…"

Sarah laughed. "I can imagine. Waterworks."

"Right. So the last couple of weeks Dr. Rollins, or Liz, became convinced that I have this untapped memory that's serving as the source for my grief. I kept trying to tell her it's my dad's death, and that I've always been a big crier, but she thought it might be something more."

"Oh man. Like…abuse or something?"

I paused. "I think that's what she was getting at."

Sarah was quiet.

I continued. "She suggested hypnotherapy. Which scared me at first. I don't need her planting things in my head, you know?"

"I've read a little about hypnotherapy," Sarah said, getting breathless. I pictured her pacing back and forth down the hallway of her sprawling rental in Burlington, Vermont with the two-car garage and long driveway. I looked around my tiny apartment with the street parking—my car got towed during street cleaning at least once a month—and was suddenly worried. Would Sarah hate the city? My anxieties were blasting me from every angle. Traumatic past, nervy present, unknown future—I was extremely overwhelmed.

"Sometimes the resulting memories aren't really memories," Sarah was saying. "They get, like, suggested to you, so you think they're real. I read about all these court cases in college…wait, sorry. Go on."

"It's okay," I said, having lost my train of thought. Thankfully I retrieved it quickly and said, "Okay, right. Today's session was the latest attempt at the whole hypnotherapy thing. She got me into this trance state, where I felt conscious, but kind of sleepy, and then next thing I know, I'm inside kind of a dream. I was reliving my childhood. It seemed like I was reliving a whole day, but less than an hour passed in real time. And it was vivid. Much more vivid than the session before."

I stopped, exhausted, and warned myself not to give anything away. I wanted Sarah to remember anything about Max on her own. I began again. "Something happened. I want to know if I told you about it. Back around the time it happened. I'm thinking—and Liz is thinking—it's a traumatic memory I've repressed. Or, it never happened, and this hypnotherapy thing is a crock of shit."

Sarah was quiet.

"You remember Maxine Lang, right?" I asked.

"Of course I remember her. I'm friends with her on Facebook for some bizarre reason."

"Oh, you are?" I asked, stunned. A small part of me thought maybe…

"Yeah," Sarah was saying, "I think she just adds people to gain followers. You should have seen this burlesque thing she posted—"

"Okay," I said, cutting her off, "I need to know something specific. When we were, like, eleven or twelve, do you remember any incidents in town that had to do with her?"

"Incidents?"

"Yeah.

Sarah murmured. "Well, yeah. Obviously the whole thing where she was attacked."

I said nothing.

She went on. "She got, like, approached or attacked or something in the Hollow. Supposedly. I can't remember exact details. She was fine though."

I furrowed my brow and said nothing at first. Then, "Why do you say she was fine?"

"Well, I mean, she was. And I remember a lot of people didn't believe there even was a man? She was hot but she was a total sketchball. You used to tell me all the time."

"Huh…" Why had I not remembered that day if it was so benign?

"Why, what about it?" Sarah asked.

"Well, according to my hypnosis-dream thing, I was there when it happened. When she got taken. We were in the Hollow. I saw the man running off and Max was all bruised and terrified. Then I recalled a second abduction in my session today. I was apparently there for that too. She was taken again."

"She was taken a second time?" Sarah asked. "I don't remember that. "Oh God, but remember she got all fucked up in high school? She became a huge slut and everyone turned on her—and she ended up dropping out after that school dance where she almost overdosed…remember that? She didn't even make it through freshman year. I wonder if she just ended up getting her GED."

I jolted upright. Images arose of Max in a mini skirt with no underwear underneath, getting pulled off the dance floor by the chaperones. "Whoa," I said, shaking my head. "I forgot all about that."

Sarah continued. "I just remember her tweaking out. The principal and teachers were restraining her and she kept yelling crazy stuff. She wouldn't let Principal Goldfarb touch her. Only the female teachers."

My stomach flipped. "You've got an excellent memory, Muppet."

"But to answer your question more clearly, Ellie, yes. I do remember someone tried to attack or kidnap her, and she became really popular from it afterwards. You used to complain about it to me on the phone." Sarah laughed. "We were both jealous that she almost got abducted. How fucked."

I did remember. But I asked again, "And you don't remember her getting abducted a second time?"

"No, I don't remember a second time at all."

I tried a different tack. "Do you remember Lauren Vine?"

"Ugh, yes, you used to complain about her all the time, too. She was so mean. You'd write me letters, remember? You sent me a poem pretending you were her, I'll never forget it. 'My name is Lauren Vine and all I do is whine.' I probably still have them somewhere. I'd tell you all the time to stop hanging out with them. But they kinda hooked you. You thought they were cool or whatever."

I shook my head to myself and said, "Your memory is insane. Either that or mine is terrible." A smile crept onto my face. "I do remember those poems!"

I would sit at my desk in my bedroom and craft ditties about my enemies. Then, with a filched book of my mother's stamps, I'd mail them off to Sarah at boarding school.

We sat quietly for a moment. Then I said, "I'm just so confused. After a certain point, Max is a blur, and Lauren is a total blur, too. All I recall is that my mom had something against Lauren's parents because they were so lenient with us. She'd go up to their door and be crazy about making sure they had their eye on us. Weird what comes back so vivid, and what's still spotty. And Max's mom—she was a piece of work. I read a bunch of old police reports on her. No wonder Max turned out the way she did."

Sarah murmured in agreement.

I sighed. "My stomach is in knots. Something's not right. My mom was being kind of weird at the beach last weekend too, so dismissive of hypnotherapy. Of the whole process."

"Well, I don't blame her, sorry to say," Sarah said. "She's professionally trained in mental health. Of course she doesn't trust this stuff."

Sarah couldn't remember much more about Max, or the Hollow, and eventually the conversation shifted from the brain-draining mess that was my childhood to the logistics of Sarah's impending move.

Then she asked about Tim. I gave a short and sweet response. "So far, so good."

"Oh, you're being mum," Sarah teased.

"Just waiting for the other shoe to drop. It's going too well."

"Don't be so paranoid, Elf. If it's good, it's good."

"Maybe," I said.

"Okay, girl." Sarah yawned. "I'm getting to bed. Love ya."

I echoed her yawn. "Lova ya, bye."

After getting off the phone, I set up another therapy appointment online for Thursday, which was in two days.

I heard a scratching sound outside my door, and made a mental note to get some mousetraps before Sarah moved in.

13

Three Little Birds

I was folded up on the futon at Dr. Rollins's office. After a few minutes of relaxing my mind and listening to soft tinkling music in the background, I lost sense of place and time, hurtling backwards and landing, once again, in 1996.

***

I'm at Lauren's house, standing on the front stoop, looking askance at my mother. "Please go back in the car? You're embarrassing me, Mom!"

She ignores me. She has marched me all the way up the steep hill of Lauren's driveway and now stands so close to me I can smell her coffee breath. She insists on speaking with Lauren's dad, Mr. Vine.

Lauren answers the door, finally, after we ring the bell for five minutes. My mother gives her a curt hello and asks, "Your mother's working, correct? May I speak with your father for a moment?"

Lauren tosses her head toward the top of the stairs and calls, "Dad! Come down! Mrs. Frites again!" Her eyes rest again on my mother, and then me. She has no interest in the ensuing exchange, so she bounds down the hall toward the back of the house. I hear the slider open up, the one that that leads to back deck. I assume Max is out there already. I make a move to follow, but my mother's hand clamps around my knobby shoulder and holds me back.

Mr. Vine clunks down the stairs in his shiny black shoes and stands wearily on the second to last step. He clutches a stack of papers in one hand, the other rests on top of the banister.

He listens patiently as my mother natters about safety, supervision. He assures her that the girls are fine—he'll be home the whole time.

She adds that she does not want me roaming in the woods in the backyard, and that she does not want a repeat of us walking to the Hollow. It's been over a month since that incident occurred, but it's still fresh in my mother's mind.

He cuts her off with a wave of his large hand, still holding the papers. "I'm not even sure the girl was ever kidnapped in the first place."

My mother opened her mouth, but he cut her off. "These girls have wild imaginations, and that TJ punk is a troublemaker. I don't believe a word out of the kid's mouth."

"But he's just a kid!" my mother says. "And Maxine, I know we all doubted her story at first, but Ellie is insistent about what she saw. A man running off in the woods. And then, the other day, Max went missing again…"

"Mo-om," I piped in through gritted teeth. "She snuck off to 7-Eleven. The cops found her. You know this."

"But you said you saw a strange man that day, too, Ellie. You said—"

I widen by eyes. "I thought I saw one, but Max was fine, Mom. She skipped class to buy candy." And also cigarettes, but I'll be damned if I tell my mother this; she'd never let met hang out with Max again. It's a miracle she is letting me now.

"See?" Mr. Vine says, his palm upturned towards me. "The cops found her. Case closed."

He goes on to say we constructed the original Hollow story for attention. He doesn't call any of us by name, just "the girls," like we all colluded and conspired to make up it all up, like there was never a whacko who had left Max beaten in the woods. I know what I saw, but I don't press it. I just want to hang out with my friends and my embarrassing mother to leave.

My mother stares at him intently, her wild hair shooting up in spirals off the sides of her head. "I'm not taking any chances."

I regard the both of them. My mother's dowdy, off-white shirt appears dirty in contrast to Mr. Vine's creased black slacks and slightly crinkled, but stark-white dress shirt. He looks—what's the word—professional? No. Rich. My mother, therefore, looks poor.

I peek around them to the back of the house, through the glass sliding door, where Lauren and Max are spared my mother's tyrannical display of overprotection. Thank God. Other mothers are polite and have tact and laugh courteously at the bad jokes of other parents, even ones they don't like. Other mothers brush aside their constant worry for their children and let go a little. Never my mom. She holds tight to the worry and wears it proud; to hell if she masks it with small talk. She "buried her husband at forty-one, and she'll be damned if she loses her children." It's her favorite line.

Mr. Vine fixes his eyes on her now, bored. He waits for my mother to say anything else. She doesn't, but turns to me and points a long, thin finger at my chest, as if she wants to tunnel it into my heart and extract it, á la *Indiana Jones and the Temple of Doom*, and says, "You behave."

I nod, my face beet red. She turns and crashes out the screen door and stomps down the hill back to our crap Subaru, which she'd kept running in case the engine wouldn't restart.

I look up at Mr. Vine, elevated on the second to last step. "Sorry about my mom," I say with a small smile, like I understand she's a coot. I know I'm betraying my own mother for the approval of some man, but I can't help it. Especially since my father died, I'm starved for male attention.

Well, Mr. Vine couldn't care less about me—this is certain. He barely catches my eye before he breathes in using seemingly all of his lung capacity. After a beat too long, he breathes out a guttural growl. He turns from me and ascends the stairs with heavy steps. I feel the lowest of the low. I don't have too many father figures in my life; my uncles live far away. They're all my dad's brothers, and so since he's dead, who are we to them, really? We don't even have so much as a friendly male neighbor. Sarah's dad is a sweet guy, a big, jovial redhead, but he travels for business so much, I barely see him.

I walk through the kitchen and slip out the slider and step onto the back deck. Lauren and Max are together on the grass, flipping through at magazines. Their heads barely lift as I amble towards them, feeling as though a lead ball is knocking around my stomach. I realize it is the first I've seen Max since she was suspended for running off to 7-Eleven, causing everyone to think our testimony from the incident in the Hollow was a total lie.

"Hey, guys," I say.

Lauren grunts. "Hey." She is stomach-down on the grass, propped up by her elbows, both palms squishing her cheeks like a deflated whoopee cushion as she scans *Seventeen*.

Words tumble out of my mouth. "So, Max, everything okay? After the other day? That was crazy." I shake my head, trying to look sympathetic and get her to spill. It's unlike me to address her so directly; I usually wait until she decides to speak to me. But right now, as much as I pretended to my mother that I didn't care so that she'd allow me to still hang out with her, I'm too curious—and honestly? Freaked out. "Everyone thought you were taken again. Like the first time."

Max doesn't answer, but Lauren looks up and says sharply, "I'm sick of hearing about this. Max was an idiot and wanted to be cool and buy cigarettes. Plain and simple." She gives Max a wretched look. "All you want is attention."

Max purses her lips and says nothing.

Lauren places the back of her hand to her forehead and forms her fingers in the shape of an L. "Loser, is what you are," Lauren says.

Max, again, says and does nothing. What happened to the sassy and brash leader of the pack? A few months ago, she'd have put Lauren in her place. Now, Max can't even make eye contact with me, let alone Lauren—she looks defeated. I realize I'm still standing, hovering over them, so I sit down. I feel helpless and confused. What is going on? It's not even enjoyable being around these two. I was used to being the ignored, often patronized third wheel to their giggling twosome. But they would always warm up to me eventually and we'd end up having fun. But something is different about today.

"Let's do a movie," Max says suddenly. She looks at Lauren hopefully. Movies are our thing. We pretend to film each other and write out lines, typically for horror films, because we are obsessed with old movies like *Texas Chainsaw Massacre* and *Amityville Horror*.

Lauren sighs and sits up. "Fine. Ellie and I will be the directors and you'll be the actress."

Lauren instructs Max to go inside and get the camera. Her father's old camcorder doesn't work—it's more of a prop in our game of pretend—but it lends a feel of authenticity.

"Have Ellie do it," Max says, not moving. She rips handfuls of grass from their roots and sprinkles them over her tanned legs.

"Ellie and I are the directors," Lauren says. "You're the actress. That means you go get the camera because we're the bosses. We tell you what to do."

Lauren stares Max down. Max waits, as if she thinks Lauren

will just drop it. When she doesn't, she huffs and makes a dramatic display of getting to her feet. The blades of grass cascade down her legs. She turns on her heel and heads into the house. I'm doubtful directors in real movies make actresses carry the equipment, but I say nothing. I don't dare incite Lauren's wrath on her home turf.

With sheets of lined paper, Lauren and I plan out the scene. We write our typical dialogue like: "Veronica Mills runs scared through the woods." "She looks over her shoulder and screams." And of course the requisite: "Helllllllp!"

Veronica Mills is our favorite character name. Mills, as in Hayley Mills from the original *Parent Trap*, not the stupid Lindsay Lohan one, and Veronica because it sounds to us like most Veronicas would be pretty. Lauren assigns me the *male* serial killer role and writes Max a slow death. Lauren is the hero and sole survivor, naturally. We use an air-camera on our shoulders while we wait for Max to come back with the real thing.

Fifteen minutes pass.

"Where the shit is she?" Lauren asks.

I turn towards the house. "Want me to go see? I have to pee anyway."

"Just pee. If she doesn't come out, then we'll do the movie on our own." As I get up she repeats, "Don't even bother looking for her. She just wants attention."

I think this is weird, but Lauren has been acting like a grade-A bitch all day so it doesn't surprise me. I go to the bathroom in the downstairs half bath next to the kitchen. But before I head back out the slider door, I see the camcorder on the kitchen table amid piles of unopened mail and JC Penney catalogs. I start to get annoyed. It's been a good twenty minutes now. Is Max pulling something again? Maybe she is so incredibly starved for attention that she ran off again. Then Lauren and I would have to go look for her, maybe even call the cops. I start to feel angry and understand Lauren's frustration. Max is exhausting.

Before I go outside in a huff and tell Lauren that Max is indeed missing, I figure I'd better be sure she's actually gone from the house. I look downstairs, the basement, and even poke my head into the garage. Nothing. I look out the front window, which overlooks the end loop of the cul-de-sac. Minivans sit in driveways under unused basketball hoops of children grown up and out of their childhood homes.

I don't want to go upstairs and disturb Mr. Vine; he'd told Lauren in no uncertain terms that he was busy working on a case and that we were not allowed upstairs. The second floor only consists of the master bedroom with his office built into it, along with a narrow loft overlooking the first floor that has a broken TV, so no one ever goes up there. But then I remember that there is a small alcove. It has a phone, a beanbag chair, and a little table. I listen hard from the bottom of the stairs. I think I hear her.

I hop up the stairs quietly, and as I pass the parents' bedroom I notice the door is cracked. I pass by it quickly, hoping Mr. Vine doesn't see me. I peek around to the alcove. No Max.

I tiptoe back to the stairs and must pass the bedroom once more. I hear a noise and stop. I peer closer through the cracked door with one eye. Max is on her knees. Mr. Vine is standing before her, his hand grabbing a chunk of her blonde hair like a handle as her head goes back and forth, back and forth. His pants are crumpled and down around his ankles. He is facing me, and would see me watching—if his eyes weren't closed.

First, I don't register what I'm seeing. I just know it's wrong. I sense my mouth hanging open, and my legs suddenly feel very weak. I turn around like one of the zombies in our pretend horror movies and slowly walk down the stairs, the noise of my steps absorbed by the carpet. Everything starts spinning. I see stars and little flying sparks that look like twinkling lightning bugs, and then it becomes cloudy. Somehow I make my way to the slider. I open the door and stand at the threshold trying to clear my sight. I call Lauren's name. There is something that catches the corner of my eye. I turn and look—it's a small, pewter-colored coat rack nailed to the wall with a string of three white seagulls painted across the top. Hanging on one hook is a bucket hat, like the kind my grandfather used to wear golfing. On another, a baseball cap. A red, faded-almost-to-pink, baseball cap.

My vision blurs, and all I see are those little white seagulls fluttering in front of my face. And that one speck of red.

14

The Interface

The tricky thing about conjuring these memories from thirteen years ago was just that: everything had happened thirteen years ago. So as terrifying as the revelation may have been about Max and Mr. Vine, there was nothing I could really do about it. Unless I wanted to call up Maxine out of the blue and rehash everything. Even then, who would I be helping? Me.

Dr. Rollins and I continued having sessions that week to talk it through, turning over every detail. I'd see my mother that coming weekend—we'd be attending a family wedding on the Cape—so I told Liz I'd use the opportunity to tell my mother what I remembered and to ask more questions.

The wedding, by the way, was an affair I'd be attending without a date. Because when it came to my present-day life—and in particular, Tim—I was continuing to be an expert at fucking things up.

***

Oliver Windig, Symbicore CEO, rested his forearms on the podium. Sweat beads dripped down his temple. He was dwarfed in height by the lanky CFO, Ron Smithers, who stood to his right. The light beamed into Oliver's eyes from the projector, causing him to blink and his head to create a large oval shadow against the white screen. As the last trickle of employees filtered in along the back of the conference room, the lights dimmed and huge block letters appeared: *Q3 Company Interface: How do we stay Innovative?*

The *Rocky* soundtrack piped through the speakers, too loud at first, causing us all to jump. Mel and I were crouched in the second the last row, and behind us, Barry's IT group was tittering and clicking and twisting their headset mics. Middle managers in the front row bopped their heads to the music as they smiled conspiratorially at one another: *Aren't we so hip?* Buster, of course, was posted up front and center.

I scanned the room. A couple members of the nattily dressed Global West sales team sat along the left wall on top of tables or cross-legged on the floor, giving each other fist bumps. They were receiving some big award today, along with fat bonuses. I swore, if the Customer Service Ninjas got a sliver of commission for all the tedious work we did for them, I could have paid off my school loans in one lump sum.

Beside the sales team sat the Database Marketing team, who wore polo shirts and sneakers. I sneaked a peek at Tim. He sat in a folding chair squeezed between two plump blondes. He caught me looking and I whipped my head forward, pretending to be interested in Ron Smithers's quarterly financials. A blazing heat crept up my neck. Mel must have followed my gaze, because she elbowed me.

Oliver regained center stage. "Who can I R.A.V.E.! about first?"

We all waited for him to select the most eager lemming, the person leaning the most forward in their seat. "You, sir," he shouted at Buster. "Your elevator pitch. Ten seconds. Go!"

"Of course," I murmured to Mel.

Buster stood, smoothing wrinkled dress pants that looked about ready to rip at the butt crack, and waited for Randy Mangs, a bottom-feeder in the HR department, to scurry across the aisle with a microphone. Randy wore a nametag that said *Interface Volunteer*.

"Poor Randy," Mel whispered. "His name tag doesn't even have his name on it. Just Interface Volunteer."

Buster tapped the microphone and spoke too close to the mouthpiece. "To a client, I'll immediately say on a call: 'We stand for R.A.V.E.! Responsiveness, Adventuresome, Valued, and Enterprising. What do you stand for? Because I'll just bet we're on the same team.'" He cleared his throat and added, "I tell my Ninjas the same thing."

A couple ass kissers from our Customer Service, including Susan Ellmore, my fish-loving cubicle-mate, cheered.

Oliver nodded his head furiously and clapped hard. "Yes, yes!"

Mel and I rolled our eyes.

Buster held out his hand, wiggling his wrist in impatience as he waited for Randy to dart back across the aisle. Randy snatched the mic and scuttled away like a ball boy at Wimbledon. Buster was preening. Some people started to clap, but Oliver cut them off and spat into his own mic, "Who's next?"

Oliver's next move was to catch someone off guard. His victim today was Peter, a sweaty contractor from accounting. "You!" he pointed. "Make me R.A.V.E.!"

I looked around, dumbfounded. Did all these people, besides Mel and me, think what this company did was important? Selling storage software? Did they find their jobs impactful? Fulfilling? Or were they just better at faking it? Was something wrong with me? For some unknown reason, I started to laugh uncontrollably.

Mel joined in, infected. Our giggles were silent, at least, but our shoulders shook. I caught Tim's eye across the room again. I looked away quickly. My complexion must have been maroon.

"Stop looking at him," Mel whispered.

"I know, I can't help myself."

"Have you talked to him about it?"

I shook my head as tears welled in my eyes. "I feel so stupid."

"He'd probably understand if you explained you've been trying to work out some issues lately. That you're going through some weird shit."

I raised my eyebrows. "I can't do that!"

"Why not?"

"It's too early. He'll think I'm a psycho. Hypnotherapy? Possible childhood abuse? That's the stuff you drop after you get your hooks into them. I don't have hooks yet. I have nubs." I held up my hand and fashioned it into a limp-wristed fist.

"I'm telling you, Ellie, he likes you—you're gonna ruin it if you don't talk to him."

"I already ruined it the other night!"

"Shh!" Susan whipped her melon head around. "I can't hear!"

Mel set her jaw and spoke through her teeth. "And I can't eat my lunch when you turn the communal kitchen into a Red Lobster."

Susan's mouth dropped open and she turned back around.

"Mel, that was mean," I said.

Mel shrugged. "Sometimes you gotta take one for the team. For the greater good."

Two Nights Earlier

After that last haunting therapy session, Liz suggested I give my brain a rest. The following week at work, my brain was doing anything but resting. I kept seeing Mr. Vine standing over Max, his grip on her blonde hair, her head rocking back and forth. I couldn't get it out of my mind.

When Mel suggested I blow off some steam at a work mixer, I was more than happy to oblige.

Buster let the Ninjas leave early by a whopping half hour, so I trotted down the sidewalk with Mel in tow. Tim told me he would be making an appearance, so I'd worn my best sweater dress. My chest felt light and fluttery. Up to this point, we'd been on a handful of dates and spoke regularly on the phone; he called me practically every night. During the workweek, our schedules were at odds, so we rarely saw each other. I was looking forward to the mixer, to hanging out with him around other people.

The rest of the office trickled in slowly. My first glass of wine bore witty comments and emboldened approaches to unknown coworkers. I felt the thrill of working among relatively young people, the same nameless faces tilted downwards in the hallways were now open-mouthed, laughing, introducing one another. *Symbicore's not so bad*, I thought. *Maybe Tim and Savannah are right. Maybe I'm in this career-confused phase of my life for a reason—so I'll be forced to figure things out. And maybe, if I play my cards right, my time in Customer Service will parlay into a better position.*

And hell, I thought shyly, *maybe it had allowed me to meet the love of my life.*

On my second glass, I looked around for Tim, casually. I didn't want to seem too desperate. He hadn't approached me yet, but he had to have seen me. Maybe he was doing the same thing. At one point, I saw him out of the corner of my eye, talking to the bartender. The tattooed brunette threw her head back in laughter at whatever he said as she slid him a drink. I wasn't jealous, for once, but felt myself smiling dumbly at the back of his head. Then I realized how creepy I probably looked and turned away.

Mel and I, along with a newcomer to the Customer Service

Ninjas, a snarky dirty blonde named Jen, stood away from the crowd. We each posed with one hand on our hips to diminish arm flab, the other hand gripping our drinks. When Jen went off to get another drink, I noticed I'd failed to engage Mel in conversation over three words per sentence. She wasn't acting like herself.

"Everything okay?" I asked.

She shrugged and peered into her wine glass.

"So, no," I answered for her.

She shrugged again and I saw her eyes drift to the pool tables in the corner.

"Ah," I said. "Trouble in paradise?"

Savannah and Mel had seen each other much more frequently than Tim and I since our initial double date. Despite this, their relationship status was just as undefined as my nascent relationship with Tim, and while Mel sniffed that she "wasn't into labels," it was clear she didn't like the looks of Savannah getting ogled by the Global West Sales guys over a game of innocent pool either.

"What's the protocol here?" I asked, tossing my head in Savannah's direction. "If she's gay and getting hit on mercilessly by straight guys, can you get mad about that?"

Mel narrowed her eyes at me. "She used to be straight. She only just came out this year. Maybe she's bi."

"Wouldn't she have told you if that was the case?"

"Maybe she doesn't know. Or maybe she's bi-curious," Mel said miserably, staring into her glass.

I couldn't help but grin. "Your gaydar is so off, Mel. You've been insisting that I'm bi-curious ever since you told me you were gay. And no offense, I have no interest in the lady folk."

My eyes followed Mel's back over to the pool table. Men of all shapes, sizes, and ages, from the frumpy IT nerds to the suited, married executives were throwing Savannah head-to-

toe gawks. It was the parting of the Red Sea as she wandered up to the cheese and crackers station.

Jen came back with a fresh beer and stifled a burp. She followed our eyes and said, "I heard she wears a band on her ring finger when she goes on client visits so guys don't hit on her. Imagine having that problem?"

Jen didn't know Mel and Savannah were dating. We didn't offer the information now either.

Mel's face twisted in anger. "There are so many sleaze balls at this company, even at nerdy software companies like ours. At the last one I worked at, my friend Tess wanted to network with this higher-up and scheduled a couple meetings with him. He apparently thought being nice equated to her wanting him. He started calling her all the time and even told her to come with him on a vacation he'd planned with his wife. He said he wanted to go with her instead because his wife was too much of a 'nag.'"

"That's messed up," Jen said.

Mel nodded. "She went to HR, but the guy made so much money for the company nothing ever happened to him. She ended up leaving. You think those types care about a ring?"

"Mel," I said quietly when Jen turned her head, "do you really think Savannah cares about those sleaze balls? She's gorgeous, yeah, but she's gay. She told you so. Take her at her word."

Mel took a deep breath and put her drink down. "I need to chill out."

I nodded.

Mel's eyes bugged as she fixed on something behind me.

I felt someone tap my shoulder and I turned. It was Tim, smiling wide.

"Hey."

An odd thought popped into my head. I wondered if he knew I'd memorized his daily schedule by now. I knew what time he took lunch, when he left work, and that he took the Orange Line train. I knew he stood on the left side of the train platform—not the right—because that's where the stairs were located and it was less crowded.

I also knew my gray sweater dress was so stifling at the moment I was forming pit stains. *Why wear grey, Ellie, why?*

"I'd, uh, I'd offer you a drink, but since the company is footing the bill that wouldn't be very chivalrous." He laughed at himself, and I laughed along.

Jen sidled up a little closer.

"Oh! Sorry, Tim. I'm so rude." I put my arm around Jen's shoulders and pushed her closer. "This is Jen. She's new."

They shook.

"And you know Mel," I said, suddenly feeling shy. I shifted my weight and tried to clear my head. I was quite buzzed.

"Are you in Customer Service too?" he asked Jen.

"Yes, we're in hell," Jen said drily. She may have been new, but she'd picked up on the quotidian absurdity of Buster's Symbicore Customer Service team quicker than most.

Tim eyes crinkled in the corners. "I know too well. I used to be in C.S. at another company."

"Did they have pet names for you? Like 'Ninjas'?" Jen asked.

He laughed. "Nope, can't say they did."

Mel, Jen, and Tim chattered more about work, but I grew more inhibited and couldn't think of anything of value to add. I bit my nails and watched.

"So, you ladies going out after this?" Tim asked. The girls looked at one another.

"Yes," I finally piped up.

"Cool. I think we're headed to the Living Room."

The Living Room was an expensive lounge lined with fashion pillows and cushy chairs. Normally, if faced with sitting awkwardly on satin pillows in public dressed to the nines, and sitting in sweatpants on my second-hand couch, I'd pick the sweatpants option. But if Tim was going…

"Love the Living Room," I said.

"Okay, well, before we leave, I'll grab you." He smiled, gave a little wave, and walked off.

The other girls waited until he was a safe distance away and looked at me with matching smirks.

"You must be happy," Mel said.

My mood was suddenly soaring. "Yeah. I am."

"Looks like your stalking paid off," Jen said. "Think he noticed you trailing him like a Post-it note stuck to his shoe the other day?" She was leaning on the table again to keep her balance.

"What?" I hissed. "Shh!" I checked to make sure Tim was out of earshot.

"He can't hear," Jen slurred, then she started giggling. She'd had double the drinks Mel and I had had, which was several, and didn't look to be lasting much longer.

I laughed along with them but grew worried. Had he noticed? I went over and over in my head what I'd said to him just then: a measly three or four responses to his questions. An ugly seed of doubt sprung up. He hadn't called last night, or texted, despite being consistent for weeks. He usually at *least* texted once before bed.

A heat rose in my chest, and tears were not far off. Maybe he invited me out as a pity offering? I wondered. And he didn't even invite me out. He invited us out, the "ladies."

Maybe I was reading this all wrong. Maybe the dates were over. Maybe I was expected to go home with him tonight—to drop trou and he'd get what he wanted, and then he'd be done with me.

"Hey!" Mel said, snapping her fingers in my face. "You alright?"

"Tim doesn't like me," I blurted.

Mel squawked with laughter. "Now who's the paranoid one?"

"Did you see that?" I insisted. "He's using me. He wants to just take me home. Or worse, he was just being nice, and he won't even meet up with us. Maybe he didn't want to completely ignore me so he just—"

"Ellie," she said firmly. "Stop."

She gently dismantled my death grip on my wine glass, and set it down on the table. "You're not allowed any more drinks."

But I needed just one more drink. I need it so that I could talk to Tim. So that I wouldn't be nervous. I told Mel this, and she shook her head. "No."

We went to the Living Room shortly afterwards, but Tim was nowhere to be found. Savannah, on the other hand, was, and she and Mel canoodled the rest of the night, the sight of which made my mood plummet even further.

I looked at my phone. No messages. I noted the time, and gauged it had been an hour since my last drink.

I texted Tim, asking where he was.

No answer.

I wheedled permission from Mel to order another drink, insisting I was "so sober by now."

A few minutes later, in between wriggling around on the dance floor, I sent Tim another text: *Where r u?*

No answer.

Ten minutes later: *Tim? Did you go home? Would have been nice to get a goodbye.*

Five minutes later: *Tim—if you don't' like me, just say it. Why waist my time? I really liked you. But if you're being a dick, then I don't need to waist my time.*

Immediately after: **Waste*

When I arrived home two hours later, I sat in a heap on my

kitchen floor. Buffalo sauce ringed my mouth, and my orange fingers stabbed at my phone.

Tim, did I do something? Tell me what I did wrong. I won't be offended.

Then, before I stumbled to bed, weeping and chuffing sobs, I charged my dying phone. But not before I stuck one last nail in the coffin in my last waking hour, two o'clock in the morning.

Duck you.

***

That was two nights ago, and here I was at the Interface, trying not to look at him. He never called me, or texted me, or so much as stopped by my cubicle. Just thinking about what I'd texted to him made me feel all clammy and mortified.

When the *Rocky* music started piping through the speakers again and the projector was shut off, everyone started shuffling out of their seats towards the exit. I considered waiting around by the glass door outside the elevator. He'd be forced to pass through to return to his desk. I could apologize to him for my ridiculous behavior.

After several minutes idling outside the glass door, whipping my head around every time someone came around the corner from the bathroom, or exited the elevator, I gave up and headed back to my desk.

As I finished my work that afternoon, I left my SymbiChat open, marking my status as available and mentally willing him to send me a message.

He didn't.

15

Memorial Day

I dropped my duffel bag at the front door and collapsed into the pilling couch cushion with a loud sigh. "The ride down was brutal. Took me four hours."

My mother was curled up in her easy chair reading through case files. She delayed a beat in acknowledging me, intent on finishing the last page. Finally, she took her glasses off, looked up, and said, "Hello, dear."

I sprung up and walked into the kitchen, opening and slamming cabinet doors, peering into the fridge. I decided on tortilla chips and brought back the whole bag and sat back down on the couch, offering my mother a handful. When she declined I said, "You're too thin, Mom, take some."

"I just ate."

I gave up and pulled my socked feet up on the couch. "So. What's up with you?"

My mother sighed. "Our office is overloaded. Heroin is making a comeback and it's causing problems down here. There's an overdose every weekend. First it was oxy, now it's H." She put her pen down. "I thought you weren't coming until late tonight. I would've had a quiche or a batch of cookies ready for you."

"I called you to tell you I got off work early…" I stopped to think. Did I?

"No, you didn't."

"Oh. Sorry. I meant to."

Then I remembered why I hadn't. I was so upset by Tim rebuffing me, I knew if she asked a seemingly benign question about my dating life I'd break down and start weeping. Then, she'd say something besides the point that would make me fly off the handle like, "Well, first of all, who, pray tell, is this Tim?"

After a few minutes of shoveling chips in my mouth and staring mournfully at the floor thinking about my *Duck you* text, my mother gathered up her manila folders and shut her laptop. "Enough work for now. It's Friday!"

When she smiled, I noticed her teeth were yellowing and that she had a couple more sunspots on her cheeks. But she appeared to be happy.

We debated over where we could get dinner and decided on a clam shack two towns away, locally owned and without a Facebook page. It wasn't a tourist trap. Yet.

My mother poured two glasses of homemade sangria and led me out to the porch. Gone were the days when she would go nose-to-nose with me like a human breathalyzer, demanding I breathe fire into her discerning nostrils.

As we sat in the warm, early summer air, I looked out at the backyard and the waning sunlight through the porch screen. It was approaching dusk, my favorite time of day. The chickadees chirped and chattered with one another. An occasional hawk swooped high above the tree tops, and I could make out the cobalt speck of a blue jay jumping between the branches of the tall pines along the backwoods. I was calmed by the quiet, the lack of persistent car honks. A neighbor was grilling nearby. A neighbor I could not see through the trees or over the high fence.

By the time I was eighteen and went off to college, I vowed never to set foot on the provincial, isolating peninsula of Cape Cod again. I couldn't wait to escape and live where things happened. Lately, though, I'd been missing the simple, serene peace of a backyard. I didn't have a yard outside the apartment building. I had a square of pavement that housed the dumpster.

My mom blew her nose and looked at me over the Kleenex, still pinching her nose. "So."

"So."

"In your last email you said you had another therapy session. After I warned you against it. For the hundredth time."

I rolled my eyes.

"Don't roll your eyes at me. Can't you understand why I'm concerned? It's dangerous and you're at risk for conflating fantasy with reality!"

"Mom, I'm not doing this—"

"Fine," she said, pushing hair out of her eyes. "I want to hear how it's been going. Do go on." She picked up her glass, the ice clinking together as she brought it to her mouth.

"Well, I remembered something huge. Something...bad." I snuck a peek at her.

She bit her lower lip and sat back, saying nothing.

"Nothing happened to me; don't worry," I assured her.

"What, then?" she asked.

"Do you remember when Max disappeared from class and everyone thought she got attacked again, but she was really just at the convenience store, buying cigarettes?"

My mom sat back and crossed her arms.

"And she got suspended and everything...and shortly after I went over to Lauren's house? You dropped me off?"

She shrugged. "I dropped you off at the Vines' so many times—"

"Well, there was this day when you dropped me off and you insisted on speaking with Mr. Vine. You gave him this whole lecture about watching us closely, especially after what happened in the Hollow."

She cocked her head.

I was getting impatient. "Don't you remember? Mr. Vine was in the middle of working in his office, and he came down, and you tried warning him about us playing in the woods after what happened in the Hollow, and he was being a major prick to you?"

She chewed her lip and muttered, "He was always a prick."

I gave up and told her about what I'd remembered, how I searched for Max throughout the house only to find her in Mr. Vine's room. The color drained from my mother's face and tears pooled around her eyes. "Are you sure you remember this right?"

"Yes."

She put her hand to her mouth.

"Nothing happened to me, Mom, don't worry."

She shook her head and her voice shook. "But it *did* happen to you. Just a young girl…and you've carried it around with you this whole time…"

"Mom. Don't cry," I urged, leaning forward over the table, grasping for her hand, which was ice cold.

She looked up at me and asked intently, "What else do you remember?

I sighed and shook my head. "That's where my recollection stops. I assume you just came and picked me up, and I was too shocked to say anything. Clearly I didn't tell you about it."

She thought for a moment. "I wish this so-called memory recall had come about more naturally. And who knows if you dreamed up additional facets of it? That aren't even true?" She looked at me hopefully.

Here she goes, I thought. "You don't get it, Mom. All of this happened, I'd just blocked it out. It's like a light went on in my head, as cliché as that sounds. Liz says it's amnesia after a trauma, and blotting out terrible events like this is common."

My mother furrowed her brows and stared into her near-empty glass of Sangria, swirling the melting ice cubes with the white and lime green striped straw. Tears continued to stream down her face.

"Mom, please don't be upset. Nothing happened to me. I'm certain of it. I guess there was an advantage to being an underdeveloped little troll back then."

My mom's mouth hung open in dismay. "Ellie, you weren't underdeveloped. You looked your *age*. Unfortunately, that was not true for poor Max."

I bristled at this. "Poor Max? It's terrible what he did to her, yeah. But she wasn't so innocent either. You should have seen the way she acted with the male teachers, like Mr. Davidson. She knew how to be, like, coy."

"Ellie, don't say that. She was a very troubled little girl."

Something inside me snapped. "She was not, Mom! She made my life miserable. Did you know that every single day she'd ask me what store I'd gotten a piece of clothing from? And if I lied, because odds were it came from Bradlees or Goodwill, she would call me out in front of everyone? Did you know she stole from every single convenience store in the town of Marshside? That she smoked butts and did gross, age inappropriate things with older boys in the Hollow when she was just twelve? Did you know she was a pathological liar?"

My mom looked down into her lap. "Honey, she had a hard home life. Her mother was on and off drugs, and her father was God knows where."

"She said her father was some big shot in New York, on Wall Street!"

My mother shook her head and said, "That isn't true. Her father...he left without a trace when Max was young."

"Wait, wait, wait. Back up. You let me go over her house

for birthday parties and stuff when you knew her mom did *drugs*?"

My mother was silent a moment, and seemed to be choosing her words carefully. "I couldn't tell you at the time, but I was assigned to their case. Max was almost taken away by Child Services countless times. I had a pretty close relationship with her mother, despite her problems. She was a sweet woman, but troubled and addicted."

My eyes bulged.

"I was under a confidentiality agreement."

"What?" I sat back in my chair, stunned.

"And as for those parties, Ellie, trust me. All the parents knew how popular Max was, we couldn't keep you all from her parties. But...we kept watch." She paused, a smirk forming, and added, "Susan Eldredge used to drive by with her lights off and peek through the windows."

"Wait. And her dad. He wasn't some rich dude?" I shook my head incredulously. "Max's mom had a BMW and Max always had the best clothes. She ripped me apart for being poor, for everyone for dressing poor, looking poor! It was her favorite insult. Besides calling everyone a 'loser.'"

My mother started to say something then stopped. Finally, she said, "I think her mother had...other means of obtaining things."

"Was she a *prostitute*?"

My mom shushed me. "Ellie, the neighbors. Calm down."

"A prostitute, on Cape Cod?"

My mother straightened her back and went on her favorite spiel. "This isn't just some idyllic little summer paradise, Ellie. You know this. The vacationers love to bomb in here every summer and treat the locals like second-class citizens and pretend it's nothing but clam shacks and sunshine. But we have drugs and prostitution and abuse," she said, her voice cracking, "just like anywhere else."

"I know, Mom. But you have to admit that's extreme."

She cleared her throat. "Let's just say Larissa knew how to provide for her daughter, and then some. Not in the most dignified ways." She smoothed her shirt. "I shouldn't even be telling you this, even now."

My head was spinning. My mother had always acted as if she and Mrs. Lang were distant but cordial acquaintances, when in reality she was making home visits at the Lang's home? No wonder Max hated me. She was probably terrified I would find out the truth.

"There is still so much I can't remember, or don't understand," I finally said. "That day in the Hollow, when I found Max lying there, did Mr. Vine go in there meaning to…meet her? Was it planned? Did they have a fight or something? Was he sexually *and* physically abusing her? She was all bloody and had a huge bruise on her face and she was lying there frozen. She was terrified. I remember that clearly."

"We'd all thought she was making that whole thing up," my mother said, trailing off. "Which is terrible, I know, but even we adults knew Max liked to lie."

"Well, Mom, I remember seeing the guy, and now I am certain it was Mr. Vine."

My mom dabbed under her eyes with a napkin. "I guess it doesn't matter now. It's over."

I raised my eyebrows. "That's it? I thought you would to want to press charges or something."

Her face darkened as she leaned in. "Do you want to do that? Do you want to give a statement to the police? Because, honey, this type of thing, so many years later, with a testimony as a result of hypnotherapy no less, goes nowhere. Especially if you can't get Max to testify. You said you don't know where she lives now, right?"

"I could find out. According to Facebook she lives in New Jersey. I've looked at her profile through Sarah's account. Max has had a million different jobs; never sticks with anything, it doesn't seem. She claims to be a 'model.'" I used air quotes. "I have no idea where Lauren is. She has no online footprint. I checked."

My mom blanched and reached across the table and put her hand on mine. "Hon, what good does this do us now? Let's talk about something else. Let's put this terrible incident behind us."

I nodded lightly, but still felt unsettled. Didn't my mother used to go on and on about being a "mandatory reporter"? Sheryl Berg, my greasy-haired classmate, wore the same outfit six days in a row and often went without lunch, hiding in the bathroom. In science one day, as her shirt sleeve slipped high on her arm, I noticed bruises, little gray spots that lined her inner forearm, stark against her milky skin. That evening, when I'd mentioned Sheryl's bruises at the dinner table, my mother clanked her fork against her plate, flew out of her chair, and said she was alerting Child Services immediately. She went on and on about her role as a mandatory reporter in Massachusetts, a role that obligated her to report abuse and neglect.

Then again, I supposed my mother was right: after all these years…what could we do? Max was alive and well. What good would it do to dredge it all up now?

"Will you promise me you'll stop allowing her to talk you into hypnotherapy?" my mother asked. "It makes me uncomfortable. By all means, talk out your issues. But it seems to be doing more harm than good here."

I nodded but did not agree. I had visions and hallucinations and lucid dreams for a reason. To unearth something I'd buried long ago. Something that was eating at my subconscious. Wasn't it better just to get it all out in the open and acknowledge the past?

"So." Her eyes crinkled at the corners and she sat back.

"I know you're not bringing anyone to Charlotte's wedding tomorrow, but I feel I should ask anyway. Seeing anyone?"

My gut felt like it had been punched. I'd temporarily forgotten about the whole Texting Tim debacle. I averted her gaze and said, "No one of consequence."

***

I burrowed under the sheets of my creaky twin bed and stared at the ceiling, at old glow-in-the-dark adhesive stars, and moped over Tim some more before falling asleep. I woke up to my mother calling up the stairs, "Ellie! Still want to go to dinner?"

Groggy, I sat up and told her I was coming. We drove to dinner. For the first time in a long time, my mother and I laughed and teased each another, stole clam strips and lobster salad off each other's plates, and shared dessert without arguing.

We talked about my mom's garden. We talked about Sarah moving in; she'd be arriving with all her belongings in a couple days. We talked about my dad, how he'd have loved to see how Jack and I were doing these days; me in the city, navigating life on my own, however difficult, and Jack thriving in college in my mom's words as a "lady killer." I swelled with pride as my mother spoke with a detached wonder about all the years that had passed and how happy she was for her children. And how happy she was, finally, with herself.

At Charlotte's wedding the following night, held at a swanky resort in Chatham, I didn't cry effusively like I normally did at weddings—drunk and wistful as I watched the father-daughter dance. It helped that I'd refused even one glass of champagne.

Not that I was the picture of bliss. At dinner, I stuffed my face with about nine different buffet pastas and barely spoke to anyone, thankful for the four-foot high floral centerpieces blocking the faces of my meddling cousins across the table.

After I finished binging on double chocolate chip cookies the size of my head, the cheek-to-shoulder slow dances to Sam Cooke started up, and then I couldn't help but brood over Tim some more. What if I hadn't ruined everything? What if I'd had the confidence and the guts a couple weeks ago to invite him? Charlotte had given me a plus one; I'd even RVSP'd for two people eight months prior in the slight chance I'd have a boyfriend. Maybe, come to think of it, that particular dick move was why Charlotte "accidentally" messed up my seating arrangement and sat me far from my mother and Jack and instead with said cousins.

What if Tim was here with me now? I wondered. Would he have laughed at Jack's incessant bouncing knee as we waited for the processional to begin? Would they have hit it off, passing time by snickering over the bridesmaid whose dress, according to Jack, was cut so short it fell "right below the cooter"?

What about my mother? She would have adored Tim, of course. He would have behaved as his polite, genuine, smiley self. What wasn't there to adore?

My mother found me at the end of the night mooning over cake, still lost in thought.

"Upset over the dance?" she asked, smoothing my hair with her hand.

She knew I always cried over the father-daughter dance. Double if it was that Paul Simon song—sweet Jesus, that made me lose it.

I shrugged. "Something like that."

The next morning, Memorial Day, I woke up late and checked the traffic at the Sagamore bridge—thirteen-mile back up, wonderful. I didn't want to go home, but Sarah was moving in, and I wanted to be there to help out, even if she'd insisted she didn't need it.

My upcoming week was more daunting. There was Tim, of course, who I was bound to run into at work—probably when I looked horrendous, hair askew after a rainy walk in from the train, or at the end of the day when the grease level on my face was high and the chances of my eyeliner still being intact were low.

Then, therapy. Liz had suggested one last hypnosis session, but I'd declined. I would go talk to her about everyday issues, but as for Max and Lauren and the incident, I told her, "I need to move on."

But secretly, I did wish I could remember how everything panned out after I witnessed Max and Mr. Vine in that lascivious act. Did I really never say anything to anyone? Not to Lauren, or Max? It was possible. But why couldn't I remember, still, anything after that day in regards to those two little girls? When did we stop being friends?

16

Move In

Sarah was standing on the curb outside my apartment next to piles of cardboard boxes and bubble-wrapped paintings strewn on the ground. Movers were extracting more furniture from the truck, with the head mover consulting with her over a clipboard.

"Hey!" she shouted when she saw me descending the hilly side street on which I parked my car. When I reached her, she squealed, clutched my shoulders, and jumped up and down. I jumped up and down along with her.

"*Elf!* We're back together again!"

I laughed. "Yes. The band's back together."

She pointed to her car, a small sedan, double-parked with its flashers on. "This okay here for now?"

I nodded as I set my heavy duffel bag down to relieve my shoulder. "For a little bit you should be fine."

"This in the bedroom too?" a sweaty mover barked from under the weight of a bookshelf.

"Yes, please!" Sarah chirped.

Slinging garbage bags of clothes over our shoulders, Sarah and I walked up the three flights of stairs to my, or now *our*, apartment. Panting as we reached the top, we had to sidestep a neighbor emerging from the unit across the hall. Sarah tossed him a cheery hello.

"Hi," he grunted through long black hair as he clomped down the stairs.

"Who was that?" Sarah asked.

"I don't bother learning their names, is that bad?" I whispered once the door shut behind me. "They go to BU, down the street. Or maybe they start going to BU and get kicked out because they don't go to class? I rarely see them coming and going and I swear, their faces change every few months."

"It's good to know your neighbors. We may need them for something someday."

"What, a keg?"

"You never know," Sarah said, shrugging.

I deposited the garbage bag in what was now Sarah's room, which was already mostly furnished. She followed my eyes and pointed to the Derek Jeter poster she'd had since college, along with the Yankees flag hung beside it. "Remember when my decor stirred up all sorts of trouble at UMass?"

I raised my eyebrows. "No, I don't remember *anything* about you getting a brick thrown through your window."

"I can't believe you ratted out those kids. They got kicked out of the dorms." She put her hand over her mouth. "I felt so bad."

"You shouldn't have. They were assholes," I said. "Fellow Sox fans or not."

In 2009, the Jeter poster didn't hold the same weight as it had the night of the brick throwing, which was in fall of 2004. It was game seven of the ALCS championship. The Sox had been down three games to none, rallied, and to about eighty-five percent of the in-state residents' delight and shock, they beat the Yankees. We would go on to sweep the Cardinals for the World Series title for the first time in eighty-six years. The win was a big deal, as evidenced by the row of riot police atop their majestic horses, tear gas ready, lined up outside our dorm. They'd arrest hundreds of students who were intent on committing low-grade acts of arson, toilet papering of trees, and in our case, tossing bricks through the glass windows of Yankees fans.

"I don't mind Jeter as much anymore," I said smiling, "or that you're a total turncoat Mass resident who loves the Yankees."

"It's because my dad likes them!" she insisted. "He's from New York!"

"Whatever," I said, perking up. "Even my *Yankees Suck, Jeter Swallows* T-shirt lost its bite by now, I suppose."

"Oh, those were so stupid."

"They were kind of funny." I smiled and looked around. "I wish you would have let me help you move."

She waved me off. "Movers are worth every penny. I've barely had to lift a finger."

As we were surveying the bare walls of the living room—Ricki had taken her parentally financed Pier 1 collection along with her to Tyler's, while I owned practically nothing—there was a knock at the door.

We didn't have a peephole, or a working doorbell, so I had to call through the door, "Who is it?"

"It's Tim."

My eyes bugged as I whirled around to face Sarah. She bugged her eyes back and mouthed, "I'll be in here," and slipped into her new bedroom.

My heart was thudding in my chest as I opened the door and faced him.

"Hi," I said.

"Hi," he said. His hands were crammed into his pockets.

I led him to the kitchen and we sat in the tiny breakfast nook. I looked at the clock on the stove; it was after three. I offered him a beer, but he declined, so I poured two glasses of water instead.

I set them down on the table and then sat down across from him. I stared at him. He stared at me. I bit my lip.

"So." Tim.

"So." Me.

"You want to tell me what your deal is?" Tim asked.

"I'm sorry."

"Sorry for…"

My face was hot. "For texting you such idiotic things."

He cocked his head. "You texted me?"

"You didn't get them?"

"No," he said.

A flood of relief. Thank God.

"My phone got stolen at the mixer. I had to walk back to the office and report it missing."

"You had to walk back to the office?" My mind was racing, as was my heart. "Oh. That's why you left."

I started to say something, then stopped.

"What?"

I shrugged.

"What were you going to say?" he asked, leaning his head in.

"I mean it sucks to get your phone stolen and everything," I said, "but why'd you just leave like that? Couldn't you have just dealt with it later? And gone and met up with me like you said you would…"

I was starting to feel indignant. He hadn't even seen my psycho texts, and he still hadn't called me in almost a week? I opened my mouth to say more, but he spoke first.

"I had to go back that night because we're a storage security software company." There was more than a hint of irritation in his voice.

"Okay…" I said, trailing off.

He dipped his head a little more, cocking it, and spoke slowly. "I'm in database marketing. They pay for my phone and I have tons of proprietary information on it. So if it gets stolen, that's a huge problem."

"Ohhh," I said. "Still, though, why—"

"Why haven't I called you?" he said, looking evenly into my eyes.

"Yeah," I said. "I texted you that night, asking where you were. Then I texted some stupid drunken things, mean things." I cringed, but then smiled, because so long as he never received them, it was all actually quite funny now. "I concluded my string of texts with *Duck you*."

Tim didn't return my smile.

"And then…at work, you haven't chatted me, or emailed me—which I would think…" I trailed off. Not having a phone does not equal being completely off the grid, I thought. There were other ways of communicating. It was 2009!

I waited for his explanation, but he seemed to be waiting for one from me.

I raised my hands up. "I don't know what you want me to say. You never told me your phone was stolen."

"And you never asked."

"But—"

"Did you email me?"

"I—"

"Did you even try to leave me a voicemail, instead of texting?"

"Well, no—"

He started speaking faster and more angrily. "Did you come to my desk and ask what's up? Did you wait around after the Interface and see what the deal was, after I caught you staring at me the whole time?"

"Hey, now—"

"I can't do all the work, Ellie. You don't act like you like me. You don't express interest. You wait for me to call, you wait for me to ask you to hang out. You've never asked me to hang out. It's been almost two months. Not once have you asked me to go anywhere."

"But you're—"

"A guy? Yes, I'm a guy. But I'm not a mind reader, and it's not up to me to put in all the effort, all the time. This isn't a question of chivalry or stupid dating rules. It's about respect. And aside from all that, I know nothing about you. You don't tell me anything about, like, your hometown, or your parents, I mean, other than that one time you got upset over your dad, or whatever." His face was red now, a shade not too far off from his hair, which was sprouting off in all sorts of directions. He had about eight cowlicks and he needed a haircut. He seemed genuinely distressed.

I was at a loss and for a few moments said nothing. Finally, I said, "No one's ever…no one's ever come at me like that."

"Like what?"

"No guy has ever cared enough I guess. About whether I have feelings for them. They lose interest, or fuck me over, and then it's done."

"Well, that's dumb," he said. "Why would you allow anyone to treat you like that?"

"I guess…"

But I didn't have a response. He was right. Why was I always waiting so passively, convinced I wasn't good enough? Convinced no one would want me, especially after they got to know me? Like they'd always eventually figure me out. It was like Max's favorite word, loser, had been playing over and over in my head for thirteen years.

Tim was hurt. It was in his eyes, and the way he kept pushing his chest to the edge of the table as he spoke, and then would sit back with frustration, unable to understand why I was the way I was.

"This whole thing with your dad dying when you were

little, I mean, don't get me wrong, Ellie. That's really sad. That sucks. But is there something else?"

I wanted to tell him everything. I yearned for his comfort and sense, for his honesty, his humor. But I couldn't do it. My voice, and the words that needed to desperately to escape, would not come.

He got up. I followed him, pleading with him to stay, telling him I was sorry.

"I'm just going to head out."

"I've been going to therapy," I blurted.

His hand was on the doorknob but he dropped it.

"I have some crap from my past that I'd repressed, and I've been working it out. If you'll forgive me, and we can still try to do this, I'll tell you more about it. I promise. I just haven't been ready. Nothing against you. I've barely told anyone."

"Right," he said. And that was it. He opened the door, looked once more at me, and shut it behind him.

My heart thudded in my chest and Sarah opened her door a crack. "Ellie, are you okay?"

"No, I think I ruined everything." I sniffed, wiping my nose on my sleeve and patting the edges of my eyes. "I'm such an *idiot*."

There was another knock at the door. Sarah bugged her eyes at me again. "Maybe it's him," she whispered.

I opened the door.

He stepped towards me, holding both arms out straight. I fell into his embrace, fighting tears. He stroked my hair and whispered in my ear, "Ellie, I really like you. I'm glad you're working stuff out. But please don't ruin this for us. We have something good."

I looked up at him, nodded, kissed his lips, and said, "I know."

17

Raggedy Anne

The next day at work, Tim asked me over SymbiChat to meet him in the lobby so we could go down the street and grab coffee.

When I saw Buster waddle into a meeting room and shut the door, I slipped downstairs.

Tim was waiting for me. "Fancy seeing you here," he said as I exited the elevator.

I smiled.

As we walked to the revolving door, we passed Susan Ellmore sitting on one of the metal benches beside a large fern. She was on the phone, and I tossed her a curt nod. She didn't nod back, miffed probably after Mel's comment about her Red Lobster at the Interface. Her eyes glossed disinterestedly over my face. That is, until she saw Tim behind me, and then her eyebrows rose ever so slightly.

We ambled up the walkway to Broadway, the main road. Tim fished for my hand in the air, and as his fingers grazed mine I kept my arm locked straight, looking around quickly.

He looked around to see what I was looking at. "What?"

I opened my mouth and started sputtering. "Sorry, sorry." I grabbed at his hand, but it had already gone limp at his side. "That was a reflex. I was just weird again," I blurted helplessly.

"You think?" he said, his eyes narrowed.

"Please don't take it the wrong way. I can't help it, but I'm protecting myself."

He looked hurt. "From what?"

"In case, you know. Just in case."

"In case what?"

"In case we break up and then everyone would know we didn't work out and people would gossip and I'd be so embarrassed."

"Ellie, you're kinda nuts." Then he smiled.

"I know."

We continued our walk, arriving a few minutes later at the coffee shop. It was typically a Symbicorean-free zone, and that was why I liked going there. As we approached the counter, I chided myself for not bringing my reusable mug, anticipating a look of derision from the barista, a dreadlocked blonde who gave almost everyone the stink eye.

Tim insisted on paying and waiting for the coffees so I snagged a table near the window. When he sat down I filled him in about Sarah's smooth transition to living in the city so far.

"So, you guys went to high school and college together?" Tim asked.

I nodded. "We were separated during grade school because she went to boarding school. Then we reunited in high school, and we both went to UMass. We were roommates all four years. I've been lost without her since we graduated."

"Does this mean you'll never stay at my place ever again?" Tim joked.

I smiled. "No, but I want you to become friends with her, too. It's required."

Tim smiled back. "Deal."

I took a sip of coffee and looked out the window at a man pacing up and down the sidewalk. His knees were knocking into the chairs set up outside, but he didn't seem to notice. He was waving his hand around, gesticulating as if in an intense conversation. My eyes kept shifting back to the window, and after a few moments I was hit with a wave of recognition. The man, tall with gray hair and donning a black suit, looked much older, but the longer I stared at his face, the surer I was.

It was Mr. Vine.

Tim waved a hand in front of my face. "You okay?"

Panicked, I shifted in my chair and said, "Yeah, I just...I see a guy I knew when I was young."

Tim turned to look out the window.

"Don't turn around!" I snapped.

Tim whipped his head back and looked at me in surprise. It was too late. Mr. Vine turned towards the window. His eyes rested on the back of Tim's head. Luckily, his flat gaze didn't make its way past Tim over to me. After a slight pause, Mr. Vine resumed his conversation and continued to pace back and forth in front of the window on the phone.

I'd been holding my breath, and the exhalation came out in a *whoosh*.

"What's the story?" Tim asked, reaching for my hand.

I snatched my hand away and put both hands on my knees, under the table. I was shaking. "He's...he's just a bad man. I don't want to talk about it right now. Maybe some other time."

"Bad man" was such an insufficient, elementary characterization, yet the words echoed in my head long after.

Tim was still looking at me, concerned.

"We should go," I said.

I pushed out my chair with the back of my legs and got up, but at the same moment Mr. Vine entered through the jangling door and marched up to the register, which was right in our path. The tables were set up too tightly together for us to wend our way to the entrance any other way. I plopped back down in my chair and watched him out of the corner of my eye.

With his phone still pressed up against his ear, he barked a coffee order to the sneering barista, snapping his fingers in impatience when she asked him to clarify his order.

"Two sugars. Two."

I realized I'd unconsciously slumped in my seat, my head tucked between her shoulders like a turtle. I started to straighten up but immediately slumped down again as Mr. Vine whirled around.

"Where are you? You're here already? I don't see you. Oh, for Christ's sake. You're making this as difficult as possible. Wave your hand!"

Mr. Vine scanned the room with the phone in the crook of his shoulder, and his eyes met mine for a split second before moving on. I thought my heart would stop.

"There you are." He was coming my way, and I put my hand up as if to scratch my eyebrow so that he couldn't see my face. He came so close his suit jacket brushed my chair as he passed. I let my eyes, but not my head, follow him as he weaved in and out of tables to get to the back of the café.

Mr. Vine was in excellent shape for an older man; tall with broad shoulders and a confident gait, he seemed to rise up on the balls of his feet at each step to maximize his height.

He sat down at a table with a very short, slight, younger woman, dirty blonde, in the farthest corner. I couldn't make out her face, which was covered by her hair.

Tim followed my eyes. "She someone you know, too?"

I opened my mouth and closed it as the woman tilted her head and her face came into view. She was girlish looking, except for the lines around her mouth and at the creases of her eyes, lines so pronounced that even from afar I could see them. She appeared worn and tired and pale.

"Not positive," I whispered, even though in the din of the

café my words would never reach them, "but I think I do know her. I think that's his…" I trailed off.

"His what?" he pressed.

"Daughter." A chill ran down my spine.

"Is she bad too?"

"No. Yes. I don't know. I just want to get out of here." I felt sick.

I glanced once more in their direction and saw a little girl's head pop up from beneath the table. The girl's hair was a paler blonde with loose curls framing her face. A spitting image of Lauren.

I observed them for a moment. Mr. Vine had not greeted Lauren or the little girl with more than a nod. No embrace. No warmth. I realized I was gaping at them now and turned to Tim; I was having difficulty processing all that I was seeing. *Is that Lauren's daughter? She looks at least six. That would mean…Lauren had her as a teenager?*

Tim wagged his head toward the door, sensing my immense discomfort, and I nodded. He grabbed the trash off the table and I stood up slowly. We made our way to the exit and I grabbed Tim's hand. He dropped it and instead put his arm around my shoulders, kissing the top of my forehead. I tried to hide within his bulk and bury my head so that the Vines wouldn't see my face, but I couldn't help myself. Once we got outside, I took one last look back through the window.

The glare of the sun made it difficult to see inside, but a few steps to the side and there they were, Lauren and her father, staring right back at me, their faces contorted with confusion, recognition—and then, I was sure of this—*alarm.*

***

I scheduled an emergency session with Dr. Rollins that night.

I couldn't get to her office fast enough, beeping at the

slowpokes on Route 9, banging my steering wheel as I got caught at light after light after light.

When I arrived, ten minutes late, I had barely sat down when I told Liz about what I saw earlier that day. We discussed the scene with Lauren and Mr. Vine ad nauseum. I didn't know how many times Liz asked, "Why are you so frightened? What do you mean they looked *alarmed*, can you explain?"

But I couldn't explain, that was the problem.

I looked at the clock, and with a rising panic I saw the session was nearing its end. I blurted that I was sick and tired of talking in circles about a time period in my memory that halted so suddenly in the bedroom of a child rapist.

"I'd wanted to bury the past and forget about it all and move on. Max was alive and well, I kept telling myself. But after seeing Mr. Vine…" I cleared my throat. "I am almost sure that the day didn't end there. Seeing him today…somehow I just know. It didn't end there."

Liz was all too eager to agree, and in anticipation of this, she'd cleared the hour after mine. I was free to stay for an extended session.

She turned on the tinkling music and began asking simple questions, and repeated that she'd cleared the appointment after mine, so *no rush*.

She started with questions about Tim, to relax my mind, distract me, and not put undue strain on my efforts at remembering the past. I told her about my relief that he hadn't given up on me. I told her it wasn't yet love, but I was close. I told her how happy I was to have Sarah so close again, and how nice it was to come back to an apartment smelling of cookies and someone I could talk to, rather than feeling lonely. I told her how everything was looking up and I was happy, if not for the lead ball knocking around my insides every time I thought of Max or Mr. Vine.

Then, in a soft, soothing voice, she asked me to describe that red hat again, and the pewter hanging coat rack from which it hung.

"There were these white, painted little seagulls that dotted the top…these three little birds…"

And then I was back.

***

Mr. Vine. Max. His pants to his ankles. Max, on her knees. Max's bloody face in the Hollow. The red hat. *Holyshitholyshitholyshit…*

I walk outside onto Lauren's porch, the sun a blinding shock to my dry eyes. Lauren is still sitting on the grass and looks up at me from her magazine. The lined notebook papers scrawled with our movie script are scattered beside her, weighted down by rocks.

"What took you so long?"

I stand over her and blurt, "I need to go home."

She curls her lip. "Why? We haven't started our movie yet."

Then she eyes the house. "Did you see Max?"

I say nothing.

Lauren's face is turning red. She looks down at her magazine, feigning boredom. Finally, she shakes her head and shrugs. "If you're gonna just stand there, go home, then."

I stare at her for a moment, incredulous. She knows. She told me not to look for Max because she knows. I don't know what to say, how to articulate this awareness, this disgust. I turn around and walk toward the house.

Lauren calls after me, talking fast. "You can call your mommy on the phone in the living room. Don't use the one upstairs."

The gall of this girl. I swivel around, my knees shaking. "Why, Lauren? Why not the phone upstairs?" I sense Lauren's confidence, her authority over me, waver.

"Just…use the one downstairs." She composes herself a bit and stands up, wiping the bottom of her jeans. "God. You are so fucking annoying."

Shoots of anger course through me and I feel like I'm about to blow, like I do around my mom, which, before now, was exclusively a housebound temper. I hear my voice take on a husky quality. "Because of what I'd see?"

Lauren's eyes flash angrily back at me. "Shut up. Go home, God."

I don't move. I feel like my feet are spiked into the ground.

Lauren's face is twisted in rage; her lip is curled all the way up to her nose now, baring her uneven front teeth. "Go home, Ellie, you ugly idiot. Anyone tell you that you have a mustache? Like a Mexican?"

I don't answer.

"Maybe people would like you if you were normal," she said. "Ever since your Dad died you think everyone should say, 'Poor Ellie, boo-hoo.'" She smiles at me, as if bestowing kind words instead of cruel ones. "But no one cares. Everyone thinks you're a freak, you know. A poser. A loser."

My voice goes from husky to almost screechy, and I'm leaning forward in a half squat, spitting out the words like venom. "Speaking of dads. Why not go upstairs, Lauren? Because I'd find Max with yours?"

Suddenly the slider opens with a long creak and shuts with a short slam. Max steps out on to the deck. She shields her eyes from the sun and squints down at us on the grass. She stands a moment, as if collecting herself, and walks down the steps slowly. She is carrying the camcorder. It is heavy and she struggles to balance it on her shoulder.

Lauren springs up from the ground and stalks towards Max, crazed and on the verge of tears. "Were you in my Dad's room again, Max?"

Max takes a half step back and shakes her head furiously. "No, Lauren. No."

Lauren turns to me. "Was she, you troll?" She is screaming now. "*Was she?*"

I nod.

I need to get inside and call my mother. I need to leave immediately. Lauren lunges towards Max and grabs her arm, causing her to drop the video camera. It crashes to the ground and the lens cap pops off.

"Stop!" Max yelps.

"You stupid slut!" Lauren slaps Max across the face, hard. I scream and tell them to stop. At first, I try to intervene, to keep them apart. But I deem the flailing hands and kicking feet far too destructive so I run towards the house, but at the top step of the deck I freeze.

Mr. Vine is standing at the threshold of the sliding door, his arms crossed. He ignores the two girls below, tumbling on the grass fighting and screaming, and instead looks down at me. Slowly and quietly he says, "Well, Ellie, what's going on here?"

I shrug and manage to slither by him. I pray he will continue on outside and stop the melee of his daughter and Max and forget all about me. Instead, he comes inside and shuts the slider. He follows me down the hall. My heart feels like it's beating so hard it will stop from overexertion. I almost pray it does.

Mr. Vine's deep voice echoes down the narrow hallway behind me. "Was that you I heard upstairs, Ellie?" I freeze.

"No."

"I think it was."

"I-I didn't see anything."

"Who said there was something to see?" I look at him over my shoulder, and his face is set in a grim, sick smile and his arms remain crossed. Before I have a chance to go any further he steps in long strides past me, blocking me from the doorway to the living room, the location of the only other house phone besides the one upstairs, as well as the only pathway to the front door.

"I'd like to go home," I say quietly, feeling sobs erupting.

"Feel free." He smiles.

I step closer to the doorway, but he refuses to budge from his wide-legged stance blocking it. I try, as my thoughts race, to convince myself that what I saw upstairs before wasn't even real. This is Lauren's dad. He picks us up from school. He is a good man. He has a wife. He has a nice car. He is an adult. I try to be sensible, to rid myself of my paranoia of what surely can't be happening and be the yielding, agreeable little girl that I am. "Um, excuse me, sir. Mr. Vine? I just need to call my mom."

In his eyes I see something horrible, something no words can explain, and before I can react his hand shoots out and grabs my arm. I take a swift step backwards so he only catches a piece of my sleeve. I don't think to yell. I am helplessly silent. I try to yank my sleeve out of his grasp but he clings and lunges at me. He grabs me by the back of the neck, squeezing the skin with his large fingers, catching stray strands of hair that are pulled painfully from the base of my scalp. I try to scream now, but his other hand silences me and cups my mouth. My whole head is contained within both of his hands, like a vise. He is sweaty and I taste his sour, damp palm. He smells of cigarettes and the brown liquid my father used to keep in the top right cabinet above the stove. Whiskey. I gasp to breathe. My mind shoots off to strange places: Sarah's dad, who grunts with approval as we get ready for school dances in our miniskirts. My father watching a movie, breathing heavily, his lap covered with a blanket, yelling at me to go back upstairs.

I then watch, as if outside myself, as Mr. Vine pulls me by

the head down the hall. My legs are almost unable to keep up— they get half dragged along the floor. He's going to rip my head off my body. He's going to kill me. The painful wrenching and twisting of my neck is unbearable. So I cling to his arm, hanging on him, trying to shift the weight off my neck and head. I'm reminded of dance class, my mom laughing when she picked me up, "You're so loose, like a rag doll!" I would take it as a compliment and laugh and think of Raggedy Anne, my favorite doll. But this hurts. It hurts.

We are about to round the corner to the stairwell and he twists my head awfully to the side again where I get a glimpse of the glass slider. On the other side of the glass stands Lauren and Max staring at me from the deck, their hair in knots, grass stains all over their legs. They watch as Lauren's father drags me up the stairs. They watch my pleading eyes in between the slits of Mr. Vine's fingers.

And they do nothing.

***

Twelve minutes. That's all it took.

I sat up with a jolt on Dr. Rollins's couch. I remembered. *That* was the last day I ever stepped foot in Lauren's house. *That* was the last day I ever saw or spoke to Lauren Vine or Maxine Lang.

No further hypnosis was necessary to remember what happened in Mr. Vine's bedroom after he dragged me upstairs by the throat. The remainder of that afternoon had come flooding back, the memory loosened and rattled out of my consciousness after a good, hard shake.

Now I understood all the present-day manifestations, the reverberations of that fateful day: me always feeling rejected and unwanted; me never having enough confidence. Me never fully trusting a male.

Dr. Rollins was pelting me with questions, assaulting my

already jumbled thoughts. "So what did you see? *What did he do to you?*"

I didn't answer.

"What happened? Work with me, Ellie, dig. We're so close—"

"Liz," I said as I sat up. "I can't do this right now. I need a break. I need some time to think about this. On my own."

Liz relaxed her bugged eyes and dabbed her moist brow with a cloth from her pocket. I knew to some degree she was using me; I was the perfect case study for her much maligned practice of hypnotherapy. I was invaluable to her struggling business, as evidenced by the lumpy futon, her constant openings, and her clunky car wedged beside mine in the driveway.

But unfortunately for Dr. Rollins, I was not concerned with her or her business.

I sprang up from the futon, placed a check on the bureau, and without looking back I shut the door firmly behind me. As I walked outside to the car, the scenes at Lauren's house—the backyard, Max and Mr. Vine—had already started losing their crispness. But I remembered what happened afterwards. Now, whether it was a good thing or not, I would always remember.

And I knew why it had been so difficult to uncover what happened that day. Why every time I closed in on the truth, I got shunted off track.

It was simple, really, and something I should have sensed already. My mother lied to me.

18

Loser

On the drive back to my apartment a pit had formed in my stomach, and Tylenol was doing nothing for my pounding headache. As I pulled up to my neighborhood, my mouth started watering and I tasted bile in the back of my throat. I choked it down, barely in time, and sweat formed on my upper lip.

A few minutes later, I wasn't so lucky. I had to swerve off to the side of the road, jerk the gear into park, and heave the door open with my shoulder. With the top half of my body thrust into the open air and my hand still on the door handle, only a dry heave escaped. I spit warm saliva onto the pavement, drew myself back into the driver's seat, and shut the door.

I needed to talk to someone. But I wasn't ready to confront my mother. Not yet. Sarah obviously came to mind, but she was working a night shift and wasn't privy to the details surrounding my last couple of eye-opening sessions. The few times I'd consulted with Sarah over my recovered memories she'd planted herself in the paramnesia camp, same as my mother: "Ellie, you might be confabulating real memories with implanted or suggested ones."

I couldn't risk Sarah doubting the veracity of what I'd recalled. I knew what was real. I wished I didn't, but now

I needed for someone to listen, without judgment, while I collected my thoughts.

My phone rang in my purse beside me. It was her, I thought, without even fishing it out of my bag to see. Sometimes when I'd be thinking of my mother, she would call right at that moment, as if some otherworldly power was at work, our intractable mother-daughter bond.

But it wasn't my mother. It was Tim. And it was time to trust him.

Tim met me at the park near my apartment. We were the only two there, and we sat down on a wooden bench still slightly damp from a rainstorm earlier that day. It was dusk, and the clouds now gathered into magnificent formations against a peach pink and raspberry red sky. As the sun retreated into a sliver of egg-yolk orange above the horizon, I gently took my hand out of Tim's grasp and rested it in my lap.

I couldn't look at him as I spoke, so I cast my down to my feet.

"First," I began, "I thought it had something to do with the loss of my dad," I said. "I thought I was insecure and drinking all the time and sad from losing him all those years ago and never dealing with it.

"Then tack on the frustration with Buster and my dead end job, I felt so overwhelmed. Like such a failure. It was stultifying. I couldn't lose the sense that I was lost and incapable of being loved and that there was something inherently wrong with me.

"To put it plainly," I continued, "I've been sad and confused for a long time, but it was the visions and the dreams made me begin to think I was going crazy. To top if off, I met you right smack in the middle of it all. I couldn't tell you what I was seeing, or feeling, or remembering. I'm sorry for not being upfront. But truth is these visions were scenes, scenes of my childhood. And they all involved this one person, Maxine. And this one man. A man I *knew* I knew, but I couldn't see his face."

I told Tim about the very first flashback—Max bloodied in the woods, and then seeing the man with the belt buckle.

Tim listened without interruption. He rested his forearms on his thighs, dipped his head low, and looked at the ground. I relayed all the recovered memories from hypnotherapy: the school field trip, my hyper vigilant mother, the first incident in the Hollow.

And then I told him what I witnessed in Mr. Vine's bedroom, concluding with the moment Mr. Vine dragged me down the hallway, smothering my mouth with his sweaty hand.

I paused and looked up at Tim, my breath shaky.

Tim met my eyes. "That's the last thing you saw during hypnosis?"

I nodded. "Yes. But…it triggered—it caused everything to flood back."

"And…what happened?"

I took a deep, shaky breath. "He dragged me up to the master bedroom, which was also his office. He was still covering my mouth so I wouldn't scream. When he finally let go of me, he threw me towards the bed and I cracked my head on the bed frame."

I took another deep breath to stave off sobs. "I was crying. He kept telling me to be quiet, to shut up. He paced and back and forth in the room. I told him, 'I'll do what Max did. Just let me go. I'll do what Max did. I won't tell.'

"He looked at me and laughed. He *laughed*. 'You think I want you,' he said. 'A little girl.' He just kept laughing, right in my face. And…I'm so disgusted with myself at this, but I remember feeling *sad*. I felt sad that he didn't want me. That he didn't want me to do disgusting, unthinkable things to him.

I was jealous that he wanted Max and not me. How sick? How fucking sick is that?"

Now I could no longer stop the tears, and they streamed down my face. Tim placed his hand on my back and let me finish.

"I was on the floor slumped against the end of the bed for a while. When he wasn't pacing across the room, he was sitting down at his desk muttering to himself. I begged him to let me go home. I don't really remember what he said, but obviously he wouldn't allow that. I tried making a run for it at one point, but he stopped me and threw me down to the floor again and smacked me across the face. He was so much stronger. I didn't have a chance." I caught my wavering breath and sniffled.

Tim looked at me, the color drained from his face. "Take your time."

"There was an almost empty bottle on his desk, whiskey. To this day I can't stomach the smell of whiskey, even though I've never had a sip. Now I know why.

"He undid his belt buckle. But he didn't come towards me at first, just stood in the center of the room, staring down at his pants and swaying a little. Then, out of the corner of my eye, I saw Max behind him, standing at the doorway. Her finger was to her lips. I tried not to look at her.

"He was oblivious though, still rambling, talking nonsense. He threatened me and said if I told anyone about Max, he'd kill me. And to make me remember that, he was going to make me pay." I choked down a sob. "He started coming toward me. He was still trying to unzip his pants but it was like his fingers were putty. Too drunk."

Tim groaned. "Oh, Ellie..."

"While he stood over me, and I'll never, ever forget this, he kept calling me a little loser. It was Max and Lauren's favorite insult. They called everyone a loser, including me. But I'd never heard an adult utter that word.

"Anyway, I tried my best to maintain eye contact with him and not look towards the door. Max had disappeared by then, but I didn't want him to see her signaling me if she came back. My eyes were fixed on that zipper then, willing it to stay zipped, willing his fingers to keep fumbling. But they didn't. He got it down…

"Then I saw movement out of the corner of my eye, a person in the doorway. I refused to look directly at them. I trained my eyes on Mr. Vine. Then I heard this strange hollow sound, *whap*, and down he went."

Tim jutted his chin out in surprise. "Max? Lauren?"

"No."

"Who, then?"

I looked at him. "My mom."

Tim's mouth dropped open. "Wait. What?"

I nodded.

"So," he narrowed his eyes and swallowed, "he didn't…"

I shook my head. "No. He didn't touch me. Thanks to my mom, he didn't get the chance."

Silence. Finally, he said, "Did she…kill him?"

I shook my head and said firmly, "No."

"How do you know?"

"We saw him."

"Who saw him? Me and you?"

I nodded. "At the coffee shop yesterday."

Tim put his hands on his head. "That guy? That was him? With the girl? And that was Lauren with him?"

I nodded.

"Holy shit." Then he said, "So he's alive, and this all means…"

I nodded miserably. "It means…"

Tim's face brightened with astonishment. "It means a lot of things. It means your mom *knew* about Mr. Vine and all this traumatic stuff that happened to you, and worse, Max—this whole time. And you said you'd asked her about it several times about what happened back then, right?"

I nodded.

"So even when you started remembering stuff she pretended not to know?"

Tears continued streaming down my face. "Yes. And told me to stop going to Dr. Rollins."

He shook his head. "That's not right."

"I don't know why she lied," I said quickly, "but I want to believe that back then, she tried to talk to me about it. I have this memory—I thought it was just a dream before, but now I'm thinking it's real—of me on my bed, my mother trying to comfort me. I had a huge lump on my head. And bloody sheets. My mom had to push her way into my room and she was trying to comfort me but I was freaking out on her. Telling her to get away from me. I wouldn't let her comfort me or talk to me or anything. I must have gone into denial mode. Then obviously I blocked it out and convinced myself none of it happened."

"But, Ellie," he said sternly. "She's lying to you *now*."

I had no response to that.

Tim ran his hands through his hair. "I'm still confused. After your mom knocked him out with the bat, what happened? She just took you away and left Lauren there with him? Clearly she didn't call the cops."

"That's all still cloudy for me. I have to talk to my mom. Get her to tell me the truth about what went on, and what happened after that. And why she lied to me. No more bullshit."

Tim looked skeptical, almost disgusted. "I hope she comes clean."

I sat up straighter and couldn't help but feel protective of my mom. I didn't want him to think poorly of her, whatever her motivations had been. "Tim, you have to understand.

She was a single mother. My dad had just died. She had no power, no money. Mr. Vine was a prominent lawyer in town. Maybe…maybe she handled this some other way."

As I said that, I was surprised with the words that escaped my mouth after: "Wait…I *do* remember. They moved." I looked at Tim and repeated, "The Vines moved!"

I sat back and stared into space. "Max was alive and well," I continued, "and got through middle school and a little bit of high school before she dropped out. Sarah confirmed that. But no wonder I had no memory of Lauren beyond that day. It's because she *moved*."

Tim shook his head and wasn't as thrilled with this revelation as I was. He was still stuck on my mom. "Your mom's a social worker, right? Aren't they required to report this kind of stuff?"

I didn't answer him. I couldn't comprehend why she didn't alert the authorities either—and due to her inability to do so, over a decade later, Mr. Vine was free living a seemingly normal life. She could have made him pay. Or did she?

19

Bock Pond

I sat in the passenger side of my mother's car in the parking lot of Bock Pond. It was around nine at night. I'd driven down from Boston in record time, but my mother worked "late." Hiding from me, was what I'd guess. Delaying the inevitable.

The radio was on low; Neil Young's crooning, nasally voice rose just above the sound of the harsh wind outside. The brief car ride to the pond had been silent.

Once she parked, leaving the heat on, I demanded, "Start with the day you dropped me off at the Vines'. You know which day. Leave nothing out."

My mother's whole body was shaking, but I felt no sympathy.

She spoke fast as she gazed out the windshield into the dark night. "I just want to start out by saying I had a terrible feeling after I dropped you off at the Vines' that day. Every fiber of my being screamed for me not to allow you to go over there. I nearly turned the car around and came back and got you."

She looked over at me and bit her lip.

I stared back at her. "I asked you about that day, Mom, multiple times. And you lied. You lied."

She stared at me, her breath uneven, as tears fell down her face.

My voice rose. "Would you please tell me why no one

called the cops and that asshole is in Boston, gallivanting around in an Armani suit?!"

She opened her mouth to speak but apparently my psyche had other plans. Right there in the car, I had my first full-blown panic attack. Gasping for air, short breaths, crying, the whole bit. My mother rubbed my back cried right along with me and waited for me to calm down.

When I had, I looked at her, shook my head, and said, "Jesus."

She nodded sadly. "It's all my fault."

"What was your part in this, Mom? Please. Nothing makes sense. Please make it make sense."

"Okay, okay. It—it started with an assignment in the spring of 1995, a case inherited from my coworker, Anne."

She handed me a folder. Inside the folder was a stack of papers fastened by a large paper clip. A sticky note was tacked to the report's cover:

Maureen, thx for taking this one over. The baby's coming sooner than we thought. You'll see this one's an open and shut case—submit to CS for processing & you're all thru. —Anne

The top page, a report summary, was organized and succinct.

Case #: 4353. Address: 41 Moth Lane, East Marshside. Name: Larissa Lang. Status: Single mother, Divorced. Prior Treatment: Rehab, one completed stint 2/13/92, one voluntary discharge, 9/29/93. Dependents: One child, sole custody: Maxine Lang. Age 11. Grade 6. Father: Jim Lang.

I flipped through scribbled notes I couldn't decipher, and my mom told me to go to the last page, titled *Recommendations.*

Final Notes: Call Child Services Immediately. Last home visit showed Ms. Lang strung out, erratic. Alimony from ex-husband—location unknown—going presumably to drugs and to her daughter's designer clothes. Other unknown sources of income not being reported to the IRS, or to me.

I rested the report in my lap and waited for my mother to continue.

"My first mistake was not telling my boss that there was a conflict of interest. Larissa and I weren't friends by any means, but we attended the same recitals, concerts, and sporting events. Only a casual hello here and there.

"But, this being right around the time your father died, I felt a connection to Larissa. I believed she was owed more than a dismissive report. I couldn't let her daughter get wrenched away from her without a second chance. I wanted to get through to her."

She took a ragged breath. "I delayed the call to Child Services. I wanted to make my own assessment. The finite nature of Anne's report made this difficult. I had to make extra visits on my own time. At each check-in, Larissa made promises of getting clean.

"One day, Larissa told me she needed to pick something up at a friend's house, but that she couldn't find her keys. 'Would you mind giving me a ride?' she asked. I was hesitant, but she just looked at me all sad, worn, beaten down, so I gave in. I knew that look quite well. I saw it every day in the mirror.

"I sat in the car as Larissa hopped out. It became clear that she was exchanging goods—drugs—in the doorway of this old, dilapidated duplex over on South Street. When she came back in the car, I was furious. I threatened to include the incident in my report. It was then I realized she was high. 'You're an accessory, Maureen,' she said. 'You just drove me to a drug deal.' Then she said to me, "You'll lose your license. I'll tell 'em you've brought me to multiple deals. So why don't you just keep your mouth shut.'

"I was stunned and scared of losing my license. Of course there was a chance my superiors wouldn't believe her, but what if they did? What if someone saw me at that house? It's right on a main road. I'm not proud of this, but...I fudged my report. As recompense, I told myself I'd do everything in my power to get Larissa clean. She wanted to be clean more than anything, but she was an addict. Her own worst enemy.

"I personally stopped in to Larissa's house and cared for her as she went through withdrawals. I took her to counseling and checked up on her off the books. Larissa eventually stopped using and put the alimony towards tutors for Max. She went back to work.

"After enduring the most tumultuous year of my own life, this rehabilitation of Larissa Lang was a ray of hope for me. It was a personal, rewarding success. I had very little to be excited about then, very few feelings of accomplishment. At home with you and Jack I felt like a failure. I could barely keep up with the bills, I was exhausted, Jack was so young. And you'd adopted this attitude; you and your brother were constantly fighting."

My heart sank. It was so hard to picture my mother younger, helpless, and grief stricken, but forced to hold it together in front of us. Forced to fiercely protect us and care for us and rear us.

"After Larissa cleaned up, we went our separate ways. Anne never returned to work after maternity leave, thank God, so she never followed up on the Lang case. Anne's replacement was assigned to make the monthly follow-up visits. After that, I never expected to see Larissa except in passing.

"Then, unbelievably, you and Max became friends. I never understood why you fell in with her. She seemed like such a brat. But I did know that the linchpin to your little threesome was Lauren Vine," she said. She rolled her eyes and added, "I wasn't sure why you were friends with her either.

"When you began hanging out with Max, I knew I had to

uphold the confidentiality agreement and be very careful with what I said and how I acted around Max's mother. Larissa and I pushed you girls to play at a neutral site: the Vines' house. I allowed this with some trepidation; I was scarcely familiar with either of Lauren's parents. Lauren's father, from the start, was off-putting and arrogant. And that mother was never around, God. I forget her name. She was a night nurse…"

She shifted in her seat and faced me. "Ellie, I can't say this enough—not in my wildest dreams had I thought for one second that Frank Vine was a pedophile. Not one second. Please, please believe that." Maureen looked pleadingly at me.

I said nothing.

My mother looked down and placed her fingertips on her forehead. "I want to make clear to you that I am not proud of my decisions. I just did what I thought was right at the time. For our family and my career, and for Max and her family, who had it even worse than we did."

"What *happened* that day? Please. Just tell me, Mom."

My mother's face turned red all the way down her neck to the lining of her blue boat neck shirt and she swallowed. "I dropped you off. You remember that."

I nodded and waved my hand impatiently for her to go on.

"Larissa called me at the house. Max had called her in tears talking a mile a minute about Mr. Vine touching her and making her do things in his bedroom." She shook her head. "As if that wasn't enough, I could tell Larissa was high right away. I asked if she'd called the cops yet. She said she didn't and she wouldn't, not in the state she was in. So I said, 'Well, I'll call them, then!' And she screamed at me and told me I couldn't. Obviously I asked why the hell not, and she told me that Frank had been 'feeding' her drugs."

"Lauren's dad?" I asked, confused. "Why would he—"

"Well, I figured this out only later, but apparently he'd picked up on the fact that she was an addict, so he supplied her with heroin to numb her out. It allowed him to more easily carry on a…relationship with Max."

"Disgusting."

My mother had that far off look again. "Larissa begged me not to call the police until I could figure out what was going on in that house." She turned to me. "I know this sounds terrible, Ellie, but there was also a big possibility Max was lying about what Frank—Mr. Vine—was doing to her. It wouldn't have been the first time she lied. The Hollow…"

"The Hollow happened. I saw him run way. Do you believe me now? For God's sake!" My voice was almost at a shriek.

My mother gave me an exasperated look. "Yes, I know. Let me finish. I told Larissa I would call the police regardless, that they would be better suited to assess the situation. That's when Larissa threatened me. She said if she was going down, I was going down. If I called the cops, she would tell them I altered the case file and that I assisted her in obtaining drugs. Plus, if the cops questioned her while she was in such a stupor, she was done. And then I'd be done. I would lose my job, my license; I'd have been shunned from the profession. Then I would have no way to support you. Things were dire in those days, Ellie, more than you ever knew."

She looked cautiously at me, but my eyes remained dry, unblinking. She swallowed. "I had no idea what I would find over at the Vines'. I brought a baseball bat and your father's gun, and I was ready to use either of them. The bat, as you may remember, was my weapon of choice." She looked hesitantly at me. "And…you do remember, yes?"

"I want you tell me. In your words."

She took a sip of her water bottle, her hand shaking as she put it down. Her teeth were chattering as well, and she turned the knob to high heat. "I sped over there. I never grasped what many people refer to as a blind rage. Not until that day.

"I got right in through the front door. I could hear him yelling upstairs. I heard a bottle smash, I heard crying. It was you. I was about to fly right up there; I could barely feel the ground beneath me. Over to my left I saw Lauren sitting on the couch in the family room, staring at a muted TV like she was possessed. She didn't even turn her head.

"Then I saw Max up at the top of the stairs, motioning wildly to me through the slits in the upper banister. I snuck up the stairs and the door was partially open. His back was to me and he was standing over you, and his belt was undone…" Maureen drew uneven, suckling breaths and dabbed her eyes and nose with a damp tissue.

"You were so smart, Ellie," she said. "You didn't look at me. You knew I was there, but you kept talking to him, kept goading him into paying attention to you so that I could sneak up from behind. Your face was so bloody and bruised. You were struggling to crawl away from him, so weak, and somehow…you kept his focus. He leaned down and grabbed your hair, you were crawling away from him at this point in a sort of crab walk…and I drew the bat behind my head, and oh God. I cracked him on the head. That sound…"

She shook her head and wiped her face on a fresh tissue that I supplied out of my purse. I held in my own tears. The sensation of Mr. Vine yanking at my hair came flooding back.

I shifted in my seat. "And after that?"

"He was completely unconscious. You were in and out, you could barely walk. I had to have Max help me bring you downstairs. Max came home with us."

"What about Lauren?"

"Lauren…I tried to get her to come with me, but she refused to come. She was yelling at me, telling us all to get out, to leave her daddy alone. She was calling you girls sluts. It was very disturbing."

"And Mr. Vine? You left him there with her?"

My mother laughed bitterly, her lips curled up in disgust. She shook her head and her voice lost all emotion. "I left a note."

I opened my mouth in disbelief but my mother cut me off. "I wrote that I would be taking Max to the hospital for a rape kit. That I would get credible proof that he was a rapist and a pedophile. I told him his law practice and his family and his entire life would be ruined unless he agreed to leave town, leave the state. I know this makes no sense right now and it was a shot in the dark to work, but I was thinking only of you and Jack and my career—which was the only way I could keep our family afloat. Not involving the police was, in my mind, the only way I could continue working, providing for you. The only way Max could stay with her mother."

"So, you blackmailed him? And you returned Max to her drug-addled mother and never even called the cops?"

"I supported Larissa, got her clean again, for good." She said this with a vehemence that me jump.

I composed myself. "So he just skipped town? Sold his house or whatever? I can't believe he just up and left like that and took his family. How'd he convince his—?"

"I told his wife," Maureen said. "I called her at work from a payphone right after I left. Believe it or not, she didn't scream at me. She didn't tell me to go to hell, which is what I expected. She just said, 'Thank you,' and hung up."

I raised my eyebrows.

She went on. "I kept you out of school for four days while you healed. I slept on the couch downstairs with the gun under my pillow. But, days later, they were gone, their house on the market."

I put a palm to my forehead. "You're lucky he didn't come after you, Mom! After us! And you allowed him to go on, and be free? Free to continue doing what he was doing?"

My mother was crying now. "I don't know, Ellie. I question it every day of my life. Every day."

I shook my head in wonder. "I just...can't believe this stuff was in some inaccessible corner of my brain for so long. Just sitting there. I knew I had kind of an unhappy childhood, but, shit. I thought it was just because of dad."

"Your memory was definitely affected, whether through emotional trauma or physical trauma. I had a nurse friend come over to make sure you didn't have a concussion, but you were catatonic for a while. You had a visceral reaction if I'd so much as utter Max's name, or Lauren's. You'd wail, scream, punch me..."

The memory in my bedroom with blood on the sheets, slapping at my mother, now made perfect sense.

"Ellie, I would beg you to talk to me but you holed yourself up in your room. Then, one day, you snapped out of it. You slipped back into your routine, made different friends at school: Betsy, Selma, Erin. And thank God for Sarah and her family once she joined you at Marshside High. Sarah and her family's stability, their generosity in those years—you weren't aware of it...but her parents did a lot for you.

"Anyway," she continued, "you never spoke of it again. And I'll admit, I never brought it up. As awful as this is, honey, with the Vines gone without a trace, and each year never hearing a peep about it again, it seemed like we could just put it behind us. Forever."

I narrowed my eyes and shook my head. What a stupid fucking risk.

"Wishful thinking, I know." My mom wrung her hands together and bit her lip.

"Very wishful," I said. "Seeing as how I saw him just the other day."

She bit her lip. "And you're sure it was him?"

I nodded. "And Lauren. In a coffee shop. They did not look thrilled to see me."

"Do you think we should call the police?" my mom asked, her eyes searching mine.

"Now? What would I say?"

She didn't hear me; she was rambling over my words, her face corkscrewed in agony. "How could I ever explain what I did or why I did it? I'm a mandatory reporter. I was required by law to report him. I didn't. I could have put another child in danger."

I instinctively put my hand on her back and rubbed it. I could feel the jutting knobs of her spine. "I don't know what you should do. You're the mom. You're the adult."

"But you're an adult now, too."

I looked up. "Wait."

"What?"

"There's still one more thing."

My mother sucked the air through her teeth. "Yes?"

"Did you ever really get a rape kit?"

She looked into her lap again and shook her head. "Larissa wouldn't sign off on it. Maxine needed a parental guardian and it would have required involvement of the authorities anyway. It was…a bluff."

We sat in that car without saying anything for a long, long time.

20

The Letter

It had been only three days since I'd seen the Vines at the coffee shop. I had marked it on my calendar. And I marked the night of the conversation with my mother. I wanted in some way indicate a shift, a new beginning. I felt completely changed.

On the counter lay some mail. It was mostly junk. Before I tossed the pile into the trash I noticed one square envelope with no return address, only my name in neat lettering. I opened it. The letter was typed.

Dear Ellie,

I can only imagine what you must have thought, seeing my father and me that day at the coffee shop. My long dead nightmares have been haunting me ever since. This letter is mostly for me; I won't deny that. To help myself heal. In order to do that, for some reason, I feel compelled to explain why I was within three feet of that disgusting, poor excuse for a man.

The day your mother flew into my house, bat in hand, my life changed forever. My own mother came home, packed two duffel bags of my belongings and took me far, far away. Her decision was calculated and she'd been planning it for some time. My father was still lying on the ground, barely breathing, when we left. I asked my mother if he was dead.

She shook her head and I'll never forget what she said: "I wish to God he was."

We started a new life. I have a wonderful stepfather, and friends whom I treated much better than you and Max. I didn't have contact with my father—and I use that term only so that you know to who I am referring—until a couple years ago when he sought me out, seeking repentance. What you witnessed, Ellie, was a supervised visit. He was intent on meeting my daughter, Charlie. She is five. I did not allow him touch her in any way, and the meeting lasted ten minutes total. The odds of you stumbling across this meeting are almost unbelievable to me. Serendipity, maybe.

What haunted me was the look I saw in your eyes. Fear. I don't blame you. But from here on out this letter is not only for me, but for you, for your peace of mind. Please know that he lives far, far away. Don't mistake how he appeared, in his typical blustery, impatient manner, his moneyed dress. The reality is that he was wearing a borrowed suit and he came to town that day on a Greyhound bus.

He attained Level-3 sex offender status in the state of Ohio in 2002 and has a rap sheet of various assault charges. You can look it all up; he changed his name to Frank Reiner long ago, and it's all documented in the sex offender database. His probation officer keeps close tabs on him, he's not allowed to go near schools or playgrounds, and he wears a GPS tracking device on his ankle at all times.

And, as much as I doubt this myself, he claims he is a changed man. There is so much more to say, but all I can bear to write at the moment is I'm sorry. I'm sorry for whatever negative effects on your life that man caused. I'm sorry because although I was just a child, even then I did not try to do more.

I'm sorry to Max, who has not written back any of the twelve letters I've sent her over the years. Maybe you can try to get through to her. If you do, please, tell her I am sorry. I wish it could have been different. You were a good friend.

Lauren Wilson (Vine)

My hand was shaking. "Sarah," I said, a tremor to my voice.

"Yeah?" she called from the bathroom. The toilet flushed and she came out.

I stood in the entryway between the kitchen and the living room and held out the letter. "She wrote me."

"Who?"

"Lauren."

"You're kidding."

I handed it to her. She scrunched up her nose when she finished. "Well, this is interesting."

I sat down on the couch, stunned. "Very."

"What do you think about it?" she asked.

I widened my eyes. "I can't. I can't process it right now. I need sleep."

The clock said it was two in the morning, and I had work the following day. Sarah rubbed her eyes. "I think that's a good idea."

We went to bed and I blinked up at the dark ceiling for hours, my heart thudding, unable to sleep. Mr. Vine was far away. He was of no threat. Lauren's life had turned out well, too.

It was all so neatly tied up, so conveniently safe and conciliatory. Lauren had changed tremendously from the rat-faced, churlish girl from over a decade ago.

I was safe, according to that letter. It was all behind us.

So why didn't I feel safe?

***

I woke up from three hours of sleep and it was Friday.

I was not hungover. My hair did not smell of vodka, and I was not worrying about what I'd said to my coworkers at the mixer the night before. I'd skipped the mixer to drive down to Marshside and find out my mother had lied to me for thirteen years.

My check-in was a perfunctory one on Buster's end, but for me, I'd been staging a comeback—and this was the day I had planned on calling attention to it. With Buster fiddling with the waist of his pants and his eyes on my left nipple I broached the possibility of growth opportunities, a possible raise, a title change, maybe moving elsewhere in the company—marketing perhaps?

Buster's eyes whisked from my chest and he stared intently at something on his laptop. I continued, on a roll, urging myself to get it all out in the open, to be bold and proactive. I told him I gleaned enjoyment out of learning about analytics and metrics at a development training a couple weeks ago. I'd made some contacts. Would he be open to discussing my future, possibly on the Enterprise Data team? Or, at the very least, would he be open to reassessing my compensation that had not budged in over two years?

When I finished, I was proud of myself. It had taken a lot of mettle for me to finally bring up. I was terrified of asking for a raise, but I finally did. And as I waited for a response, and didn't get one after an agonizing pause, I realized he hadn't heard a word I said.

He looked up, finally. I couldn't pretend to smile. I couldn't even look at him with a neutral expression. I was angry; the heat flushing my neck and face could kindle a large fire.

"Is everything alright, Ellie?"

"Did you listen to one word I just said?" I asked, my hands gripping the table. "One word?"

"Of course, Ellie, you're talking about growing. And the executive team wants us to grow all of our Symbicoreans to their best potential. But I have to add that attitude goes a long way..."

And there Buster launched into a diatribe about his own ascent at Symbicore, his hard work, his relationships, his this, his that. This account was a cherry-picked version of his rise here; I knew from Savannah's inside track that he was inherently unlikable and impudent when he didn't get his way. A "squeaky wheel" was how she described his rise at Symbicore, along with the tiny fact that his cousin was the Chief Operating Officer.

"Buster," I said, trying to keep the exasperation from my voice, "the last couple months I have done everything I can to improve. I've tried to remain patient amid the effects of the recession. Four quarters in a row we were promised bonuses, and we received nothing. Last quarter you said the budget committee had allocated funds for merit increases. None of us have seen a dime.

"My numbers are highest on the team. I've networked and spoken to other managers. And they all say I need to work with you, I need to have your support. Will you at least give me that?"

It was the most direct and honest I'd ever been with him. And it was all true. Call it lofty, but ever since meeting Tim, and getting to know Savannah through Mel, I'd felt energized at work. Customer Service was a stepping-stone, I finally understood.

"Raises are earned," he honked. "Respect is earned, and when you have leadership skills like I have—"

"You know what, Buster?" I said, cutting him off. "I'm done here today. You're not supportive. You want to keep me here, keep me down. You want to keep all of us down."

"Now, Ellie, this attitude will not get you—"

I stood up, pointed two fingers into my eyes, and said, "And my eyes are up here."

With that I left, the glass door hissing shut behind me in the most undramatic fashion. I was shaking, not for the first time that week. As my adrenaline dissipated, I regretted my outburst and became acutely aware of my life unraveling bit by bit. *What have I done?* I thought as I returned to my cubicle. *Will he fire me?*

When I got home from what felt like a neverending day at work spent hunched in my cubicle talking to no one, not even Mel, I took out my laptop and logged in to Sarah's Facebook account. She said I could use it anytime to view Max's profile. I navigated to Max's *About* section, and unbelievably her phone number was listed. Judging from the amount of *Baby, you fine* messages plastered all over her wall from men in wife beaters, I figured this was intentional.

She picked up on the first ring, which I hadn't expected, and I was thrown in to a babble fit. "Hi, I hope you remember me, ah, I'm Ellie…from middle school—"

"Excuse me, what?" she barked. Her voice was harsher, scratchy, like her mother's. I guessed she still smoked.

"Max—it's Ellie."

"Ellie who?"

"Ellie Frites."

She paused. "Okay…"

"I, um, I wanted to talk to you."

"Clearly, you called me."

She tripped me up. I wasn't sure how to proceed, she'd already reduced me to the same stammering nitwit I was at age eleven.

I took a deep breath and said, "Max…I know it's been so long, but I wanted to apologize to you."

"Apologize, for what?"

"Well, wait. Let me back up. First, I wanted to thank you, then to apologize. For what happened at Lauren's that day."

She was silent. Then, "What's that got to do with anything

now? This is so weird you calling me out of the blue like this. Do you not have a life?"

"Max, I wanted to explain that I repressed the memory." I thought for a split second she didn't know what that word meant. "I blocked it out. The whole day. Whole weeks. The day at the Hollow when he attacked you in the woods, the day at Lauren's when I saw...everything. It took years, but...it all came back. I went to a therapist and we worked things out and I remembered."

"Congratulations, you remembered me giving some old-ass man a blow job."

"I...well, yes, but I remembered what happened afterward, with you calling my mom, and—"

"I saved the day." She laughed, but with a bitter edge. "And what's this about apologizing?"

"Max, I guess I'm ashamed to say that still, I have no idea..." I cleared my throat. "I have no idea how we even stopped being friends. So, I wanted to—"

"You..." she said softly, then stopped.

"I...what?"

"You abandoned me. You dropped me."

I frowned. "I don't remember that."

"Well, you did. You ignored me. Went over to those losers, Betsy and Selma, formed a little group of you own. You'd trash me all the time."

"Please believe me. I short-circuited or something, and must not have been able to handle being around you. Too traumatic."

"Too traumatic," she said flatly. "For you."

And I did remember, now. All it took was to hear her voice again to remember. To remember the pit forming in my stomach every time Max came into view at school. To remember grabbing Erin or Selma and snickering at Max as we walked past her. I thought I was turning the tables. Getting her back for being so awful to me. At likely the worst possible time in her life.

"God, Max, I'm sorry," I continued. "And I'm so thankful to you for calling my mom that day, and helping her stop him from doing anything…else."

She sighed. "Is that all?"

"No…" I said quickly. "It's not. I got a letter from Lauren recently."

She snorted. "What's that little bitch up to."

"She actually…she sounded really nice in the letter, really apologetic, and said her dad's all fucked up and lives in Ohio and has gotten into trouble over the years—"

"Huh, trouble."

"Want me to read it?"

I took her silence as a yes, and read it out loud.

After I finished, she said, "I could still fuck him, you know."

I cringed. Some things hadn't changed. "Max, that's terrible. Why—"

"Not in that way," she said, impatient. "I mean, I have proof."

"Proof?"

"Are you deaf?' she barked again. "Proof."

"Okay, what proof," I said, getting testy myself.

"He used to make me put my underwear in a garbage bag. He so very nicely provided me with these garbage bags so that his 'stuff' couldn't be traced on any of my things. So he'd buy me new underwear, like, women's underwear, to replace them. At twelve years old I was walking around in Victoria's Secret thongs."

I remembered the flattened black garbage bag beside her, unused, the day she was attacked. "Oh," I said softly.

"That day you found me in the Hollow," she said quickly. "That's the day I told him I liked TJ. I told him I wanted someone my own age." She laughed, without any humor in her voice. "And he didn't like that."

"So that's why he beat you. Why you were bruised, bloody."

"You got it, genius. And a couple days later, when he came to my house again, shooting my mother up so she was high as a kite, he made me do stuff, like he always did. He didn't hit me, told me he was sorry, all that. Told me he loved me, even.

"I managed to keep one of the bags. This is only a day or two before the day your mom cracked him over the head with the bat. I was so stupid back then, but at least smart enough to keep one of the bags. Has his DNA all over it."

"Are you going to report him?"

She scoffed at me, her breath heaving into the mouthpiece. "And what would that do? Sounds like he's already in deep enough shit. I'd only use it to get something out of him. To make him pay."

"Um, okay. Well—"

"Yeah, *well*," she mocked my voice, "sounds like we're done here. You said sorry, you forgot you abandoned me, blah, blah, blah. Thanks for letting me know his life is in the toilet, though. At least that makes me feel better."

"Me, too," I whispered.

Before she hung up, I added, "Wait. Before you go. Lauren said she wrote to you a bunch of times. To say sorry, too. She didn't include her return address, but if she writes me again...do you want me to get it from her? So you guys can talk?"

"I don't want to hear from that fuck-up," she said. "She knew what was going on and she did nothing. She can rot in hell."

"So, you haven't gotten her letters?"

"No. But I move a lot. Don't you start trying to be my pen pal either. We're done here."

I rolled my eyes to myself. "You're right. We are. I just needed to get that off my chest."

"Well, how nice for you."

She hung up on me. I didn't know what I expected. Did I think she'd cry with me? Thank me? She hated me then, and she hated me now. And for how I treated her in the end, maybe I deserved it.

I had to say I was impressed she kept evidence though. Just in case. I could call Maxine Lang many disparaging, unflattering names, and she'd deserve them. But I'd never call her stupid.

21

Detective Frites

A month passed since my conversation with Max, and my life fell back into a drama-free, hallucination-free rhythm.

Though at work, things could have been better. My relationship with Buster was irreparable after our spat, and I was looking for new jobs like mad. Lucky for me, the hiring freeze had lifted, and positions were opening up in the marketing department. Savannah and Tim were trying to pull strings with their department heads, helping me set up coffee meetings with hiring managers. Savannah's nickname should have been Savvy, because she sought out key contacts who she knew couldn't stand Buster. Of whom, to my pleasant surprise, there were several.

"Hang tight," she told me. "I'll get you out of there."

To my mix of pleasure and sadness, she'd already plucked Mel from ninjaville and helped land her a job as an account manager on Global East. It turned out Mel's honesty and assertiveness translated well in the business world. Once Savannah coached her not to be such a "snarky know-it-all," Mel was fitting in quite well with the fist-bumping sales force. I was left in the dust, though, and missed her terribly. She was usually too busy to even message me on SymbiChat.

The month of August also brought my twenty-fifth birthday, and Tim took me to dinner to celebrate. Additional sessions with Liz—no more hypnosis, just straight talking—were helping me work out my trust issues.

As a bonus birthday gift, Tim paid for a hotel room at Chatham Bars Inn for me and three girlfriends. Tim's uncle worked in their hospitality unit and he got a deal. I invited Mel, Savannah, and of course Sarah, to accompany me on a girls' weekend.

I didn't tell my mother I'd be down the Cape that weekend; our relationship was still strained, but we were on our way to a mending it. I still called her every week; I still visited her. It was a work in progress. But for that weekend, I wanted to pretend I didn't grow up on that peninsula with my mother four miles away. I was a tourist for once.

After the girls and I dropped our bags in our own private cottage surrounded by blue and white hydrangeas and the most meticulously groomed, verdant grass I'd ever seen, we headed down to the pool. I'd cocktail-waitressed at that same pool during summers home from college, and I relished in the reversal of fortunes. Well, even if I was staying in a heavily discounted room, and my day job was more menial and less fun than slinging drinks to rich and famous people.

My phone rang as I sipped on a Miami Vice. It was my mother. I walked to the far perimeter of the pool where the cabanas were empty and no children were scurrying around. I had to answer; she'd give me grief for the abrupt cut of the last ring—the fast track to voicemail.

I stood behind a large, limb-splaying aloe plant and picked up. "Hello?"

My mom's voice was trembling. "Ellie, listen to me." She cleared her throat. "Maxine Lang was found dead."

My voice caught and I felt the hairs on my arm stand up. I could hear a high-pressure noise, perhaps from an open car window. "How...how do you know?"

"Her obituary made it into the *Marshside Chronicle*. It was vague; it didn't say cause of death. So I did the Google of her name and remembered you said she lived in New Jersey. I found the police report on it. There was also an article in the Hoboken local paper, online."

"Can you read it to me?" My heartbeat quickened.

A car door slammed. "Yes. Let me just get inside. I was just at the library."

"The library? What were you doing there?"

"Ellie, I'm just…you know, I'm just looking around, using their computers. Making sure Frank Vine is where Lauren claims he is—"

"Mom!" I said. "You're still obsessing over this?"

"Let me just read off the article about Max, and you can tell me what you think."

"Okay," I relented. *Max is dead*, I thought. *Max is dead. What does that mean?*

It could mean nothing, I told myself. I thought of her hoarse smoker's voice, her gaunt face in her Facebook profile, a face that looked like it had done its fair share of drugs.

I heard keys jangling, the creak of the front door. Then the door slammed. "Hang on…"

I balanced the phone in the crook of my neck and shifted my feet on the hot tiles that surrounded the pool.

Twin boys came out of nowhere and launched themselves into the pool beside me, their dual cannonballs crashing loudly, soaking my back.

"Where are you?" my mother asked.

"Chatham."

"You didn't tell me that."

"I don't tell you everything. Doesn't feel very good, does it?" I couldn't resist that one, and immediately regretted saying it.

"I've been apologizing nonstop, Ellie, and you're not making this any easier on me."

"Sorry, Mom. Seriously. I shouldn't have said that."

"Okay, right here," she said breathlessly. "I've got it up on my laptop. This is what it's titled: *Massage Therapist Found Dead in Hoboken Apartment*. The article is dated four days ago." She clucked her tongue and spoke some of it under her breath as she scanned the article. "It has not yet been ruled a homicide, but suspicious activity hasn't been ruled out either. Few details were provided. There's a picture of Max from her Facebook page, I think. Oh, geez. It's provocative. Her breasts…oh my. They couldn't have chosen something a little more…chaste?"

"Is that all it says, Mom? Stop talking to yourself."

"Alright. It says she lived alone and was found by a coworker after she hadn't shown up to work in three days. She worked at a salon."

"Mom, it doesn't necessarily mean anything. She could have overdosed or something."

My mother gave an exasperated sigh. "It's possible, but…the timing with the letter…and the fact Lauren knows your address…what if her father—"

"Mom, her dad lives in Ohio. He's broke, and he's got a freaking GPS ankle bracelet. He's of no threat. We looked him up the Ohio sex registry, remember? Everything Lauren said added up. Plus, all that happened over a month ago now."

"I just don't feel good about this, Ellie."

"Well, what do you suppose I do, Mom? Call the cops? Tell them my mother has a 'bad feeling' about some child rapist we never reported? So I saw him in the coffee shop. Big deal. He's done nothing to me. Or to you, after all this time."

She said nothing.

My tone turned tender. "Mom, just let me enjoy my birthday weekend. I'll be back in Boston tomorrow. I'll have Tim watch my apartment when I'm gone, and I'll ask him to be there when I get back if that makes you feel better."

"What is Tim's number? I'll call him and tell him. His last name is McDonnell, right?"

"I'm not giving you his number, Mom! You only met him that one time, for five seconds. I'd like to keep it that way for now."

"Ellie, please, I just want—"

"Mom, I'm sorry, I love you, but I think you're overreacting without having all the facts. Max was rough. She partied hard. Who knows how she died. If it was a suspicious death, the article would have said so."

My mother wasn't convinced. And despite the words coming out of my mouth, neither was I.

***

The girls and I lounged by the pool the rest of the day, and I didn't mention anything about Max. I didn't want to drum up needless speculation and drama that would put me on edge for the remainder of the weekend.

But after dinner that night, a raucous meal at the Squire, I turned my phone back on. I'd shut it off earlier to avoid my mother. Four voicemails from her appeared, plus one text from Tim. *Call me back, Ellie, please. NOW.*

I left the girls without a word; they were busy dancing to the music blaring out of the jukebox. I shouldered past more bodies streaming inside from a long line outside, sweating and bumping and swaying in the weak A/C.

I went outside and called Tim back before even listening to my mother's messages.

He picked up on the first ring. "Ellie, your Mom and I found out some scary shit today."

"Ugh, she called you?"

"She called me this morning, I guess after talking to you. And I'm glad she did. Ellie…you need to hear me out. Are you somewhere safe? Are you somewhere you can talk?"

"I'm at the bar. Outside. Tim, you're scaring me."

"Okay, I hate to take you away from your friends, but you need to hear what we found out today. We may need to call the cops."

"I'll get Sarah and we'll walk back to the hotel. I'll call you back."

***

Back at the hotel, with Sarah promptly falling fast asleep on the double bed we were sharing, Tim told me all about his fruitful day of sleuthing, in cahoots with none other than my mother. He spoke fast.

Maureen wanted to be sure this time she wasn't overreacting, that this time she would be smart. She told Tim that some nights, she would wake to pangs of anxiety knifing into her chest. She'd be convinced her son or her daughter was in trouble. Other nights she would open her eyes, her cheek squished into a tear-soaked pillow, with me at the forefront of her mind. More often than not, her premonitions or intuition were validated. I would call her the next morning, crying softly over the phone, "I've been feeling sad, Mom, I don't know why, I can't stop crying and I can't sleep…"

Jack wasn't as forthcoming. She'd be the one to give in and call him, panicked, and even then he would divulge only maddening tidbits of near accidents. "Yeah, we were on the roof the other night, drinking a bit. Oh, yeah, and Denny almost fell off—oh come off it, Mom, I said so no one got hurt!"

Today, she told Tim, was such a day. Something wasn't sitting right. After seeing the article about Max, she'd become intent on finding more information on Lauren Vine. She searched fruitlessly for any trace of her. She used her maiden name, Vine, and then what she assumed was her married name, Wilson, the name with which she signed the letter. Not knowing where Lauren lived, or her occupation, the results from the two very common, generic names proved too overwhelming and she gave up.

When she revisited the very brief newspaper articles about Maxine's death, she grew frustrated, unable to glean any further information, and called me, in hopes that I would recognize the dangerous coincidence.

"After she talked to you, Maureen scoured the Ohio sex offender database one more time," Tim said, "re-checking the entry on Frank Vine that she'd found earlier. She found him under the changed surname provided by Lauren in the letter, Reiner. Lauren had said he changed his name. And, at first, Lauren's story still added up.

"What bothered Maureen was that the photograph wouldn't load next to his rap sheet. Just a blank white box with a red X and the text *Unable to Load*. She reported the bug to the customer service email listed and requested, as was her right to such public information, that they supply her with the mug shot of Frank Reiner. She said she wanted it ASAP.

"That's when she found my number and called me. She apologized for bothering me, for concerning me, but she was worried. I told her I was, too."

"Okay, so what exactly did Nancy Drew and Ned find out today?" I tried to keep my voice light, though I was feeling anything but.

"Your mom was kind of stuck, like, frustrated she couldn't find anything on Lauren. She thought that was too weird. Then I asked if she remembered anything about the mother, maybe? Like what's her role in all this, you know? Maybe she'd lead us to the father. And she said she remembered Lauren's mom's name started with a C, but it wasn't coming to her. Then she remembered: Claire. She tried both Claire Wilson and Claire Vine and saw reams of results. A couple databases captured family information, street name, siblings, and offspring, and occasionally, occupation. She tried a few of the phone numbers that matched her name with 'nurse,' remembering that Claire had been a night nurse. Dead ends. I tried, too, but those names are way too common. I wasn't coming up roses either.

"Maureen and I were calling each other throughout the day, but she called me back all excited this time because she found a Claire Wilson who was a nurse with a husband, David, on Spring Lane in West Hartford, Connecticut. Maureen tried the number and got an answering machine, a bright, sunny voice greeting her. She thought it might be her, but wasn't sure. She didn't leave a message.

"Then she looked down at the junk mail on the coffee table—an AARP newsletter and her annual employee catalog. This gave her an idea. She Googled the hospitals—she's so funny—she said 'did the Google.'" He chuckled.

"Yes, I know, she does that," I said, my heart still pounding. "Go on."

"So, anyway, she Googled hospitals in the Connecticut area and tried to match the name. An old hospital staff newsletter PDF popped up for Beth Israel Deaconess in Hartford. In it, she found a photo of Claire Wilson."

"Oh my God. She found her," I murmured, somewhat impressed.

"Yes. She called and left a message this time. She asked for Claire to please call her back, it was urgent; she needed to speak to her about her daughter. Then…minutes later…she got a call back."

And according to my mother, by way of Tim, this was how that call went down.

The phone rang. Maureen rushed to the phone hanging on the kitchen wall. Caller ID: Wilson, 202-555-5352.

"Hello?"

"Hi, um," a woman cleared her throat, "Maureen? This is Claire Wilson. Formerly, uh, Vine. Returning your call?"

"Claire. It's been some time. I'm sorry for disturbing you. Thank you, thank you for calling me back. I just...I can't explain it any better than that I have a feeling something isn't right."

Claire said nothing.

"You see, Ellie was recently contacted by your daughter. She'd seen Lauren and your ex-husband in a coffee shop up in Boston. Afterwards, Lauren wrote her to explain why she was seen with your ex-husband, understandably, after what happened all those years ago. Anyway what is tugging at me is that I saw that Max Lang died and—"

"I'm sorry, what?"

"Apologies. I'm talking too fast. I said Max Lang was found dead—"

"No. I mean, yes, that's terrible about Max," Claire said. "But...what you said about Lauren. You said Lauren wrote to your daughter? Ellie saw her?"

"Oh, yes, after she saw her—"

"And when was this?"

"Over a month ago."

Claire's voice was cold, flat. "Well, isn't this interesting. I haven't seen my daughter since 1996."

"What?" Maureen frowned. She fingered her necklace nervously. She could hear Claire breathing on the line. "Lauren said in the letter that she moved away with you, and that her father lives in Ohio..."

"Do you have this letter?"

"Yes, I have a copy right here." My mom of course had a copy of it glued to her, readily available on the table in front of her. She'd read it a million times.

"Can you read it to me?" Claire asked.

When Maureen finished reading, she heard a TV shut off and a sigh.

"I need to sit down."

"If you haven't seen your daughter since '96, does that mean she didn't move away with you?" Maureen pressed.

"She did move away with me. I took her from Marshside that very day you called me at work. Back in '96. I had emergency bags already packed. But," she snorted, "our exodus didn't last long. Lauren ran away after a few months."

The cops must have returned to Marshside, searching for Lauren, Maureen thought, her heart pounding so hard she could feel it in the back of her throat. "You must have involved the cops, then? Did they know about your husband? She was likely with him, right?"

"Yes, of course I involved the cops. But they couldn't locate him either."

"And the cops never came back here, to Marshside? To look for her?" Maureen could hear her voice growing shriller.

"The cops did go back to Marshside. They questioned people who knew her. Teachers, friends."

Maureen buried her head in her hands, cradling the phone in the crook of her neck and shoulder. "No one ever questioned me or Ellie. It never got around town that Lauren was even a missing person."

"Well, first off, they were convinced she just ran away with her dad. I'm not sure how hard they even looked. We'd gotten into a terrible fight beforehand. All we did was fight in those days." Claire sucked in her breath, exhaling slow and hard. "Second, I never named you or your daughter. Consider it a thank you, for giving me the impetus to leave that day. And for cracking that bastard over the head and almost killing him. I wish to God you did."

Maureen hit her forehead with her palm. "I didn't even think to search a Missing Person's database to find information on Lauren. I have access to one through work, for God's sake." Maureen frowned, angry at herself for all that wasted time conducting elementary Google searches.

Claire didn't seem to be listening, unaware of Maureen's resurfaced regrets, her horribly too-late hindsight. Claire's mind was also in 1996, in her own world. "When we moved, we changed our name to Wilson and I foolishly thought he wouldn't find us that way. Turns out he did. Or, rather, Lauren found him. That's what I believe happened, anyway." Claire got quiet, and spoke softer. "To say those years were a living nightmare would be a severe understatement."

Maureen's mind raced, trying to piece together what she could. But it didn't make sense. "Wait. I don't understand, Claire. The cops, they didn't follow through, they didn't find anything? It sounds like they just…gave up on a missing person's case because they figured she was with her dad. But weren't they motivated by the fact that your ex-husband was a child molester?"

Claire sucked in her breath. "That…no. I…I didn't mention any of that to them."

Maureen started to protest, but Claire cut her off. "I knew he was a creep, Maureen. He'd had affairs. But Lauren swore up and down to me he never touched Max. The thing is, we don't know what really happened that day. We never will."

"But we do. Ellie saw—"

"Enough," Claire said briskly. "I can't think about that right now. What's done is done. No use debating it now."

Maureen was nonplussed about Claire's denial, but she couldn't focus on that right now. She pressed on. "Claire, tell me something. According to Lauren's letter, Frank Vine, or so-called Reiner, is a sex offender who lives in the state of Ohio. Are you saying that's a crock of shit?"

Claire sighed. "I don't know anything about Frank. The only truth—what I know to be true, anyway—is that Lauren has a daughter, my granddaughter, named Charlie. She is five years old. She started sending me pictures when Charlie was a baby. But that's it. No word of where she lives. No contact.

And certainly no contact with my asshole ex-husband. Reiner, or Vine, or whatever his name is now."

"Oh, good God." The hairs on Maureen's arms stood straight as pricks. She thought of Ellie saying the three of them were together in the coffee shop. What did that mean?

"Maureen, that letter is full of lies. I have no idea why she would write it. But, I also know my ex-husband brainwashed her all those years ago. He was a selfish, dishonest, alcoholic asshole and she refused to see that. If Ellie does talk to her again, can you let her know that her mother loves her and misses her?" Claire sniffed. "I want to be a part of her life. Will you have her do that?"

Maureen agreed but her mind was on another plane. She thanked Claire and hung up.

***

"The letter was made up?" I asked. My mind was spinning.

"There's more.

"More?"

"About midday, Maureen called me back. She tried calling you…"

"And?" I pressed.

"Check your email, I forwarded you something."

I sifted through my inbox. I glanced over at Sarah passed out over the covers, fully dressed, snoring lightly. Text notifications streamed in from Mel, informing me that she and Savannah were heading back soon, along with, *Everything okay?* I ignored them.

Tim's email was a forward from my mother's account. Scrolling down, I saw the original sender, custservice@ohio.gov. The email read:

We apologize for the inconvenience. We have restored the missing image file of Frank Reiner. [click here]

I tapped on the hyperlink with my finger, and the Ohio Sex Offender website appeared on my browser. I magnified the entry on the screen and tapped on the picture. Staring back at me was Frank Reiner: same height and build that matched the physical description of what I saw in the coffee shop. Aged sixty, height six-foot-three, weight two hundred and twenty pounds, brown hair and brown eyes. But the face staring back—dark, hooded eyes beneath a half moon of bare scalp, the head itself large and round atop rounded shoulders, was a man that in all absolution was not the Frank Vine I knew.

22

Neighborly Love

I hung up with Tim and packed my bag so I could have a fast exit the next morning. Sarah was still sleeping, and when Mel and Savannah finally stumbled into the room, I made sure I was curled up beside her, pretending to sleep. I hadn't the energy to rehash everything Tim had told me.

In the morning, while Savannah and Mel slept soundly, I stirred Sarah from her slumber and led her to the bathroom. I whispered an abridged version of what I'd learned from Tim the night before, and told her I was sitting on some startling information from my mother: Max was dead.

"She's dead?" Sarah said, widening her eyes at me in the mirror. Then she put her hands on her hips and gave me a look not unlike the dubious death stares I'd receive in college after confiding naïve gems like, "He said he wasn't into labels, so I'm like, cool with it" and "He said she was just a friend and that I'm crazy, and maybe he's right and I'm overreacting…"

"It's too coincidental, Ellie," she said now, shaking her head. "You talked to Max on the phone what, a couple weeks ago?"

"Over a month. Sar, it could have been from anything, right? Clearly she's involved with drugs and sketchy guys. Maybe it was an overdose."

She sighed. "She did post that video where she was doing lines of coke at like three in the morning, which I only saw because I was bored on my night shift. The one she deleted in the morning."

"The one where she had the mascara all down her face and her mouth was kinda frothy, like she was foaming at the mouth, and that guy was—?"

"Oh, no–that's the other one," Sarah said. "I'm talking about the one she deleted in the morning—I don't think you saw this one."

I scrunched up my nose. "Oh." Sarah and I had taken to checking in on Max the last few weeks, curious about what she was up to. Upon closer examination, her life was shadier than we'd ever thought.

We stood in silence for a moment. I kept stealing glances at Sarah as she slowly packed her toiletries, mentally urging her to agree with me, tell me everything was going to be fine.

Finally, she said, "Ok. I guess it's possible. It could have been an overdose. Or she was murdered by one of those dudes in her videos with the tear drop face tattoos. It could have been anything like that, really."

Instead of soothing me, my stomach dropped as I thought about the letter. "But Lauren lied about her father. Why the hell would she do that?"

Sarah bit her lip. "I don't know. That's definitely sketchy."

I didn't wish to alarm the other girls, so we left a note for Mel and Savannah that instructed them to stay for as long as they wanted to, but that I wasn't feeling well and wanted to get a head start back to Boston.

Sarah drove me back to our apartment mostly in silence. Exhausted from the lackluster sleep after speaking with Tim, I snoozed on and off, my temple resting against the cool window. When we arrived outside the apartment, I got out, dropped my bags on the sidewalk, and slammed the car door shut. I had to step back from the car and nudge my bag onto the grass so a young mother jogging behind a running stroller could get by.

It was late afternoon, warm but not too hot. Sarah leaned over the console and called through the passenger window, "Do you want me to walk in with you?"

I stooped down and rested my forehead against the top of the car door. "Tim will be here any minute."

Sarah creased her forehead. "Okay, I'll be back as soon as I can. Hopefully parking's not too bad."

I nodded, watched her drive off, then yawned and stretched my back. I looked up at the facade of my building, at my bedroom window on the third floor that faced the street. I thought I saw a shadow, a tiny movement of the blind. I stared a little longer, but saw nothing. A zephyr passed and goosebumps pimpled my arm.

I craned my neck and looked down the street both ways for Tim's car. No sign. I took out my phone and called him. When he picked up I blurted, "Sarah just dropped me off. She's off to find street parking, but it could take forever for her to find a spot. Are you on your way?"

"Two minutes. Hang tight."

"I think I'm going crazy. I thought I just saw someone in the window."

"I'll walk inside with you. Don't go anywhere."

I sat down on the curb. I felt unclean. My hair was unwashed, and despite brushing my teeth twice, a film on my front teeth had built up from eating carb-heavy meals with lush desserts, sugary margaritas, and mudslides.

I could hear Tim before I could see him. He pulled up in his Jeep, the engine whirring. The oversized wheels propped the body of the car high off the ground, so he had to swing himself down from the elevated ledge. He landed hard on the pavement.

I ran up to him now, wrapped my arms around him, and

squeezed. I was on the verge of tears as I spoke into his shoulder. "I've been paranoid Mr. Vine is following me. Any guy who's tall, or has grey hair, I think it's him. Do you know how many tall, grey-haired people there are?"

Tim extracted himself and held the sides of my shoulders and looked into my eyes. "I'm glad you're safe. I worried the whole time you were up there. I don't blame you for being freaked out. Especially after what I found out today."

"Good God." I put a hand to my forehead. "What'd you find out today?"

Tim looked around and I became aware that I'd been doing the same. Up the street, down the street, through windows, at passersby.

He rubbed his cheek. "I just don't see why you or your mom hasn't called the cops yet. It's crazy to me."

"Have you talked to her today?"

He nodded. "You haven't?

I curled my lip. "I'm sure she's all jittery and crazy…she'd just make me feel more panicked."

"She called me twenty times today. Twenty."

"Pretty standard."

"Well, at least I got through to her. She thinks you should call the cops, too, Ellie."

"I want sit and think about this. It's been one day since we found out Lauren's letter was bullshit. I just want to sit down and make a plan. Figure out how to approach this."

Tim sighed. "Okay—"

I fingered the handle to my suitcase. "Can we go up now? Make sure no one's there?"

He sighed. "Of course. And I don't mean to lecture. I'm just worried about you. I hope you know that."

He looked down at his flip-flops and hooked his thumbs in his pockets. "It's because…I love you."

My eyes widened. The words "I love you, too" were on the

tip of my tongue, but they wouldn't go any further. My eyes landed on a bumblebee hovering over a small patch of grass next to my bag. I couldn't say it back. Not yet. Not when I was in this state, I thought. Soon.

He cleared his throat and grasped the handle to my duffel bag, hoisting it over his shoulder. He picked up my suitcase easily in his other hand. His face was red. He smiled weakly. "Okay. Uh…guess we should just go upstairs, then."

I opened my mouth to say something, anything, but he brushed by me and held the door open. I went in and stood at the bottom of the steps and looked up at the small shared hallway between my unit and the college kids' across the hall, which, judging by lack of foot traffic or noise the last month, was vacant for the summer.

He held his hand out. I gave him the key, and he clomped up the stairs and went inside first. The apartment was so small that confirming an adult male wasn't lurking in every nook and cranny took all of two minutes. No one else was there.

"So, you said you found out more?" I asked, holding his hands in mine across the table.

"Well, now that we know that the whole name change to Frank Reiner is a load of crap, I started poking around for Frank Vine again. Like your mom said, there was nothing on him online. So, I went old school and found out where he works."

"Old school?"

"You'd never guess…the *phone book*."

I raised my eyebrows.

"It was just his business address. He's a partner at Shiner, Vine, and Brimley, up in Marblehead. It's forty-five minutes from here. They don't have a website. Conveniently."

"He's been that close, this whole time? Forty-five minutes?" My eyelids felt weighted by bricks. I looked around;

the apartment was so quiet. Tim watched me, biting his lip, but said nothing.

"You know what, I just want to lie down," I said. "Sarah will be here soon, and I'm just going to double lock my door tonight and keep my old softball bat by my bed and sleep on it. I'm hungover and dirty and can't keep my eyes open. Tomorrow I want a fresh, rested view of things."

Tim shook his head. "You shouldn't put this off. I don't feel comfortable leaving you here alone."

I got up from the table and started pacing the kitchen and running my hands through my hair. "It's fine. I'm fine. I have my phone, and I won't answer the door for anyone. Plus, like, there is still a chance Max died on her own, completely unrelated to Mr. Vine or Lauren. Yes, Lauren's letter was full of lies. But…maybe…"

"Maybe what?" He looked at me incredulously.

I threw my hands in the air. "I don't know. I have no explanation for it, I guess. I'm just so beat right now; I can't think straight."

Tim got up. "This is crazy. I'm not leaving you alone. I'll get my stuff out of my car and park on Comm Ave."

I touched his arm. "Sorry, but, Tim, I'm serious. Do you mind sleeping at your place? I want to sleep alone tonight. So I can think."

"Are you sending me away because of what I said before?" he asked.

"What?" My face heated up.

"Nothing. Never mind."

His face was redder than mine, surely, approaching the color of the maroon Roman blinds over the A/C unit. He straightened a picture hanging on the wall, a scenic beach landscape picture Sarah had hung. Then he made his way over to the door, his posture defeated and his hips cracking. His hand lingered on the knob without twisting it. He turned to me. "Call me if anything happens. Like, immediately." Then he pointed to the deadbolt. "And lock this."

"I will." I followed him and we kissed awkwardly goodbye. I locked the door and texted Sarah, who answered that she was grabbing some snacks for the three of us so we could all hang out tonight, if I didn't mind her being a third wheel. I told her Tim wasn't staying over, that I was too tired. I didn't mention that the three unreturned words from earlier still hung in the air, and that I regretted every second of not returning them. I had this uncanny sense that I'd made a huge, irreparable mistake.

**

When Sarah came back, I'd already been dozing off in my room. I heard her close the freezer door and step quietly about the apartment, likely trying not to wake me. I roused myself out of sleep and stood in my doorway and rubbed my eyes.

She walked over to me. "Sorry I can't enjoy ice cream with you, Elf, I'm just so tired. My shift's in just a few hours."

"Oh my God, don't even worry. Sleep."

I went back to bed, tossing and turning, until finally I fell asleep.

Some time later I woke up to piercing screams. *Sarah.*

I shot up out of bed and clutched my phone, dialing 911 with my finger hovering over the send button. I was trembling all over. I tiptoed to my closed door and put my ear to it. She'd stopped screaming.

"Sarah? Are you all right?" I called out, my voice shaking. Silence.

I opened the door a small crack and peeked through and looked down the hall.

Her bedroom door opened slowly and it creaked.

When it opened all the way I saw she was smiling. "Sorry," she called out, "there was a *mouse!*"

I let out a huge sigh of relief and opened my door all the way. "You scared me," I said, clutching my chest. "So badly."

"Sorry." She winced. "You told me you had a mouse and I totally forgot."

"He's harmless," I said, smirking, and Sarah rolled her eyes at me. She was already in her scrubs, ready for another night shift. She had max gotten two extra hours of sleep.

"This must have been such a long weekend for you," I said. "Thank you for coming down and celebrating even though you must be so exhausted."

"I love you, Elf. Of course I'd come celebrate with you."

Sarah begged me to lock the deadbolt, as Tim had, and left for work.

It was barely dark, but as soon as I lay down in bed I fell asleep again, having light but colorless dreams. I woke up periodically only to fall right back into a slumber. I was awoken abruptly by footsteps on the stairs. It had gotten dark and I turned on the light. I grasped for my phone. I had two texts from Sarah.

I went all the way there and realized I forgot my work badge. AND I can't find my keys. I'm locked out, let me in?

The other, only a few seconds before.

Nevermind, found them!

I recognized Sarah's signature stomping up the stairs. Our senior year, Sarah had taken the attic bedroom of our sprawling, falling-apart house on Main Street, and I used to swear she spent half her days walking around with ankle weights. I would joke that I never heard a human lack as much grace as her.

There was a rustling and keys dropped outside the door.

I turned the light on and rubbed my eyes. I wanted to remind Sarah to deadbolt the door behind her. The keys jangled; Sarah was likely fumbling over which key.

I giggled and called out, "Should I just let you in? You've got more keys than the super."

As I exited my bedroom Sarah burst into the apartment, her eyes wild. She looked like she was smiling, eyes wide. I clutched the doorframe, still dizzy from getting up from sleep and was about to ask her what was so funny.

Then, as if in slow motion, my perception of Sarah's demeanor shifted, and I started to see that Sarah's face was contorted in horror and fright. She was not laughing.

The reason for the look on her face presented itself, large and looming and red-faced. Behind Sarah stood Frank Vine.

23

Serendipity

Sarah sprang forward, pushed from behind. Mr. Vine gripped a small gleaming knife in his left hand and was holding it to her throat. His other hand covered her mouth, pulling her head back close to his chest. His lip curled in a sneer as he nodded his head, eyes on me. "Don't scream."

I couldn't if I tried. I was frozen. He shuffled Sarah forward into the foyer. I shifted on my feet nervously, and with a couple small steps retreated backward. My phone was inside my bedroom on the nightstand and I could see the hot pink case in my peripheral vision. *I might be able to just make a quick grab for it,* I thought hurriedly, *or maybe jump out the window. Three stories are nothing.*

I took one more step back…

"Don't move another inch." The voice came from a small-framed dirty blonde with a scrunched up face who appeared behind Mr. Vine. The girl smiled, her lips thin, her teeth a greyish-yellow. "Hi, Ellie."

Dark spindly ink peeked out from beyond the neckline of Lauren's beige blouse and the top of her hands were etched in the same black, swirling tattoos. She had dark circles underneath her eyes, stark against the unhealthy pallor of her skin.

"Nice fancy city apartment you got here," she said, looking around. She had deep creases in her forehead, around her mouth. Although from far away she could have passed for a slight, underweight teen, up close she looked much, much older than twenty-five. I stared at her and gripped the doorframe for balance and was suddenly very aware of my limbs and how loose and weak they felt. My throat was raw, dry from sleep.

I choked out, "Why are you here? What do you want?"

A small thought emerged in the back of my head; how this scene seemed surreal, dream-like, so much less real than the lucid hypnosis sessions.

My eyes met Sarah's, whose cheeks were warped by Mr. Vine's gloved hand gripping her face. He shifted her around with force. I saw a flash of myself as a small child, staring through the creases of his hot, moist fingers as he wrenched my neck back and forth, pulling me down the hall and up the stairs.

Lauren turned to her father. "Let me do it, Daddy."

"We discussed this. You do nothing. You watch."

She pouted, turned to me, then walked towards me slowly. I stepped back.

"Stay put," Mr. Vine barked, and it wasn't clear who he was speaking to. My mind seemed to be working in slow motion. But one thought shone bright: I had at least twenty pounds on Lauren. I could take her. Then, just as bright: but what about Sarah? He'd kill her. The possibility hung in the shrinking distance between me and Lauren, who was stalking closer to me, slow, step after step. She appeared to hold nothing in her hands. No weapons.

Her father's voice halted her. "Step back from her, Lauren. I told you to disappear into the furniture. You're a fly on the wall, a passenger. You hear me?"

She was within three feet of me now, her eyes dancing up and down my face, forehead to chin, down to my feet, her beady eyes stopping at my waist. She smirked. "You're still ugly. An ugly, ugly girl."

Hardly uglier than you, you fucking rat, I thought furiously, but swallowed my words, my throat sandpaper. I tore my eyes away and looked wildly at her father, then back at Sarah's despairing expression. I was tortured by the possibility of overtaking Lauren, she was so close I could reach out and touch her. Slap her. Strangle her. Should I do it? Should I?

These questions felt miles away. *This can't really be happening*, a voice whispered. *This is happening. Do something.* But I couldn't.

So we all stood staring at one another, sweating, breathing copious amounts of hot air into the cramped apartment. Droplets fell along Mr. Vine's temples, beads of sweat pooled in my décolletage, my breasts barely held inside the old camisole I'd worn to bed.

Mr. Vine wiped his temple with the knife's handle and turned to his daughter, who was still sizing me up. "Turn that A/C on and pull the blinds down on that window. Now."

Lauren swiveled on her heel and walked over to the window unit beside the couch and fiddled with the buttons, tapping them harder and harder. She slapped the whole unit in frustration. "It's broken."

"It's not broken," I called to her.

"Miss Know-it-All," Lauren said, sticking out her tongue. "You fix it—"

"She stays put," Mr. Vine grumbled again.

I felt like we had been in this standoff for hours, but it had probably been only a few minutes. I turned my head slightly towards my bedroom. If only I could—

"Get the phone out of her room," Mr. Vine growled. "I see her eyeing it."

Lauren nodded. "I see her too. She thinks she's smart?

She thinks it's a movie? Remember those movies we'd make, Ellie?" She smiled wide. "Those were the days, huh?"

I nodded, regarding her carefully.

Lauren sneered back at me. "You were a sneak. A snoop. A—"

"Shut up and get the phone, Lauren," her father's voice boomed.

Lauren slithered past me, and I could have grabbed her hair and slammed her lying, trashy head into the doorframe, *whack*. But I didn't. I feared too much for Sarah.

Lauren picked up the phone from the nightstand and read the screen. "Awwww, it's that ginger boyfriend of yours. You got a little message." She dangled the phone as she walked past.

I tried to snatch it but Lauren was too fast. She walked backwards to the vicinity of her father and Sarah. "Too...tired...to...come...over," she said as she typed. "Every... thing's...O...K." She tapped the screen once more and held up the phone and wiggled it. "That should do it."

"Why did you write me that letter?" I asked, the question eating at me, the next question even more so. "Why now? I just don't understand..." My voice was imploring but surprisingly steady.

"Daddy wrote that letter. Idiot." Lauren laughed and tossed a glance at her father, but he was busy struggling with a squirmy Sarah. Every time he repositioned the knife in front of Sarah's neck, every time it got close to scraping the hived, goose bumped flesh, I jumped. I felt so foolish and helpless standing there. I thought of all the movies, all the hostage situations I'd seen on TV where I'd think, *Why doesn't that guy watching just fucking do something?*

I bit my lip and looked forlornly, helplessly, at Sarah. "Hang in there, Muppet, we'll get through this."

Sarah nodded back, tears still falling.

"Shut up with your pet names, you ugly bitch," Lauren snapped.

Lauren's pupils were completely dilated, like perfect circular blots of oil. My eyes fell to her arm, where her sleeve had slid back slightly. There were purple bruises, track marks. Lauren sneered at me and pulled the shirt cuff lower.

I'd never felt so ineffectual in my life. My arms hung limp at my sides and my head was on a swivel, watching Lauren, watching Mr. Vine, all the while trying my best not to look at Sarah's face, for when I did, it sent a prick into my heart. Sarah's silent tears were wetting Mr. Vine's gloves, droplets plunked soundlessly onto the hardwood floor. A sob arose in my throat and I dried my palm on my pants.

Mr. Vine stared at me now while he spoke to his daughter. "She's looking jumpy. Take the gun." He jutted his hip out. "Don't do anything, unless you have to. You can come out of the passenger side for this. Come get it."

Lauren skipped over to her father like a schoolchild and reached into the inside pocket of his jacket. She took out a pistol and held it up with a grin.

I tried to will my body to stop trembling and piped up again. "You…you didn't answer me. Why now? After all this time? You could have come after me or my mom years ago."

He grinned with the same slick, twisted stretching of lips as that awful day in his bedroom, when he swung from moody and solemn to excitable and manic and crazed. Here, though, he seemed a bit more subdued, and with a gun in the picture, this comforted me a slight bit. His daughter, on the other hand…

"Serendipity," he said.

I noticed his nose had gotten redder over the years. An alcoholic's veiny red nose. My eyes shot to Lauren, who put her hands on her hips, the gun loose in her right hand. The nozzle was pointed down at the floor.

"Speak English, Daddy."

I pressed him further. "Seeing me at the coffee shop you mean?"

He repeated, "Serendipity."

"So…you were never after me? It was just…dumb luck that you saw me and so you decided, hey, I think now would be a good time?"

It didn't make sense. Lauren and her father exchanged amused looks, but neither spoke. I shifted my feet. "And then Max. Did you kill her?"

Sarah's eyes went wide at this, her tears torrential, and her intermittent, muffled shrieking had been reduced to a guttural monotone moan. She'd stopped struggling, and now stood limp, leaning back against his body. I couldn't distinguish her sweat from her tears.

He grunted as he repositioned her again. "Well, I couldn't let her go out and do anything stupid, could I?"

I cocked my head. "What do you mean, stupid?"

Lauren took another step toward me, the gun still dangling in her hand. "Daddy's minding his business at the firm. Gets a call from Max the Whore. Guess who put it into her head that she could blackmail him? That she could make some *threats*? All because poor little Ellie Frites went to therapy and remembered all about her big bad childhood!" She drew out the last word.

My knees shook. Max said she'd only use the old bag of evidence, the clothes encrusted with his "stuff," to make him *pay*. Max must have sniffed out the lies in Lauren's letter and tracked down Frank Vine in one fell swoop, while my mother and I naively took Lauren at her letter's word and believed he was walking around Ohio with a GPS ankle bracelet. Max was shrewder than us all, and it got her killed. And now my stupidity would get *me* killed, along with my best friend.

Lauren continued. "Whore thought she could get some

money out of him," she laughed and looked up at her father, "and found out he was a lawyer with a big house on the water. Threatened to go to the cops if he didn't give her major cash. Even though she was the dumb slut who tricked Daddy back then." Lauren pointed the gun at my head and mouthed, "Pow, pow."

"Put that down and don't be stupid," Mr. Vine said. "Not yet."

She lowered the gun, but her bony wrist was noticeably weak and the gun flailed unsteadily in her grip. "Why now," Lauren said, in a high-pitched mocking voice. "Why now, she asks."

She started laughing hysterically and shook her head. "And we're going after your mommy next."

"No," I said, my voice shaking. "Leave her alone."

Mr. Vine snarled at me and said, "You sealed your fate when you called that little whore in New Jersey and drummed up this mess. You could have just let it be. It's all your fault, really."

"All. Your. Fault," Lauren said, giving the gun a shake with every word.

"Is your kid with your Dad?" I blurted.

Lauren curled her lip. "What do you mean? My kid's not here. Stupid."

"No, I mean did you get *pregnant* by him." I nodded at her father.

Sarah's head shifted in as great of a nod as she could manage, with the knife still set against her neck. She was encouraging me to say more. Stir things up. Get them off their toes.

"Are you fucking kidding me?" Mr. Vine's voice bounced off the walls of the small apartment. "I'm not some sick piece of shit!"

"Bullshit," I spat. "Max was a child—"

"Max was a whore," Lauren hissed. "A whore who thought she was a grown woman. She seduced Daddy—"

The knife trembled in his hand, cleaving tiny bloodletting cuts on the side of Sarah's throat as he spoke. "She was a mistake that cost me my family. And almost my career." His face was sweatier now, redder. "I'd started over again. A new life. I'd remarried and had a wife I loved. And that little bitch told her everything. Called her up and mailed her pictures from the fucking '90s." He shook Sarah as he spat, "And she left me."

Lauren's chapped lips peeled back from her crooked, beige fangs and whispered to me, like we were friends, "I'm glad she's gone."

"Shut up about her, Lauren, you little cunt!" her father erupted, pulling Sarah with him as his enormous body lumbered to and fro in anger.

Lauren sniffed; the gun was still bopping around in her grip. "You loved her more than me."

He turned his head towards his daughter. "Would you stop with this? If I have to tell you one more time—"

I seized this moment before I could talk myself out of it and lunged at Lauren, surprised at my own speed.

I knocked the gun from out of her hand and it fell to the floor with a hollow crack and then slid into the entrance of the kitchen where it spun and stopped. I collapsed on top of Lauren and we struggled together on the ground. For a split second I wondered what my next move would be. The first move was only predicated on if I retreated into my bedroom to get my phone or jump out the window, then Lauren would readily shoot me in the back, so obtaining the gun from her frail grip had seemed the only alternative. Turning it on her would have put Mr. Vine in a bind. This was all theoretical of course, because now, the gun was out of reach and Mr. Vine still had Sarah, the gleaming knife wedging deeper and deeper into her throat.

Lauren scratched madly at my arms and face from beneath me, grabbing chunks of my hair, ripping it right from the root. With my head in the midst of whiplash I struggled to keep Mr. Vine in my peripheral vision.

His complexion transitioned to a uniform color now, a flushed burgundy to match his nose. With one swift movement, the knife, firm in his grip, grazed the right side of Sarah's bare neck where the chain to her cross necklace rested above her collarbone.

He won't. He won't really—

"Don't!" I screamed as he sliced the knife clean across Sarah's neck, scarlet red seeping out instantaneously, forming rivulets down the fabric of her shirt and over the gloved hand that clutched her firm.

Sarah's eyes bulged in horror, fixing a hollow gape on me. Then her eyes lost sentience. I heard a reflexive, tormented cry escape my own throat. "No!"

Mr. Vine thrust Sarah's body to the floor where it crashed on the hardwood in an unforgiving thump. I walked on all fours towards the kitchen, towards the gun, scrambling forth as Lauren snatched at my ankles like a scuttling crab buried in sand. I kicked one leg back, hard, and in doing so banged my knee against the floor, producing a blinding pain. Lauren still had me in her grasp. But I was dragging her with me at this point and was getting closer in distance to the gun.

As I crawled, slowly, Mr. Vine was on foot in hard, long strides. I finally escaped Lauren's skeletal grip and burst forward with all my might until my fingers grazed the cold metal of the mouth of the gun. But Mr. Vine was so close, so very close. *Move!* I told myself as his shadow cast over me. I teetered backwards and fastened the gun in my hand until I managed to point it up at him from the floor as I lay on my back. I'd never touched a gun before, and this fact jammed my heart into my throat as I prayed there was no safety, prayed there was no lever I had to pull. Then as he ascended over me—blotting out the rest of the room—I fastened my finger around the trigger and pulled. The kickback shocked me more than the deafening crack, my hands numbed by a jarring vibration I hadn't expected.

His body blew back stiff and straight, almost in slow motion, like a fell tree.

Then a scream. I didn't know the source of the scream, me or Lauren. Lauren. From the ground with the gun still in my hand, ringing and stinging, I watched as Lauren shakily rose from the floor, whimpering, bleating. *She's bleating like a stuck pig*, I thought dazedly.

"Daddy, Daddy." She bent over him and ran her small tattooed hand through his hair tenderly. Then, as if just remembering I was there, she jerked up and crashed over to the door. I made no move to stop her. I stared, rapt, as Lauren's sneaker slipped on Sarah's blood that was streaming in a wide line towards the doorway.

Lauren had to shake her other shoe from a clump of Sarah's hair. She stumbled up to the door. Through tears she fiddled with the door locks confusedly. I continued to gawp, confounded by the unreality of the last what, ten? fifteen? minutes of my life. The door opened with a sharp thrust of Lauren's bony hip, and she was gone.

I stood up, my legs like jelly, a persistent buzzing in my ear. I saw little dots like lightning bugs and I had a pounding headache. Out the corner of my eye I spotted bright pink and walked slowly over to my phone that at some point was dropped on the floor.

I averted my eyes from Mr. Vine's hulking body splayed on the hardwood. I forced myself to kneel down to check his pulse. Nothing. As I stood up, I tried my best not to look at

Sarah's blood-lined face, her slit neck. I turned away from her and called 911 and spoke slowly, my voice cracking every few words. The sobs came later.

24

Those Three Words

Sirens.

As I neared Sarah's body I relented. I had to look down. I stooped over Sarah's lifeless corpse and held my hand out, but it just hovered in the air. But then I saw her hand twitch.

"Sarah!" I cried out. "Sarah!" I was screaming; I couldn't believe it, her eyes had gone vacant in such a way that I was convinced she was dead. But maybe...

I ran to the bathroom, slipping on the blood, and grabbed a towel and held it to Sarah's neck. I tapped lightly at her neck, fearful that if I pressed on the wrong spot I would burst an artery of something and make things worse. I felt the faintest, slowest pulse on her wrist; I had no idea what I was doing. Was I making things worse? I had heard the sirens, but then they'd stopped. Where were they?

Right then, the door burst open and my heart leapt into my throat. I looked up helplessly; I was unarmed, my two hands pressing the already sopping towel to Sarah's neck. I'd left the gun on the floor across the room like a moron. How could I not think she'd come back?

But it wasn't her. He shook his dark hair from his eyes, which widened with horror as he regarded the morbid scene on my hardwood floor.

"You," I said, "how are you here?"

"I live here!" he said exasperatedly, pointing across the hall. "Are you serious?"

"I haven't seen you—"

"I'm studying most of the time, holed up in there. I'm in med school."

"Oh."

He kneeled down beside me. "Another towel?"

"In there." I pointed to the bathroom.

He softly nudged me out of the way. "Go get it."

When I came back he applied the fresh towel with more pressure, checking her pulse.

He wagged his head toward Mr. Vine. "What about him."

I shook my head.

"I heard sirens," he said, looking at me. "Then saw they went to the building across the street. They must not have the number correct."

I was frozen.

"Go down there and speed this along for her at least. Get them up here, *now*!"

I sprang up, my legs almost giving way, and made my way out the door, taking care not to step in more of Sarah's blood. When I descended the stairs and reached the bottom step, I looked out the half-moon window above the main door, through which red and blue lights flashed.

Two cops and an EMT burst through right then and asked me fast questions. I pointed up the stairs and told them my neighbor was helping her. As they shot up the stairs, I called out, "Hurry, he cut her throat," in a voice I didn't recognize, though I knew it was coming from my lips.

I called to the trailing officer with a blond goatee. "Wait."

He stopped and turned to me as the other two went on ahead. I started rattling off Lauren's description but he cut me off, telling me they'd seen bloody footsteps down the street, and there were plenty of witnesses who saw her and gave her description. Police were in close pursuit.

"Why don't you come outside with me." He led me to another officer, who asked my name and gently guided me towards the street. He informed me that my mother had called in a missing person's report because she had a "bad feeling" after I hadn't picked up my phone all day. They didn't heed her warnings; it hadn't been a long enough period of time to do a wellness check. Luckily, Tim had called the authorities as well; he'd been suspicious of Lauren's misspelled text back to him.

The officer scratched his goatee. "He said the text message had emoticons? And that it was a surefire sign you hadn't been the sender."

I barely comprehended the barrage of additional voices that came streaming from all directions that were offering questions, instructions, and assurances. I was outside of myself, numb, absorbing none of it.

The image of Mr. Vine slicing Sarah's neck so effortlessly bore into my skull; I'd never forget that scarlet necklace branded on her skin, forever and ever.

The goateed cop ushered me further down the street, away from a small crowd that had gathered. I could see Tim waving his arms and standing on his tiptoes and shuffling around the stiff badged arms that tried to hold him back. I thought I saw Mel's wild dark hair, but she was enmeshed in a crowd of chattering voyeurs and I couldn't focus my eyes well enough to see for sure.

Then I saw my mother standing off from the crowd, her tiny arms hugging her tiny frame, coils of hair springing from her temples. She was crying. Tim followed my eyes and sidled up to my mother, and he put his arm around her. I broke away and ducked under the police tape and ran to them.

"Mom," I gasped.

"Honey." Tears streamed down her face.

We hugged and I kissed her wet face and I told her I loved her and I was about to turn to Tim when a man and a woman, detectives whose names I would never recall, firmly grasped both my arms and told me to come with them. Once extracted from my mother, they deposited me back on the other side of the tape. A few feet away I heard my name and turned back.

Tim had slipped through somehow, and he strolled up beside me and put his hand on my back. "They got her," he said into my ear. "I just overheard. Cops found her in an alley a few blocks down, crying and muttering to herself. It's over, Ellie."

"Sarah…" I whispered. "He got Sarah."

"Is she okay?"

"I don't know," I choked.

A racket came from the apartment right then, a clanking sound and voices shouting, and we both turned.

A stretcher crashed through the entrance to the building. A body bag.

"No!" I wailed. "Sarah."

Another stretcher emerged, this one, I was elated to see, was Sarah. There was a mask over her face, and there was blood, but I could see her hair.

"Will she be okay?" I called out to anyone and everyone. "Will she be okay?" I screamed.

The EMTs carrying her brushed past us and one spoke out the side of his mouth. "Miss, we don't know. She's in very bad shape."

Tears sprung from my eyes and a heaving sob escaped my throat and I turned back to Tim, but the detectives tried to dip me into an unmarked car. I resisted and called his name.

His head bobbed over an officer trying to direct him back toward the crowd. "Yeah, El?"

"I love you."

25

Too Legit to Quit

Two Months Later

Buster's eyes wandered to the base of my V-neck. I bugged my eyes and he flicked his upwards and blinked, shifted in his seat, and said, "Ellie. You know why I called you in, correct?"

"You wrote me a detailed email. Then you copied what you said in the email and pasted it into the calendar invite. Then you sent me a message in the CRM. To which I was required to check off *Received*. I checked it off."

"Good," he honked, leaning back in his chair, crossing his bulbous arms. "Now, I know you've suffered a personal...upheaval of sorts. And we at Symbicore understand that. But we also want our employees to remain at the top of their game, to focus on what's best for the Symbicore family." He tossed a nod through the glass to someone passing by. I saw out the corner of my eye the person didn't return his greeting. "We need to address your steep decline in productivity the last month or so."

"Oh?"

"It shouldn't be any sort of surprise, Ellie. Your numbers have declined. Let me ask you a question, to make you understand. Do you know what an ally-oop is ?"

I gritted my teeth. "Mmhm."

He cleared his throat. "Oh, you do. Well, quite frankly,

Ellie, you've not only been missing your ally-oops, you've been missing your free-throws."

I pictured myself hurling a basketball at his forehead because I also knew what a bank shot was; I was not some daft fucking nincompoop from planet Mars like he seemed to think. I also knew what a colossal waste of time this meeting was. *How small must you feel*, I thought, *how desperate*.

I waited with my hands folded in my lap.

"First order of business is we're going to put you on yet another R.A.V.E.! rehabilitation plan." He shuffled some papers on front of him. "Get you back up on your feet. We'll look at time management and check in on your queue three times a week. I think we'll have to monitor any afternoon coffee breaks," he narrowed his eyes, "to assure that you're maximizing your work periods effectively and not, you know, running off fraternizing with certain members of the Database Marketing group."

His words seemed to drain out his nose. "Now, I hate to say this but, if your numbers don't improve, this will serve as grounds for term—"

"I got another job, Buster. On the Analytics team."

Buster sat back and raised his eyebrows. "You…okay. That's interesting." He crossed his arms. "That technically isn't possible. I didn't sign off on a transition plan."

"I've met with several of the department heads, and I have mentors, like Savannah Carlson, backing me that served as my references. We talked to HR, and they said I don't need your permission. The transition plan policy was done away with last quarter, actually, when the hiring freeze was lifted. I'm surprised you don't know that." I paused. "Actually, I'm not surprised. You haven't allowed anyone to progress out of this department, and you've spent no effort or energy on mentorship, so I guess," I chuckled, "how would you know?"

He gripped his pen hard and started chewing on the end. "Now, Ellie, the problem here may be your attitude—"

I smiled. "I would say your lack of leadership is the problem here. You provide no incentive for us to do better."

"I hardly think any of this is appropriate talk—"

I cut him off. "You're right. I'll reserve the rest of what I have to say about your managerial worth for my exit interview. That's a new policy, too. Even if we change positions internally, we give exit interviews."

I pushed my chair back with my hamstrings and walked to the door. Over my shoulder I called, "I'll print out my resignation letter and put it on your chair. I start my position next week. Thanks so much for all your help. I'll be sure to tell HR all about it."

Buster glared at me.

I walked out to the hallway and took out my cell phone and called my mother, my heart pounding.

"Are you all right?" my mother blurted when she picked up on the first ring. I supposed a random phone call in the middle of the day, after everything that had happened, was not the best idea.

I looked around for Buster, and whispered, "I gave my notice. And also just the *tiniest* bit of shade."

She whooped and said she was proud of me, that she'd take me out to a nice dinner. Maybe Jack could come home for the weekend to celebrate, too. Jack, who was none the wiser to the whole Vine business up until the incident at my apartment, had been coming home to visit more often from his summer classes.

When I got off the phone with my mother, I started a group-text that included Tim, Mel, and Savannah. My finger hovered over Sarah's contact, Muppet, but I stopped myself. I felt tears sting my eyes and swallowed a lump in my throat.

Me: I gave my notice. Play hooky and celebrate?

Mel: So happy for you! I'm in.

Savannah: Yes! I wish I saw Buster's face. In.

Tim: You deserve it. Love you. I hope you had Buster the Buffoon quaking in his too-tight Wranglers. I'm in, too.

Me: Meet me at the train stop in an hour. See you turds soon.

I printed out my perfunctory resignation letter. Before shutting down my laptop to return to IT, I opened up my email.

From: <ellie_frites@symbicore.com>
To: Muppet <sarah_mupetta@email.com>
Subject: Life Updates

Consider this my last correspondence as a Ninja. I'm coming to see you.

***

Sarah emerged from her coma three weeks ago, sporting a ghoulish scar across her neck. It was fading to a tongue-colored pink as the weeks passed, but it still served as an overt reminder that she was just millimeters away from dying at the hands of a child molesting psychopath. She joked that if it were 1996, she'd just wear a choker necklace to cover it up. I told her if it was 1996, I'd have told my mother to take my father's gun and shoot Frank Vine in the fucking head rather than merely bopping him with a baseball bat, setting off this unspeakable chain of events.

Sarah, always looking on the bright side, told me she was glad it happened. I told her she was insane, but she insisted that she not only lost fifteen pounds from eating through a feeding tube for weeks, she gained a boyfriend out of the deal. Turned out the neighbor across the hall—his name, I finally figured out, was Dan—saved her life when he applied the towel pressure to her neck before the EMTs arrived. I guessed me tapping the towel to her throat like a fairy wand was not a life-saving technique.

Dan visited Sarah in the hospital every day while she was in her coma, and he helped her with her physical therapy after she woke up. Apparently, he'd had a crush on her for weeks prior to the incident. Their odd schedules found them crossing paths at all hours of the night, and he hadn't the guts to talk to her or ask her out. Not until he saved her life, that is.

"It pays to know your neighbors," Sarah said to me when I got to the hospital, where she was still recovering.

I nodded and smiled. "Yes, Muppet, it does." Then I added, "It pays to know your enemies, too. Especially if you last saw them thirteen years ago and they write you fake letters and they try to come to your apartment and kill you."

"Speaking of, what's the status of Lauren? Did she go to court yet?"

"They're trying her for accessory to murder. She goes to court next week; she got out on bail. Her mother's a moron and paid it, and she thinks she can get Lauren back in her life this way. Plus, the judge took pity on her because there was a kid involved. My lawyer warned me that the sentence might be shorter than we'd like."

Sarah shuddered. "That's not good."

"No, but we have to just wait and see. I'm sure we can get restraining orders and stuff if she ever gets out. My thought is that without her Dad, she's a helpless, deranged druggy. A little varmint, in my opinion."

Speaking of varmints, we moved out of our mice-infested apartment after the melee. Tim had helped move both Sarah's and my belongings into a two-bedroom condo in South Boston near the water. We decorated Sarah's room, Derek Jeter posters and all, while she finished her recovery.

Down the street from us, ironically, lived Tyler and his new roommate, Ricki. One morning as Tim was leaving and

I was kissing him goodbye on my stoop, I sensed someone watching me from across the street. It was Ricki, hair disheveled, in sweatpants. When our eyes met she turned and shuffled back down the street. I pulled a Jenny Cummings and shouted, "Hi, Ricki!"

She didn't look back. I had to smile.

After visiting Sarah at the hospital, I headed back towards the office and met Tim, Mel, and Savannah at a sports bar. They had a cake waiting for me. Savannah provided even more cause for celebration: she heard from a reliable source that Buster was in the hothouse for not being a R.A.V.E.!-worthy manager and failing to meet his goals, one being E.Y.E.: Empower your Employees. Not to mention, many accounts aside from my own had trickled into HR regarding his constant nipple gazing.

***

Full of cake, I took the train back to my apartment and sifted through a pile of mail. Junk, bills, catalogs.

One, stuffed in between the *PennySaver*, looked to be a card sheathed in a blue Hallmark envelope, no return address. I flipped it front to back before opening it to be sure. It must have been hand delivered. It was a Father's Day card.

I was suddenly reminded of a dream from just the night before. I'd dreamt of my father. He was off in the distance, in the grassy field, beckoning me. His face was scruffy, his hair was thick, spilling out the sides of his Red Sox hat. He had color in his face. "Honey," he called. "Come here."

I ran and ran, and then I tripped. I got up. I continued to run, and the strangest thing happened—this time, I reached him. He held his arms out, and I collapsed into his chest. "Daddy."

"Ellie." He took me gently by both shoulders. Then he leaned into my ear. "Everything is going to be *okay*."

And then I'd woken up, my pillow wet with tears. Still

smiling as I thought of my father, I opened the Father's Day card. It was blank. A piece of paper fell out onto the ground. I picked it up. The letter was typed, just like the last, and my heart careened into my throat.

It was one line.

```
Wanna do a movie, Ellie? This time, YOU die.
```

Acknowledgements

I'd like to thank my very first reader, Emily Dumas, for her kind insights into what at first barely resembled a book. I'd like to thank my second reader and first editor, Amanda Karby, for her heartfelt feedback and diligence. I'd also like to thank my best friend Beth for her exhaustive edits on numerous drafts and for being the best friend anyone could have. My other readers: Caitlin Butler, Mandy Darnell, and Lindsay Leete, much gratitude. For my cover, thank you to the lovely Cara Sylvia, who also picked up a lot of my slack in other arenas. And thank you to my husband, Mike, who was never allowed to read this manuscript but to whom it's dedicated. Mike is my lifeboat in more ways than I can do justice mentioning here.

About the Author

Nicole Barrell resides in Massachusetts with her husband and dog. This is her first novel. Her website is nicolebarrell.com.